THE SWAMP ANGEL
THE COMPLETE CASES OF
CALHOUN, VOLUME 2

THE SWAMP ANGEL

THE COMPLETE CASES OF CALHOUN, VOLUME 2

EDWARD PARRISH WARE

INTRODUCTION BY
ROBERT SAMPSON

ILLUSTRATED BY
F.M. FOLLETT

COVER BY
LEJAREN HILLER

POPULAR PUBLICATIONS · 2024

TABLE OF CONTENTS

INTRODUCTION BY
ROBERT SAMPSON

WEST OF THE Mississippi lie the Sunken Lands of northern Arkansas—a swampy tangle of mud, snakes, vines matting together a density of bushes and trees. Here channels of black water wind. Mosquitoes cloud. There are shanties by carpets of lily pads and shabby boats. The sun is heavy and the humidity strangles.

Over the Sunken Lands hovers the thick stench of vegetation decaying in heat. Through the tangle prowl quaint old swamp rats, inseparable from their rifles. And here slink thieves, murderers, and such blood-soaked riff-raff as add violence to a frontier environment.

The scene is ferocious. And through it moves Ranger Jack Calhoun, Chief Inspector of the U.S. Rangers, his beat the Sunken Lands. Calhoun's official title varies, but he, himself, does not change. He is the lead character in Edward Parrish Ware's short story series that was published in *Flynn's Weekly* and *Flynn's Detective Fiction Weekly* from about 1926 to about 1935.

The stories are in that most simple of forms—the tale of the single good man against the forces of lawlessness. Packs of human vermin, in this case. Out into the wilderness Ranger Calhoun paddles. His mission is simple: Bring in those killers.

Since their condition on return is not specified, Calhoun brings them in dead, often as not. He wears a pair of .45 revolvers and carries a rifle. Since these are stories of danger and violent action, his weapons grow white-hot through the chapters.

At the series' beginning, the action is not so lethal. In "One Good Man" (September 18, 1926), Calhoun goes after a pack of thieves who fled into the swamp. Sheriff Lundsford, the resident thick-head, red-necked, blow hard, collects a posse and paddles fiercely off in the wrong direction.

Calhoun reasons out where the quarry is, then slips down on them by night. He slugs them down, one by one, shooting only once. Then brings the whole batch back to the glory of the U.S. Rangers.

You expect this sort of competence from Calhoun, who once remarks that he is "hard-boiled without much conscience."

That isn't Calhoun's real opinion of himself. It's something Edward Ware read in *Black Mask* and thought it would be nice added to Calhoun's character. For Calhoun is tough but not hard-boiled. Not really. He is too sympathetic to young love and feminine feelings to be without conscience. On the whole, he's a competent professional of the type described as "bad news."

In "The Negative Clue" (November 20, 1926), he Sherlocks around the swamp, pondering why Old Razorback, who has been arrested for a double murder, didn't just throw the bodies into the mud. Why did he try and bury them?

Because he didn't do it, obviously.

If that story is run-of-the-mill, "The Panther" (July 9, 1927) is hard-nosed, unblushing suspense. It moves at an unrelenting pace—no introspection, no psychological finesse, no complex character building.

Just a continuous pressure of danger, fear, and physical violence.

That infamous outlaw, The Panther, is running amok in The Devil's Bowl region. Calhoun is ordered to bring him in. And The Panther's gang, too, while you're at it. Thereafter, Calhoun:

—finds a wounded man, almost dead, marooned on a mud island in the swamp.

—is fired on by an ambusher with a rifle.

—disguises himself as a swamp rat and bluffs his way into The Panther's camp.

—is interviewed by the tough leader, who conceals himself in shadow, only his white hands showing in the lamp light.

—discovers an imprisoned woman.

—gun fights his way free.

—returns with a horde of Rangers for a brutal fire-fight and slaughter of the outlaws.

—discovers that the man he saved on the mud island was actually The Panther, displaced of command by the more bloody faction of his outlaws.

—allows The Panther and his sweetheart to escape, since they assure him that they have reformed.

Although faint elements of mystery occur, this is basically an old-fashioned adventure story. In another climate, Hopalong Cassidy could have handled the same assignment in the same way and with equal gusto.

"The Grave on Number 10" (August 10, 1929, *Detective Fiction Weekly*) tells how an old drunk sees a night murder and burial out on a mud island. He blabs about this at all the bars, ends up in that same grave. Calhoun, full of intuition, locates the grave and uncovers a clever identity switch and a second murder.

From mid-1929 on, the stories cease their effete posturing and hunker down to straight blood and violence. "The Red Record" (September 14, 1929) suggests that Ware had been mightily impressed by Hammett's "The Gutting of Couffignal" (*Black Mask,* December 1925). The Jungle Butcher, a crazy outlaw, has declared war on the Arkansas river counties. He is methodically murdering and burning his way along the Mississippi.

The first part of this story sounds as if it were rewritten from a Western Story novel. It is full of horses, six-guns, posses. Horsemen gun down the only witness. In an old, board hotel, Calhoun walks into a gun trap. Pistol battle in the halls. A henchman grips his bullet-smashed arm. From a horse-drawn cab, a treacherous shot. Then the mysterious girl is whirled away.

So far, this is another job for Hopalong Cassidy. Now, however, the story veers toward the Mississippi. Trailing the girl, Calhoun comes to a wharf, is attacked by a gang. He battles free. Escapes in a boat. Is alone on the River.

Almost drowns.

Blunders into the Headquarters of The Jungle Butcher by luck. Is captured. Tied up.

The Butcher announces that he will attack and destroy Barfield's Point. After that, he will amputate Calhoun's hands and nail them above his door.

Down the river they swoop, about 150 men on a couple of riverboats.

At Barfield's Point, they rage ashore.

It's like old days at Northfield, Minnesota. The Rangers are waiting there, a rifle in every window.

Massacre.

While the streets fill up with smoking brass, Calhoun saws loose his bonds on broken window glass. Grabbing up a gun, he cleans up on those of the gang surviving the ambush. He captures The Butcher and the story ends with the banners of Good floating high.

As the 1930s progressed, the Calhoun stories gradually shortened. Stripped-down plots packed in ever more action. In "Calhoun's Way" (January 18, 1930), the sheriff suspects a meek bookkeeper of robbing a bank. But Calhoun grows a set of whiskers and runs down the real robber, just as he's sailing off for a new and merry life.

"Satan's Sink-Hole" (August 25, 1934) redoes the opening of "The Panther," although in summary. A masked man has marooned this poor naked fellow on a mud island. "Sign these papers or die." But Calhoun has been investigating back at the poor guy's cabin. Through the swamp he comes, just in time to gun down the leering fiend and save valuable timber rights.

Now the stories are published less frequently and are more familiar. They melt into the great pulp magazine sound. Violence haunts Calhoun. Everywhere danger lurks. Let his attention wander and his skull is slammed.

Searching the swamp for missing men, he finds a dead man peacefully leaning against a tree. ("Killer in the Cane," January 19, 1935.) Immediately Calhoun is slugged, pitched into a bottomless bog. Using his belt, tie, and a helpful tree branch, he barely escapes. Is immediately recaptured and imprisoned in a shanty. There a smart city gangster has terrorized a girl and her father into hiding him out. He is running a buried treasure racket, luring fools into the swamp and killing them for their money.

The girl frees Calhoun. But they are trapped in the cabin. The gangster has set fire to the place and lurks outside, his weapon cocked. While the murderer gloats, Calhoun slips through the roof and kills him with a single, long-range pistol shot.

Down into black swamp water the blood runs. Over the corpse, Calhoun stands, tanned face expressionless. In the silence, a fish splashes. Circular rings spread silently across polished water. Another cartridge, another death, another triumph for Inspector of U.S. Rangers, Jack Calhoun.

It grows dark. Over the body, Calhoun stands motionless. He will not move until the next story. He stands immobile, without feeling, lifeless as the corpse at his feet. In 1926, he was a vigorous, if shallow figure. In 1935, he is an efficient killer, one among many in the bloody pulps. Here he will stand, unchanging, waiting, until Edward Parrish Ware feeds another sheet of paper into the typewriter and the story begins again.

— Robert Sampson

THE PRICE OF PELTS

*Deep in the Wilderness of the Bayou
Country the Natives Maintained a Fierce
Resistance Against Civilization*

1

BUZZARDS AFTER CORPSES

"STROUD!"

The rawboned, gray-haired man, walking leisurely along the high sidewalks toward the post office at the east end of Deer Lick's one business street, halted abruptly, cool eyes upon the speaker. He had observed the latter's advance in his direction, and interpreted it accurately.

"Well, Hilliard?" he queried, glance level with that of the man, almost a counterpart of himself in so far as size, age, and general appearance went, who faced him about ten paces distant.

"You have proved yourself a better man than me in one thing," Hilliard said evenly. "You've beat me in the fur game—now see if you can beat me to the draw!"

That was all. No argument or discussion—simply the challenge hurled across those intervening ten paces.

Stroud never moved, but his eyes followed the swift dip of Hilliard's right hand toward the waistband of his trousers, where the unbuttoned vest hung loosely; saw the fingers of that hand grasp the butt of a revolver, and the long, blue weapon whip out. Then, with a flash of his right hand, incredibly swift, he swept the skirt of his coat back, reached his own gun, and fired from his hip.

Hilliard, hit squarely between the eyes, spun about, then sagged down to the walk. His gun wavered between fingers which were no longer capable of using it, then thudded onto the planking.

Hilliard was fast—but Stroud had been faster.

There was nothing of the bearing of a victor in the big man who stood so still, his body bent forward slightly, eyes peering at the sprawled figure in front of him. Like a statue he stood, gun ready for a second shot.

A tiny stream of smoke curled lazily from the muzzle of his weapon, was caught in the whirl of a sudden gust of wind and blown backward into the gray face. Stroud coughed, strangled by the acrid fumes, then walked slowly toward Hilliard, his boot heels tapping hollowly upon the walk.

After the report of the revolver a profound silence hung over the street, and the *tap, tap, tap* of those boot-heels sounded like the blows of a hammer on the head of an empty barrel.

Stroud bent over the body of Hilliard, then straightened slowly. His bullet had gone true. Hilliard's death had been instantaneous.

Four doors down the street, Henry Pliler, who dealt in nets and traps, thrust his head cautiously through his partly opened doorway, glanced at the tableau in the middle of the walk, perceived how matters had fallen out, and started hastily toward where Stroud was standing.

From other buildings men came hurriedly, and by the time Pliler had reached the scene of the tragedy there were some two dozen citizens close on his heels.

*A bullet whined like a hornet above Cal's
head and Ben Stroud crumpled up*

"Hilliard came gunning for me, men," Stroud told them quietly. "I beat him to the draw. That's all."

"Old Lee ought to of knowed better than try to draw ag'in' you, Ben! I saw th' play!" Pliler declared. "Always was a kind of fool, old Lee. Hard-headed, and mean, too, if you asks me!"

"Mean is right!" seconded Dave Hawkins, Pliler's store assistant. "I'm awful glad it wa'nt you, Ben! Deer Lick can git along mighty well without sich as Lee Hilliard—but we'd all miss you p'intedly, and that's a fact!"

Others echoed Dave's sentiments, while Stroud stood silent. As the comments thickened, both in numbers and quality, his face underwent a transformation. Suddenly he raised a hand and spoke.

"Pick him to pieces, buzzards!" he blazed. "He's dead and can't help himself! Time was, and not more than five minutes ago, when every damned man of you would have tucked his tail and run to cover rather than face Lee Hilliard with gun in hand! Lee's' dead now—died like he lived, and that means game as hell. If I'd fallen, instead of him, you'd all be saying the same things to him that you're saying to me—and you know it! Boot lickers!"

He paused, and the crowd, intimidated by the whip-lash tongue, waited silently—many longing to slip away, but none daring to make the move.

"I killed Lee Hilliard because I had to," Stroud went on. "I knew I'd have to, sooner or later, or be killed by him. Now, let me say this: If there's any amongst you that feels you've been cheated out of a chance to get Lee—and it seems that most of you have got something against him—I stand ready to fight any or all of you in his place. And," he went on, speaking slowly and giving his words time to sink in, "I aim to shoot the first scoundrel that says a word against Lee that he can't prove! Understand?"

He waited, compelling an answer from the crowd by sheer force of his personality—plus fear of him.

"Yes, Mr. Stroud," Pliler said faintly, seeing that the speaker's hard blue eyes were fixed unwaveringly upon him. "I reckon there won't be nothin' said, if you say not!"

Stroud, unutterable contempt in his seamed face, turned on his heel and walked rapidly back to the store whence he had come a few minutes before.

2

LEAD WILL FLY FAST

DEER LICK'S FUR war was over.

On that morning of March 1, 1890, Bennett Stroud had chalked his quotations for the day on the bulletin board in front of his general store and warehouse, advancing the price of prime muskrats to forty cents—five cents better than the figure for the preceding day. At the same time, though unknowingly, he wrote the word "finis" upon the record of a two-year struggle between Leander Hilliard and himself.

At an earlier date the two merchants had been partners, controlling the hide output in the Deer Lick district; that meant the control of practically all the fur-take in the whole of the L'Anguile Bayou section of Northern Arkansas. Both were hot of temper, and aggressive to the point of absolute cruelty.

They fulfilled the prophecies of their friends, after a few years, by falling out with each other, thereafter going separate ways in business. That might have been well enough, since they were better off apart, but for the fact that each strove thenceforward to destroy the other and establish himself in control.

Two years before Hilliard had started advancing the

prices of pelts—raw hides of the wild animals so plen-
tiful in the L'Anguile Bottoms. At that time muskrats
were selling at ten cents; they had never been higher than
that figure, and sometimes lower as befits the poorest of
fur-bearing animals, from a market point of view. Stroud
had seen the raise and gone his enemy five cents better—
advancing the prices on all green hides in proportion.

Thus the war began. It resulted in wiping out Hilliard's
finances, and, finally, Hilliard himself.

The trappers of the district had swerved first to Hilliard,
then to Stroud, and back again—according as one outbid
the other. Each buyer had, of course, his friends and
well-wishers, but such friendship did not blind the parti-
sans of either to their own interests.

It is true that had either merchant at any time called
his friends to arms in his defense there would have been a
bloody war involving practically every able-bodied man on
L'Anguile Bayou. Neither did, however, and those on the
side-lines contented themselves with watching and arguing. Now that Stroud controlled the situation, the parti-
sans of the dead Hilliard were, for the most part, careful
to conceal any disappointment they felt over the outcome.

After all, Stroud was in position to dictate in the matter
of furs, and furs were meat and bread to the swampers.

As for punishing Stroud, legally, for killing Hilliard,
there were two reasons why it would not be done. Firstly,
Stroud had shot in defense of his own life. Secondly, there
was no law in the L'Anguile country, other than men made
for themselves and maintained if they were able.

Bennett Stroud would not even be arrested.

But punishment would, in all probability, overtake the

slayer of Hilliard—justifiable though the slaying was—and overtake him speedily.

"Huh!" exclaimed Henry Pliler, albeit in low tones, when Stroud's broad back had receded to the vanishing point inside his own place of business. "I reckon old Ben better be savin' up his powder and lead, 'stid of wastin' it in Lee's quarrels! He'll be needin' of it in one of his own, torreckly!"

"Yeah!" agreed Hawkins, equally soft of voice. "When Jim gits here—an' that'll be jist as soon as steam-train an' stage kin fetch him, atter he hears his pap has been kilt—I reckon Ben'll have his hands full, 'thout botherin' about none of us!"

The crowd, which still lingered on the scene of death, nodded agreement. Henry Pliler, though not by any means so important to Deer Lick and the swampers as Hilliard had been and Stroud now was, nevertheless was a considerable figure in the wilderness. His opinions were not openly disputed. Many trappers and fishermen had credit with him, from season to season, and credit was sometimes—nearly always, in fact—highly necessary in the L'Anguile country.

"Hen shorely has got th' right of it," Bullhead Brown, a grizzled fisherman, began. "He do beat all fer goin' right to th' heart of things, does Hen. I allow that Jimmie Hilliard will start burnin' powder th' minute he steps outen th' stage frum Crampton—leastwise, he will effen thar's anybody in sight to sling lead at!"

The arrival, at that moment, of Benjy Ford, who conducted the only furniture store in the village and was, in addition, the local undertaker, put a stop to conversation.

Aided by willing hands, he lifted the body of Hilliard and bore it slowly down the walk and into his store.

Then Deer Lick settled down to await the arrival of Jim Hilliard, old Lee's only son.

3

A NEW WORD TO THE BOTTOMS

INSPECTOR JACK CALHOUN, of the Government Rangers stationed in the Sunken Land district of Arkansas, poled his dugout slowly up Bayou L'Anguile in the direction of Deer Lick. Being on his way from Hulet's Point, then his headquarters, to the headwaters of the bayou, a hundred water-miles away, he did not hurry.

There was no call for hurry, since the trip was to be one of inspection only. The ranger, but lately assigned to the L'Anguile country, desired to have a working knowledge of the territory.

"Deer Lick lies just ahead," he reflected, calling up a mental picture of a plat of the country which he had studied recently. "I'll make it there shortly before dark, and find a bed in some house or other. Maybe give the place a look over to-morrow. It being a sort of metropolis, hereabouts, I can't afford to pass it up."

He pushed on, and, shortly before dark, put in at the landing in front of the straggling street which constituted Deer Lick. Making the painter of his boat fast, he stepped ashore, and immediately became aware of a stir in the village.

A hundred yards away he could see a large group of men.

They were gathered in front of a tumble-down building whose gable flaunted the fact, in red paint, that it was Deer Lick's post office.

"Looks like the whole town is out there," Cal mused. "Waiting for the stage from Crampton, I'll bet. Yes, that's the answer. Guess I'll join 'em."

He walked slowly toward the group, and as he neared it he suddenly sensed something which seemed to set this particular group apart from the ordinary. There was a certain restless watchfulness noticeable in the conduct of the individuals gathered there, and the inspector surmised that something unusual was afoot.

"I'm one man which never licked Ben Stroud's boots— an' never sold him a single damned piece of fur, atter he split up with Lee!" came a loud voice from the crowd.

"Now old Lee air daid, an' Ben Stroud in th' saddle, I still clings to Lee! I am onable to feel any happiness account th' way things has fell out, an' I ain't pertendin' to be glad it war Lee as died, 'stid of Ben. I did like Hilliard, and I don't like Stroud!"

Calhoun paused at the edge of the crowd, listening.

"I'd be keerfuler how I talks, Gobbler!" cautioned some one.

"Let them as has ears open 'em up an' listen!" cried Gobbler. "I ain't fearin' none of 'em! Fuddermo', I has this to say: I ain't got nothin' on this here earth but my trapline an' my tree-dawgs—erbout twenty of them las' named critters, when I counted 'em up las' week—but I'm bettin' everything that young Jim will settle up for old Lee's killin', an' leave not a dang thing to be wished for!"

"You better keep yore mouth shet, Gobbler Brisco!" came another warning from the crowd. "Ben kin cause you a lot of trouble marketing yore furs, in case he don't like th' way you air shootin' off at th' mouth! You wants to remember that!"

"I remembers whut I wants to remember, an' I furgits whut I wants to furgit, Henry Pliler!" Gobbler retorted. "I ain't as rich as Ben Stroud, ner as eddicated— but I'm jest as mean! Ever bit an' grain as p'izonous! Anybody which don't believe it kin find out—easy!"

The speaker's record stood behind him in the assertion, and nobody publicly questioned it. To have done so would have brought about another killing. He continued to raise his voice in praise of Lee Hilliard, and in condemnation of Ben Stroud. The latter, it goes without saying, was not among the gathering. It would have made no difference to Gobbler, had he been there, be it said in justice to the old trapper.

Calhoun had heard enough to put him on the alert. Something tragic had happened recently in Deer Lick, that was clear. What was also clear was the apparent expectation, evinced by the gathering, of further tragic events. That crowd was expecting some one—and expecting him to act immediately he arrived in town.

The ranger was on the point of breaking through the knot of men, and demanding information, when the rattle of a dilapidated hack drew his attention to the upper end of the street. Two minutes later the stage from Crampton, the railway town twenty miles away, came to a stop before the post office.

"Thar he is! Thar's Jim!" Gobbler Brisco shouted as a young man leaped to the ground from the rear seat of the vehicle.

Jim Hilliard was built along rugged and serviceable lines. About five feet and nine inches tall, he had bone and muscle to match. His face was clean-shaved, tanned, and had the look of one who had always dwelt in the out-of-doors.

His eyes, under strong brows, were blue in some lights, gray in others, and inscrutable at all times. Straight as a young ash, he walked with the light, springy tread of a woodsman.

The fall of a pin could have been heard, after it became known positively that Jim Hilliard had arrived.

The young man wasted no time in talking. After a brief "Hello, men!" he went directly to the furniture store wherein he knew his father's body lay. At the door he turned and spoke:

"I'll go in alone, boys," he told them.

No one offered to follow, but all hung around the door, awaiting his reappearance.

That is to say, no native followed. One man, however, pushed his way through the crowd, gained the door and entered behind Hilliard.

The man was Jack Calhoun.

Jim Hilliard stood beside the coffin in which the body of old Lee lay. For a long five minutes he stared down at the bearded face, then looked up and into a pair of blue-gray eyes—eyes that looked straight out from under straight brows.

Above the eyes was a broad forehead, creased a bit with the lines of thought, and above the brow was a thatch of tawny hair. The mouth was wide and the lips thin. Altogether, it was a homely but friendly face into which the young man looked.

Something about the costume the stranger wore drew Jim Hilliard's attention. It was new to him. The six-footer before him was clothed in a uniform of some sort— trousers and tunic of brown stuff, high-top boots and wide-brimmed Stetson. Moreover, a pair of six-guns hung in holsters about his middle.

"Who are you?" Hilliard demanded.

"Calhoun," was the quiet answer. "Inspector of United States Rangers. I'm stationed down at Hulet's Point—but," significantly, "my jurisdiction is as wide and as long as the L'Anguile Bottoms."

"Well—what about it? Why come in here?"

"I heard fragments of conversation from various members of the gathering which greeted your arrival," was the quiet reply. "It seems you are expected to shoot a man in revenge for the death of your father."

Jim Hilliard looked straight into the eyes of the speaker—and found them as unreadable as his own.

"And if I should do so, or contemplate doing so? What about it?" he asked.

"I shall prevent it—if I can," came the answer, and the voice of the speaker was not nearly so quiet and friendly as it had been. "Failing that, I shall arrest you and take you to jail. Do I make myself quite clear?"

"Arrest me!" exclaimed the young man. "Why—well, I have been away from here during the past year. Attending to business of my own in Memphis. Maybe I have got out of touch with conditions in the Bottoms. At any rate, when I left here the word you have just used was strange to our ears. Since when has the law begun making arrests on Bayou L'Anguile?"

"Since a few months back, when I was ordered to take a force of rangers and carry law and order into the Bottoms," Cal informed him. "A good many arrests have been made since I came. I'd like them to be as few as possible, since I have nothing but good will in my heart toward the natives of the country.

"It rests with them, however. If folks just will break the laws, we must arrest them. Now, what I want to know is this: What, besides the sad duty of burying your father, did you come back to Deer Lick for? Did you come to kill?"

Jim Hilliard's inscrutable eyes never left Calhoun's, nor did they waver by so much as a flicker of an eyelash. "I came to bury my dead," he answered. "And then, if I find that he was foully dealt with—that he was killed without being given a chance—I mean to kill the man who done him in! I'd kill him, even though you and your entire gang of officers were present to see it done! I'd kill him—then go and hang for it, if such should be my fate! Now—are you answered?"

"Not fully," Calhoun replied. "In case you learn that your father died in an attempt to slay another—as the fragments I overheard tend to show—what then?"

"In that case I shall let the matter pass," was the reply. "If father drew first, and was not badgered into doing it by Stroud, and then fell before a faster gun, I shall do nothing. That's what I came to find out."

"Remain here for a moment," Cal ordered. Going to the door, he summoned two men by name.

"Will Henry Pliler and Gobbler Brisco step inside?" he requested.

Both men looked at him in surprise, but immediately complied.

"Pliler," Calhoun bade the merchant, "tell Jim Hilliard how his father died."

"He war kilt by Ben Stroud, in course."

"Who drew first?"

"Hilliard."

"Who started the fight?"

"Lee went gunnin' fur Ben."

"Now, Brisco, you tell your version of it."

"I'm th' friend of th' Hilliards, father and son, an' I aims to tell th' truth—bad as I hates it," Brisco said. "Ben broke Lee in th' fur war, an' Lee started out to git him. Ben kilt Lee, after Lee had his gun out. That's th' solemn truth—bad as I hates it!"

Calhoun looked meaningly at Jim Hilliard.

"Are you satisfied?" he asked.

"Yes," was the answer. "I'd take Brisco's word about anything."

"Then am I to understand that you will take no action against Stroud?"

"Not unless Stroud starts it."

"Fair enough," Cal told him. "I'm going now to see Stroud."

He turned toward the door.

"Say, who in hell air you?" Pliler demanded. "What air you doin' in this thing, anyhow? What air you goin' to see Stroud about?"

"Hilliard will tell you who I am," replied Calhoun. "I haven't got time to answer idle questions. As for what I want with Stroud—I am going to arrest him."

4

WHO FIGHTS AND RUNS

THERE WERE MEN in the group outside the furniture store who knew to what organization Calhoun belonged. They had heard of the coming of the government men to Hulet's Point, and the consequent solving of the mystery surrounding the dynamiting of the government levee. Had the inspector announced his identity, many would have recognized his name.

Cal did nothing of the kind, however. Instead he asked where Ben Stroud might be found.

"Don't know," Dave Hawkins replied. "Ben went back in th' swamp, this atternoon, an', so fur as is knowed, he ain't come back yit."

"Reckon he aims to pick his own time to die!" called a voice.

Darkness had come on, and Cal could not make out the person who had spoken.

"Ben ain't afeered!" some one answered hotly. "If he's dodgin', it's because he don't want to kill th' boy—that's whut! He didn't want to kill old Lee, but war forced. Now, I take it, he's waitin' around in th' hopes that Jim's friends will make it clear to him how his pap come to be kilt. Then maybe Jim will look at things different. But Ben ain't no dodgin' coward, that's whut!"

"Where does he live?" Cal asked.

"In th' back of his store building."

"I'll see if he is there."

But Ben Stroud was not in the room in the back of the big, dark building. Cal returned to the furniture store, saw Jim Hilliard go up the street and enter his father's place of business, accompanied by Gobbler Brisco and Tom Barbee, the latter the elder Hilliard's clerk for many years. After that the crowd gradually melted away.

"Guess I'll wait around," Cal resolved, and went to the landing and sat on the gunwale of his boat. "It's better to prevent a killing, than to punish a killer. Besides, the slaying of Hilliard must be looked into. Stroud ought to be back some time to-night."

At hourly intervals, up to eleven o'clock, Cal proceeded to the rear of Stroud's store and knocked on the door of his living room. He got no answer, and saw no light in the place. Still he hung on.

At length twelve o'clock came, and the inspector made another trip. Apparently he was the only person awake in the village. No one was on the street; even the dogs had ceased to howl, and were slumbering.

Standing upon the door log, Cal reached up and rapped on the panels of Stroud's door.

"Who's there?" came, the query in a deep voice from inside.

"It is Inspector Calhoun, of the rangers, Mr. Stroud," Cal replied. "I want a few words with you."

There was silence for a moment, then a lamp was lighted and a hand presently fumbled at the lock of the door.

"Jist a minute, Mr. Inspector," Stroud told him. Then the door swung open and the big frame of the hide buyer stood out in clear silhouette in the portal.

"Back, Stroud!" Cal cried, answering to something which prompted him inside. "That light behind you—"

Crack!

The report came from the darkness behind. A bullet whined like a hornet above Calhoun's head—and Ben Stroud, breaking at the knees, sagged forward, then crumpled in the ranger's arms.

"I—I'm killed, Mr. Inspector!" the dying man gasped. "The—price—of pelts—went—too high! This—is the—result! I'm sorry—damned sorry—about—Lee! He—was a—good fellow, and—I hated—to kill—him! Had to—though! Now I—reckon—Jim—"

His voice weakened, stammered, then grew silent.

Calhoun was holding a dead man in his arms.

Though Deer Lick may have been asleep, it slept lightly. Calhoun had barely time to carry the body of Stroud up the steps and place it on a bed in the room, when persons began to arrive. Some pounded on the street door of the store, others came to the rear.

Evidently the men of Deer Lick had gone to bed with the expectation of something happening—and happening to Stroud.

Calhoun explained what had occurred.

"The shot came from behind," he said. "The bullet passed above my head, and struck Stroud, who was outlined in the doorway above me, in the breast. He died two minutes later."

The natives looked at each other. Finally Bullhead Brown spoke, and in his voice there was an ominous note.

"I war a friend to th' Hilliards," he said. "I wanted Jim to shoot it out with Ben—but, damn his yaller hide, I thought he'd be as game and as square as his dad war, an' give Ben a chance! Never did I suspeecion he'd crack down at him from th' dark, an' drap him out lak he done!"

"Same here!" muttered Foxtrot Halliday fiercely.

"Reckon somethin' had ought to be done about this here piece of deviltry!" Bullhead went on. "What you-all say, men?"

Calhoun, well knowing the mob spirit, incipient though it was in this instance, quietly disappeared. On the sidewalk he ran rapidly to Jim Hilliard's door and pounded on it. The store was dark. He dashed to the back door, where Lee Hilliard had lived, even as Ben Stroud had done, and beat on the panels with his fists.

No answer. With a powerful kick he sent the door crashing open and stepped inside. Striking a light he surveyed the interior. It was empty of human presence.

A swift examination of the lock betrayed the fact that the bolt had been shot, and that no key was in it. The door leading into the store was also locked, but a key was in a hole on the inside. The two windows of the room were down and latched. Jim Hilliard had undoubtedly departed by the back door, locking it and taking the key with him.

Where had he gone? When had he locked that door—before, or after, the fatal shot that killed Stroud?

When Gobbler Brisco showed up in the back room, his

face whiter than was its wont, he found Calhoun standing in the center of the floor, his face unreadable.

"They're aimin' to mob Jim!" he gasped out. "Whar at is he?"

"Gone."

"Gone whar?"

"I don't know. But, since he is gone, it follows that there will be no lynching."

"Do you-all reckon Jim done it?"

"You know him better than I do," Cal replied non-committally. "Do you think he'd shoot Stroud from ambush?"

Brisco scratched his head in thought, then replied:

"He wouldn't, ordinarily," he said. "But—well, maybe he was afeered, account of you bein' here, to shoot Ben in th' open. That bein' th' case, an' him plumb honing to shed blood fur blood, he mought have done it underhanded. Yes, he mought."

Cal said nothing. He was listening. Many feet were hastening toward the store, and soon a crowd of angry men pushed into the room, while others, having broken the store door open, came in from that direction.

"Whar at is Jim Hilliard?" demanded Henry Pliler, who appeared to be the leader.

"What do you want with him?" Cal asked, looking the merchant in the eyes, his own beginning to glint with small lights which might have warned the mob leader to tread carefully had he known the man better.

"Well, I don't know that it's any of your business!" Pliler exclaimed in angry tones. "Nobody invited you into this thing—but somebody air goin' to invite you out!"

"Who—for instance?"

"Me, if you wants to know!"

"Yes!" Bullhead Brown shouted. "An' more of us, too! You-all git outen here, an' let we-all an' our business alone!"

"We don't want no damn ranger runnin' things fur us!" snarled Dave Hawkins. "We air plumb able to take keer of ourselves! What you say, men?"

Calhoun did not wait for the reply. He knew when men were at fever heat and ready to act with violence. With a flip of his right hand he snatched a gun from its holster, and fired. Fired at the lamp, and plunged the room into darkness.

When he fired he leaped backward and dashed into the store. Up the aisle between the counters he sped, out upon the walk, thence to the bayou. Before the startled, struggling men in the back room succeeded in getting out, and gathering their wits together, he was slipping silently away in his dugout.

But he was not headed upstream. No. Calhoun was racing down the bayou toward Hulet's Point—and his rangers.

"Somebody once said something about 'he who fights and runs away, will live to fight another day!'" he said to himself, a grim smile playing about the corners of his mouth. "Well, I mean to fight another day—and fight hard!"

5

AN AMBUSHED ATTACK

HULET'S POINT WAS thirty miles down Bayou L'Anguile from Deer Lick. The course lay through heavily timbered swamp, with here and there the stilt cabin of a native among the trees.

Cal poled on as swiftly as possible. At the junction of Dead Man's Slough—so named because of the finding of the corpse of an unidentified man in a fish-net at the slough's mouth—he swung across to the right hand bank.

Where the slough entered there was a break of cypress trees and knees, making it dangerous to navigate that portion of the bayou at night. The moon was now up, and the stream, save where the overhanging trees on shore threw it into shadow, shone silvery white. Cal nosed his boat into the moonlight, and headed it across to the bank.

Crack! Crack!

Tiny jets of flame, spearing the darkness of the shore, showed briefly at a point a hundred yards down the bayou and on the right.

Cal felt a stinging sensation in his left side, followed by a hot trickle of blood a moment later.

"Hell!" he ejaculated. "Somebody's trying to pot me from cover!"

With a powerful sweep of his paddle, he swung the light craft into the shadow of the shore, then crouched low, eyes ahead.

Crack!

Again the night was stabbed with a dart of flame. A bullet sang uncomfortably close to the ranger, and his own gun roared an answer.

Two more shots followed in quick succession, Cal shooting at the flashes, then no more. The ranger crept ashore, drew his dugout up into the brush, and hastened back into the deeper timber. Reaching a spot where the moonlight shone down in a small clearing, he stripped and examined his wound.

"The devil!" he exclaimed, relief in his voice. "Just barely broke the skin! Close shooting, though, and by moonlight at that! Wonder who did it? Jim Hilliard?"

Cal knew that Hilliard could not be very far away from Deer Lick, and that, in all probability, he had departed by way of the bayou. Water leaves no trail. Cal, in the moonlight, would be recognizable a good ways off.

Had Hilliard, thinking himself pursued, fired those shots? The inspector could arrive at no satisfactory answer. He had looked into the face of Jim Hilliard, and had found nothing displeasing there. Certainly the young man did not look like a killer, and an underhanded one at that.

Still, there was something in what Gobbler Brisco had said. Maybe Jim, full of the desire to avenge his father, had killed Stroud from the darkness. If he had done so, then lost his nerve and fled down the bayou, he would certainly be quite capable of shooting him, Calhoun, from the bank of the stream.

Cal filled a pipe and sat down in the shadow of a tree, there to wait till dawn. While waiting he smoked and thought.

Dawn came—and Cal had found no answer. He still was not sure that Jim Hilliard had killed Stroud.

"I'm a fool," he argued with himself. "Just a plain fool! Ben Stroud kills Lee Hilliard in a gun fight. Everybody predicts that Jim, the son of Hilliard, will kill Stroud. Jim arrives at Deer Lick—and Stroud dies from a bullet shot by—Jim Hilliard! Of course! That is logic! Therefore Jim Hilliard must be apprehended and made to answer for a dastardly crime! Come on, Calhoun—get busy!"

Returning to his dugout, the inspector got in and dropped downstream. He kept close to the shore, and anchored, as nearly as he was able to do, opposite the point where the little spurts of flame had appeared in the night. He went ashore—and his purpose in waiting until daylight became clear.

Like a well-trained hound nosing out a trail, Calhoun began looking for signs. Presently he found what he sought—four empty rifle cartridges. They were of .38 caliber, and had been lately fired.

He found something else, too. Something that caused him to straighten up in surprise.

In the soft mud of the bayou's bank were footprints.

"It don't seem credible!" the inspector argued. "But it is none the less true that a woman stood in this spot last night, and did her damnedest to shoot me up!"

For the tracks were those of a woman—a woman whose small feet were incased in moccasins.

"Moccasins argue that she is a native," Cal reflected. "But what woman, native or otherwise, would want to kill me?"

Concealing his dugout, Cal set off on the trail of those moccasins. Owing to the soft character of the soil near the bayou the imprints were clear enough for Cal, experienced as he was, to follow. Back into the timber they led him, circling southward and finally approaching the bank of the bayou again at a point a mile below where they started.

"Humph!" exclaimed Cal, pausing in a thicket of buck-rush and looking over the tops at a small stilt cabin which stood a hundred yards away. "I know where you are, my lady—but not who you are!"

Like a snake he wormed his way through the brush which grew almost up to the cabin, then, with entire lack of ceremony, he leaped to the door log, pushed the door open and entered.

The inside of the cabin was in gloom, and through the murk the inspector looked into the startled eyes of a woman—a young and startlingly lovely woman!

6

WOMEN AND HOUNDS

"GOOD MORNING!" CAL greeted. "Don't trouble to reach for the rifle on the bed. You won't need it. Where's all the men folks, that you have to do the shooting for the family?"

The girl stared at him, speechless for the moment.

Cal grinned. "Isn't it rather nice, now, to suddenly discover that you haven't committed murder?" he asked. "Bet you regretted it, last night. Didn't you?"

"I—I don't know what you-all mean!" The girl found her tongue at last. "Don't know nothin' about any murder! What you-all mean, bustin' in here?"

Calhoun glanced at the girl's feet, and his grin became wider.

"Moccasins," he remarked, pointing. "Mud stained, too. Now see here, sister, I'm willing to forgive that little scratch you gave me last night, and the intent behind it, but you'll have to come across with a few trifling bits of information in return. I know you tried to pot me from the shore of L'Anguile, last evening—and I want to know why. Willing to talk?"

The girl's dark eyes blazed into Cal's for an instant, then shifted quickly to a .38 caliber rifle lying on the foot of the bed.

The inspector crossed over and took the gun up. After a moment's scrutiny he laid it back again.

"Haven't cleaned it yet, eh?" he commented. "Well, it's too late now. Why did you crack down on me?"

"I—I didn't do no such thing!" came the vehement denial.

Calhoun's face grew serious. When he spoke again the banter was gone from his voice.

"Do you want to go down to Helena and be put in the government jail?" he asked. "Trying to murder a United States Ranger is a mighty serious offense. You would probably be sent away to a place called Leavenworth, and kept there until those black locks are all streaked with gray, and the roses in your cheeks are like snowballs. I'm giving you a chance—are you going to take it?"

The mention of jail caused a frightened look to flit over the girl's face; her eyes suddenly became intent upon the floor, and her fingers, clasped convulsively together, trembled.

"I don't want to go to no jail," she replied finally. "What you-all want to ask me?"

"That's better," Cal applauded. "In the first place, what is your name?"

"Nan."

"Nan. That's pretty, but not entirely satisfying. What else goes with it?"

"Brisco—Nan Brisco."

"Oho! Any kin to Gobbler?"

The girl nodded. "He's my pappy," she replied.

"Did you know who it was you were trying to kill—that

it was a fellow by the name of Calhoun—a ranger?" Cal proceeded.

"Y-y-es!" Nan Brisco faltered, giving her questioner a frightened glance.

"How? Who told you to be on the lookout for me?"

The girl was silent.

"Come, now, Miss Nan Brisco," Cal insisted. "You've confessed to last night's escapade. Better tell the rest."

Nan's head suddenly came up, and her dark eyes again shot fire. Her hands no longer trembled, for they were clenched into two small fists.

"I ain't tellin' you who did!" she cried emphatically. "I done it—I mean I shot four, maybe five, shots at you, last night! If you-all wants to take me to jail for that, jest go ahead and take me! But don't ask me no more questions, which I'd die rather than answer!"

Cal considered her gravely for an instant, then his tongue changed to one of sympathy.

"I don't blame you," he told her. "Giving away on yourself is one thing, and giving away on somebody else is entirely different. How long have you known Jim Hilliard?"

The question, asked so suddenly, caused the girl to recoil, and her face to go white. Her lips trembled, but she did not answer. She merely stared at Cal.

"Jim Hilliard. That's the answer," the inspector commented calmly. "You shot at me because you thought I was trailing Jim. Gosh! I'd like to have a pretty girl do a thing like that for me! You must love Jim a lot. A girl would have to love a man a lot to be willing to kill for him! Loved him a long, long time—haven't you?"

The tears sprang into Nan Brisco's eyes, and her hands

came up to hide them. Cal waited silently. To torture the girl was by no means pleasant for him, but there was no other way. Presently he spoke.

"Did Jim kill Stroud?"

Down came the hands, and the weeping woman became, in a flash of time, a dry-eyed tigress.

"No!" she shrieked. "He never kilt Ben Stroud! But you devils—you rangers—would lock him up in a stinkin' jail, then hang him for it! You wouldn't keer whether he was guilty or not! You'd hang him, and not even take the trouble to find out who was guilty! That's why I shot at you-all last night.

"Jim didn't tell me to do that—he just said that you would probably come huntin' of him, and for me not to answer no questions! I shot at you without no orders from him—and I done it because I don't think it would be wrong to shoot sich as you—a hound that looks like a man!

"A hound which is tryin' to track down a man that ain't done nothin'! I shot at you—and I wish to God I'd 'a' kilt you!"

The girl, in her rage, was beautiful. Cal waited calmly until she ceased speaking, then, sitting down on a chair, he took out his pipe, filled and lighted it.

"Nan," he said, after a puff or two, "if I were the sort of dog you think I am, I wouldn't blame you for wanting to kill me. I wonder, now, if I can convince you that I'm different? That I'd rather die myself than cause the execution of an innocent man? It's a fact.

"If I should ever learn that I had hounded a guiltless person down and sent him to the gallows, I'd—why I'd resign from the force, and then go off somewhere and—I'm not quite certain, but I think I'd keep one of my guns to blow my brains out with. That's how I feel about it."

Cal's quiet voice seemed to have a soothing effect upon the girl. When he ceased speaking, she looked intently at him as though she strove to read his face—to learn from it whether or not his words had been sincere.

"Did you come a-huntin' Jim?" she asked at last.

"No. I wasn't even sure that he had left the village. You see, I had to leave in a hurry—"

He broke off abruptly, leaped agilely to his feet, whipped out a gun and covered a man who hesitated in the doorway back of him—a man who was in the act of bringing the muzzle of a rifle to bear upon him.

"Come right in, Gobbler!" Cal invited. "Lower that gun until it is looking at the floor instead of me, then walk in and make yourself at home!"

7

IF HE IS INNOCENT

GOBBLER BRISCO, CRESTFALLEN, lowered the muzzle of his rifle to the floor, then came in slowly.

"Whut air you-all doin' in my cabin?" he asked, pausing on the sill.

"I'm merely a guest, Gobbler," Cal replied. "Stopped by to learn who lived here, and inquire into the possibilities of getting some fried hog and a cup of coffee for breakfast. Hang your rifle on the bed, alongside the little .38. There, that's better.

"If you've got a short-gun, anywhere in your clothes, just let it stay there—snug and nice. I don't believe you can beat me to the draw—and if you make any sudden motion after your hardware, I'll plug you between your eyes. Get all that?"

Brisco's face became redder than the wattles of the gobbler after which he had been nicknamed.

"You-all done said you come here fur breakfast," he replied, sitting down. "Onless you has lied you ain't in no danger. I shorely wouldn't kill nobody, just fur stoppin' in, neighborly like, an' eatin' a snack with me. Nan, git th' coffee pot a-bilin', an' some grub in th' pan. This here ranger ain't th' only one which is hongry enough to eat a yearlin', hide, hair, an' hoofs!" Nan turned obediently to her cooking, after one quick, pleading glance toward Calhoun—a glance he understood. It said, in effect:

"Are you going to tell him about Jim, and what I tried to do to you last night?"

Cal shook his head negatively—just a mere ghost of a shake. But the girl caught it, and a quick flush of gratitude dyed her cheeks.

"Now, Mr. Ranger, mebbe we-all kin talk a little," Gobbler suggested. "In th' fust place, I never had no notion of pot-shootin' you-all when I crope up to th' door an' seed you a-settin' in my house. I jes' nacherally didn't onderstand, an' I war puttin' myself ready fur whatever mought happen. That's whut."

"I'll take your word for it, Gobbler," Cal conceded. "I saw you long before you got to the door—out of a corner of an eye which I wasn't devoting to your daughter. Wasn't a chance in the world for you to pot-shoot me, after I caught the first glimpse of you. Now—let's talk."

Silence fell between the two, during which the sound of bacon frying could be heard. An aroma of coffee boiled into the room from the lean-to kitchen at the back.

"What happened after I left Deer Lick?" Cal inquired, flipping a dead match into the open hearth.

"Th' fellers all hunted fur you, found out that you'd made a clean git-away, then turned to a s'archin' fur Jimmie Hilliard. But thar wa'nt hide ner ha'r of Jimmie to be seen. He'd got plumb away, too. Finally ever'body went back to their shacks, an' slept on matters."

"How do they feel this morning?"

"I left afore I found out," was the answer. "Nan war here by herself, an' I had been gone away too long as it was."

Cal considered that, and wondered if Gobbler was being quite frank with him. It occurred to the inspector that Miss Nan was quite capable of taking care of herself, be her father gone ever so long. He made no comment to that end, however.

"Do you believe Jim Hilliard killed Stroud?" he asked suddenly.

The trapper's face grew grim. "Bad as I hates it, I does," he replied. "Jimmie lost his haid, I reckons, an' shot Ben from th' dark. I kaint figger it no other way. Who else would 'a' done it? Who, besides Jimmie, had hate in thar heart ag'in' Stroud?"

Cal shook his head. "I don't know," he replied. "Maybe you can tell me. Who else hated Stroud—anybody you know?"

"Well, thar is fellers in th' swamps, an' in Deer Lick for that matter, as hadn't no cause to love Ben," he replied thoughtfully. "Ben always driv hard when he had th' lines, an' no mistake about it. Fur instance, I hated him like p'izon!"

Cal looked up and met the keen glance of the trapper, his own eyes and face noncommittal. He nodded slowly.

"Yes. I understood that from your talk last night," he remarked. "I'd considered that, too. You made quite a lot of hot talk about Stroud, after he killed Hilliard, and you made it while under the belief that Jim would put Stroud away.

"When you found out that Jim meant to let the matter drop—you heard him so express himself—if he learned that his father had been killed in a fair fight, you might have got busy on your own hook. Stroud might get you, later, in return for your openly expressed enmity. Maybe you played safe—and got Stroud."

Brisco got slowly to his feet, eyes bulging and face gone pale. He stuttered for an instant, then found his tongue.

"Damn you, air you makin' out that I mought of shot Ben Stroud?" he shouted. "Air you tryin' to fasten his killin' onto me?"

"Sit down, Brisco," Cal bade him. "I'm just showing you how easy it is to cite circumstantial evidence enough to hang any sort of crime on anybody you choose—the same sort of evidence there is against Jim Hilliard. Jim had a reason for killing Stroud.

"After your loud talk against Stroud, betting that Jim would get him, and all that, you, too, might have had a reason—and a good one. Ben Stroud was quick with a gun—and he hadn't much respect for human life. Yes, you might have had a reason."

Gobbler dropped back into his chair, staring mutely at Cal.

"Now," the latter continued, "think again, and see if you can't dig up somebody else who might have had a reason—a reason either for putting Stroud under ground, or getting Jim Hilliard out of the way."

Gobbler scratched his grizzled head and combed his beard in deep thought. At length his eyes lit up with a gleam of what Cal took to be suspicion. It was but brief, however.

"I—no, sir, I can't figger nobody whut had it in fur Ben, that is, had it in fur him strong enough to shoot him frum th' dark," the trapper answered slowly. "No, sir, not airy one."

"How long has Miss Nan and Jim Hilliard been engaged?"

The question, so sudden and unexpected, took Brisco completely by surprise. His jaw dropped.

"Hu—why, whut has Nan been tellin' you-all?" he demanded.

"Nothing. That is, nothing about any engagement. I just guessed it. How long?"

"Well, they been sweet on one another since they war kids, I reckon," Gobbler told him. "They got 'gaged with one another when Jim went off to Memphis to git him a job thar war some money in. Old Lee war a failin' then, an' he wanted Jim to go. I reckon they meant to wed with each other, come th' time Jimmie war able to support her."

"I don't blame Jim one bit," Cal declared. "Nan is about the loveliest flower in the whole swamp land, I'm thinking. Being she is what she is, it stands to reason that other men wanted her. Name over some of them."

The old man grinned. "Thar's so dang many, I shorely couldn't spar' th' time to name 'em!" he laughed. " 'Sides, my memory ain't that good."

"Name some who now live at Deer Lick."

"Hum. Thar's Dave Hawkins, Johnnie Niles, Lafe Sears, Henry Pliler, Humpy Larrison, Sloughfoot Jackson, Squinteye, Bones—"

"Hey! Stop!" Cal called out. "Sounds like a list of casualties gathered from a battlefield! Who among those named still seem to have hopes?"

"Well, Sloughfoot and Johnnie Niles, they got into a

sort of a argyment, awhile back, an' Johnnie shoots hell outa Sloughfoot, then snook outen th' country because he war afeered Sloughfoot's friends would git him. I reckon Sloughfoot an' Johnnie both mought be said to have give up. Th' rest of th' gents named, all bein' on the ground an' in good health, air still hanging around, and give signs of hopin'."

Cal grinned. He could well imagine that they would hang around.

"Dave Hawkins, now. He was in town last night, when Stroud was shot. I saw him, and heard his name called. Who is Dave?" he asked.

"Dave is a crony of Hen Pliler—works fur him, too."

"And Pliler?"

"He sells nets, traps, an' sich like, to us trappers and fishers. Pretty big potatoes, is Hen. Biggest in Deer Lick, now. Lee an' Ben war bigger—but them bein' gone, that leaves Hen th' biggest."

Cal nodded. Just then breakfast was announced, and he followed Gobbler into the lean-to. When both men had eaten, silently and to their full capacity, Cal arose. Looking steadily into the fire-flushed face of Nan Brisco, he said:

"If I knew where Jim Hilliard was, I'd tell him not to run any farther. I'd tell him to return to Deer Lick; to get there tomorrow afternoon. He won't be in any danger from a mob—there'll be those in the town who can and will handle any mob that shows its ugly face. I'd tell him all that—provided he is innocent. If he's guilty—well, run where he will, he'll be caught and brought back. Deer Lick is the safest place on earth for him, right now. Yes, if I knew where he is hiding, I'd tell him that, and not lose any time about it."

Ten minutes later be was speeding toward headquarters in his boat.

8

WHERE THE SHOT WAS FIRED

WHEN THE CITIZENS of Deer Lick awoke in the morning following the killing of Ben Stroud, they discovered that, some time during the night, a group of strangers had arrived quietly and taken possession of the town. All the newcomers were dressed alike, in uniforms similar to that worn by the lone ranger whom they had sought so diligently the night before.

That same ranger was no longer hard to find. He was, in fact, very much in evidence.

Deer Lick supported three saloons, and supported them well. Into one of them, which was conducted by Eli Banks, Calhoun walked. He was accompanied by one of his men.

"I'm putting a man in your place, Banks," he told the proprietor. "He is not to interfere with your business. Briefly, he is to see that all disturbances which might result in loss of human life are kept down. Tell your customers about it. Also, all your gambling tables, cards, dice, and the like, must go out the back door, and go this morning. No more gambling. No more brawling. There has been too much bloodshed here lately, and it's going to cease—beginning now."

Cal turned on his heel and departed. In each of the

remaining saloons he posted a man, and repeated, in substance, what he had said to Banks. The three saloonists took counsel together hurriedly then, after it was made known to them that the inspector had a dozen armed men with which to back up his orders, they submitted to what they felt was the inevitable. The law was coming into Deer Lick.

"Been expecting something like this to happen," Eli Banks explained to a customer. "Been expecting th' gove'ment to turn its eyes in this direction—an' now it's happened! Folks is gettin' sort of crowded for land to farm, in other sections, an' th' gove'ment is settin' up an' takin' notice of some of th' finest ground in th' whole nation. It's right here in L'Anguile Bottoms. Yes, sir! All it needs is drainin' an' it'll grow anything!"

"Whut's to become of us trappers?" a swamper wanted to know. "Ain't we-all got no rights? Does we have to give up our lan' an' our livin' jist to make a lot of furriners happy?"

"Don't none of you-all own th' land you air livin' on, do you?" Banks asked.

"No."

"Belongs to th' gove'ment, don't it?"

"You-all knows it does, well as I do," was the surly reply.

"All right. If th' land belongs to th' gove'ment, an' gove'ment takes a notion to put it to some good use— ain't that jest what's goin' to happen?"

"Lissen, Banks," the swamper said grimly. "Afore I'll give up th' ground I been a-livin' on since I war a mite of a boy, I'll make 'em a present of my dead carcass to fertilize with! An' I ain't talkin' jist to hear my head rattle, neither! I means it!"

That conversation was repeated around the town, and before night many swampers had called on Cal in his headquarters in an empty cabin on the bank of L'Anguile. They wanted to know when the government was coming to take their land away.

"Nobody is going to lose his land," Cal assured each caller. "As a matter of fact, this whole section is now open for homesteading. One hundred and sixty acres free to each man for the settling. If you want to hold what you have, why don't you file on it? Then it will be yours. If you sit still and let some other fellow homestead you out of what you have, whose fault will it be? Think it over."

There was much muttering and grumbling, and Cal, recognizing the signs, knew that a storm might break at any moment. It would break fiercely sooner or later.

In the meantime, he had two things in mind. One was to make Deer Lick bow to the law. That had to be. The place was far out of hand. To permit the citizens to go ahead as they had done in the past, settling their grievances against each other with gun or knife, simply would be folly. One rotten spot soon ruins an otherwise sound apple—and Cal's particular apple had many rotten spots.

The second task, which fortunately went hand in hand with the first, was the ferreting out and punishing of the man who had killed Ben Stroud. That had been a cold-blooded murder. An unarmed man had been shot in his own doorway, and the safety of the district demanded that the perpetrator of that deed be speedily brought to account.

Cal hoped that the message he had sent to Jim Hilliard, through Nan Brisco, would prove fruitful. If Jim Hilliard was innocent, then he would show up in Deer Lick. If guilty—well, he'd have to be brought in.

In the meantime Cal had a bit of investigating to do.

Lee Hilliard's body had been buried shortly after the rangers arrived. The corpse of Stroud lay in the room in the furniture store so lately occupied by the man he had killed.

After noon of the day of his arrival Cal went alone to the undertaker's. Left alone with the body of Stroud, he made a careful examination of the wound—particularly the course of the bullet which killed him.

"It ranged neither up nor down," was his conclusion. "Must have been shot from some place of even height with the doorway of Stroud's room. That ought to give me a lead."

Quitting the undertaker's, Cal summoned Tom Murdock, a particularly useful young ranger, and together they repaired to the rear of Stroud's store.

"Stroud stood on the sill," Cal pointed out. "I stood on the door log below. I had to reach up in order to rap on the panel. Now, Tom, what do you make of that?"

Murdock surveyed the lay of the ground immediately back of the store. It was grown up in weeds and brush for a distance of two hundred feet, approximately, and then the forest began. Beyond the weeds and in the edge of the forest four cabins were visible.

"Well," Tom answered, "a man, shooting at Stroud from that weed patch, would be a lot lower placed than his target. Did you trace the course of the bullet in Stroud's body?"

"I did. There was no upward trend."

"There would have been, had the bullet been fired from

the ground," Tom commented thoughtfully. "It went straight in, eh?"

"Exactly."

"Well, then, it was fired by somebody who perched in the branches of one of those trees over yonder—else from one of those four cabins. Couldn't have been done from any other place."

"Right!" Cal approved. "Now, you stand in the doorway, and I'll try and get a line on the place the bullet came from. It should not be hard to do. Stroud stood squarely in the doorway. Do you stand as he did."

Murdock took his place in the door, and Cal disappeared into the weed patch. Half an hour later he returned.

"Well?" Murdock queried.

"The bullet was fired from the cabin directly across the patch from us, else from the woods behind it," Cal informed him. "Couldn't have come from any other point. I stood in the doorway of each cabin, and from the central one only could I have sent a bullet into you. Come along now, and we'll examine the trees back of the cabin. We may find something there."

"Who does that central cabin belong to?" Murdock asked, as they entered the forest.

"A chap named Dave Hawkins," was the reply. "I learned something else, too, from the native woman in the cabin below. There was no one in Dave's place. I learned that Gobbler Brisco usually stops with Dave when in Deer Lick—and that he was in Dave's cabin the night Stroud was killed."

9

TO BECOME A HANGING ROPE

MURDOCK WAS SILENT for a time after Cal's disclosure. Then: "I remember, inspector, something you told me when I first joined up with the organization; it was this: 'Don't be taken in by the obvious.'"

"I repeat it," Cal replied. "That's why I'm searching among these trees. Any fool would know that an investigator, provided there should be one, would inevitably arrive at the conclusion that the bullet which killed Stroud came from the doorway of the central cabin back of his store."

"Well, would he not, being wise, figure that the investigator would reckon that as obvious, and disregard it?"

"Maybe he—the killer—did not give the investigator credit for so much shrewdness," Cal replied. "Maybe he wanted the trail to lead to that particular door. What then?"

"He'd still be hid, anyhow," Murdock reflected aloud. "If investigation led to Dave Hawkins's cabin, it certainly would not lead to a certain tree—"

"And here, if I'm not mistaken, is the tree!" Cal exclaimed, stooping over the loamy soil directly below an oak ten inches in diameter. See!"

"Boot prints!" Murdock ejaculated. "And, by the Eternal, a boot heel stuck in the earth in one of them!"

Cal pointed upward to where a limb extended above the point under inspection, about fifteen feet from the ground. "He hung from that limb, then dropped to earth," he said. "It rained the night before Stroud was killed.

"I know, because I was caught out on the bayou and got a good soaking. Those tracks were made since the rain, either last night, or night before. It doesn't follow that Stroud's murderer was in this tree, or made these tracks; but, having in mind that bit about not being misled by the obvious, I'm going to assume for the present that he was in this tree and did make those tracks."

"Kind of funny that he'd run off and leave his boot heel," Murdock remarked thoughtfully.

"Bear in mind that he had to hurry in order to be where he should be when the hurrah was raised," Cal told him. "Also, being excited, he might not have noticed the loss of the heel until he'd got a few yards away from the spot. He wouldn't know just where to look for it, and to strike a match or make a light would be, under the circumstances, extremely dangerous."

"He could have got it next day, couldn't he?"

"Surely. Still, take the thing home to yourself. Say you had killed a man from this tree—would you willingly return to the spot, taking a chance on being seen here, so soon after the deed?"

"Would his presence here mean anything to whoever might see him?"

"There is something called conscience inside all of us, Tom," Cal replied. "The feeling of guilt undoubtedly throbbing inside the killer would cause him to imagine all sorts of things. Any one seeing him here might not attach any importance to it, but to the murderer it would be different. Standing on this spot, he'd be apt to view his presence here from his own guilty standpoint, instead of that of the observer. Still, you will say, that boot heel is very important.

"He should not leave it here. Not at all, I answer. The chance of any one looking for a sign among these trees, when it would seem infinitely more probable that such sign should be sought in the central cabin, would strike him as being remote. If found, what would it signify? What would it prove? Nothing. He would be a fool to come nosing over here, searching for that heel. No—he had a better way. At least, it would seem a better way to him. And I'll bet I'm right."

"What way is that?"

"He'd destroy the boots."

Murdock considered that for a moment.

"Very likely you are right, Cal," he agreed. "What then?"

"A lot. First, I'm going to climb that tree."

Cal immediately began to shin up the oak, hugging it in his arms and propelling himself upward by the power of his legs. When he reached the first limb he perched upon it and considered the situation. Presently he began picking something from the bark—several objects—and dropping what he found into his pocketbook. After a bit he climbed higher, and presently he called down softly.

"I've got a good view of Stroud's back door," he said. "And a comfortable place to rest while waiting. That killer knew I was determined to see Stroud, and he figured that, sooner or later, I'd find him in, and that Stroud would show up with the light behind him. He climbed up here and waited."

After a bit he climbed down. "You see, Tom," he said, "I've got a double motive for wanting to run this killer down. Punishment, of course—and then, there is no denying that if I hadn't called Stroud to the door he might be alive to-day."

"Yeah," Murdock replied. "But this chap who wanted Stroud's life so badly would have got him soon anyhow. No trouble for a man who is willing to shoot from ambush to make his kill, Cal. That can always be done."

"Guess you are right, boy. Guess you are. Still, I've got that double motive just the same. I'm going to get that killer, Tom."

"What did you find on the tree trunk?" his assistant inquired.

"A few threads of wool," was the reply. "Rubbed from the trousers of the man who killed Stroud. I wouldn't be at all surprised if those few flimsy threads do not become, a bit later, a hempen rope around the killer's neck. That boot heel is important, of course, but these threads, unless I am greatly mistaken, will hang our man."

10

WOULD-BE SON-IN-LAW

THE NEXT MORNING Calhoun took to the bayou in his dugout and proceeded downstream to Gobbler Brisco's cabin. Murdock had been instructed to make certain investigations during his absence, and in the meantime there was little the inspector could do. A visit to Brisco's might develop something.

On coming out of the brush in front of Gobbler's door he halted at sound of voices. Standing in concealment behind the trunk of a gum tree which shaded the roof of the cabin, he listened.

"So you air bent an' determined on havin' a skunk like Jim Hilliard for a son-in-law, eh?" The voice had a familiar ring, and Cal, after a moment's thought, placed it. Henry Pliler was speaking. "A feller which shoots his enemies from th' dark! One which will soon have a rope around his neck! That's th' sort of man you air goin' to let Nan marry, huh?"

"I reckons, Henry Pliler, that it ain't none of yore business who Nan marries with!" came Gobbler's voice in hot retort. "You ain't got no chance with her—an' never did have!"

"That ain't so!" Henry declared. "Nan had jist about

49

made up her mind to wed with me, when Jim Hilliard finally up an' asked her to marry with him. She figgered, of course, that Jim would be rich one of these days, seein' that his pap was a big man in the deestrick. I wa'n't rich—jist tryin' to git ahead, an' not travelin' very fast! Yeah, she agreed to marry with Jim, account he was goin' to have money an' a lot of influence. That's th' onliest reason!"

"Nan ain't here right now," Gobbler told him. "So in course she kain't dispute that. She will, though, when she gits back. She never did have no notion of marryin' with you!"

"Wharat is Nan?"

"That ain't none of yore damned business!"

Cal heard a chair squeak, as though its occupant arose hastily. Then Gobbler spoke again.

"Better set down, Henry, an' take it easy. As long as I let you-all set in my cabin, an' don't throw you out atter th' things you has said, you better make th' most of it. You ain't no match fur me, even if you air a young man. Effen you thinks you is, jist try me once!"

The chair squeaked again, and Cal surmised that Pliler had taken Gobbler's advice.

"Lissen, Gobbler," came in persuasive tones from Henry. "I want you to look at this thing reasonable—an' not be always thinkin' about fightin' with somebody! I didn't come here to fight! I come to git Nan to promise to marry with me—an' here you-all air talkin' about throwin' me outen yore cabin! Is that any way to treat a man which aims to be yore son-in-law? I asks you!"

"You ain't goin' to be no son-in-law to me, Henry!" Gobbler declared. "In th' fust place, Nan marries who she wants to marry—an' she p'intedly don't want to marry with you. In th' next place—whut has you got, that you think you kin take care of a wife? I asks you!"

There was silence for a moment, then Pliler answered slowly.

"I got a lot more than you-all thinks I has," he replied. "A lot more."

"How come? Ain't yore whole entire stock an' th' buildin' it sets in under chattel mortgage to Ben Stroud? Didn't you-all borry th' money from Ben to go into business with, an' did you-all ever pay it back? Not that I ever heerd of!"

"You don't hear everything, Gobbler," was the reply. "I paid out to Ben—an' I got his release. Got th' mor-gage paper, an' his signature writ on it. Now," triumphantly, "whut you sayin' to that?"

"I says I thinks you air lyin'," was the instant retort. "You-all ain't made enough money to pay off. With th' price of pelts skyrocketin' like all git out, account of Ben an' Lee's war, you-all wa'n't gittin' a holt of no fur at all. Couldn't trade any in for traps an' nets, lak you did afore, because you couldn't meet th' competishun. Wharat did you-all git th' money to pay Ben out?"

"I got it!" Pliler declared, his voice rising. "Got it, an' paid out! I got Ben's signature on th' release! They ain't no way of gittin' round that, is they?"

"I reckon not—if you-all has got it," was the answer. "But that don't make you no more welcome to me as a son-in-law, nor to Nan as a husband! An' that's settled!"

"Rather have a murderer, eh?" came in scathing tones. "Rather have a skunk like Jim Hilliard—"

"Don't say that no more!"

Cal started, recognizing the voice of Nan. If her father had told the truth about her being away, then she must have returned by the lean-to door. At any rate, she was inside the cabin.

"Nan!" It was Gobbler speaking.

"I mean it!" cried the girl. "Jim Hilliard ain't no skunk, an' he never shot Ben Stroud."

"Whut did he run for?" Pliler demanded.

"For reasons which he considered good!" Nan exclaimed. "An' he didn't run far, Henry Pliler. Now you git outen this cabin, an' don't you never set foot inside it agin! If pappy won't make you git, I will!"

"Put that gun down, Nan!" came in stern tones from Gobbler.

"She won't shoot," Henry Pliler laughed. "Nan—"

"You've got jest one minute to git out," came in cool tones from the girl. If you ain't gone by then you won't ever know you air a liar about me not shootin'—because you'll be daid!"

At that juncture Cal thought it wise to interfere.

"Hello!" he called, stepping from behind the tree and clubbing his rifle with which to ward off the hounds, should they be about. "Hello, Brisco! Are you at home?"

Gobbler appeared in the doorway. There was relief, mingled with surprise, in his face.

"Come right in, Mr. Ranger," he invited. "Air you-all huntin' another snack?"

"Not this time," Cal laughed, entering the room. "How are you, Miss Nan? That breakfast of yours was so good, however, I wouldn't refuse— Oh!" He broke off upon Pliler.

"I beg pardon, but you've got company. Mr. Pliler, is it not? Perhaps I'm intruding."

"Henry war about to go," Gobbler told him, glancing significantly at Pliler. "Sorry you-all kain't stay no longer, Hen," he grinned. "See you some other time."

Pliler, his face red and scowling, moved toward the door.

"Yeah," he said, pausing on the sill, "you'll see me agin, Gobbler—an' so will Nan."

With that he was gone.

Cal crossed the room to a window and watched Pliler until he disappeared from view, then turned upon Gobbler.

"I heard a lot of what was said in here, awhile ago," he told him. "Glad I did. No comment, either from you or Nan. I've got some questions to ask—and I want answers! Get that?"

Nan sat down, the rifle still in her hands. Gobbler gave Cal a glance full of astonishment then, stayed by the look in Cal's eyes, he, too, sat down.

"I'll admit that I'm in the middle of a riddle that seems impossible of solution," the ranger went on. "I want all the help I can get. I hate to believe Jim Hilliard guilty of so cowardly a murder, and I'm trying to believe that you, Brisco, did not do it—"

"Me!" Gobbler gasped.

"Pappy didn't!" cried Nan.

"Hush!" Cal ordered. "You hated Ben Stroud because Ben was the enemy of Lee Hilliard, Gobbler. Hate is often the one and only motive back of murder." He paused, then went on slowly: "There are three suspects in this case—Jim Hilliard, Gobbler Brisco, and Henry Pliler—"

"Pliler—Henry Pliler! Why, whut makes you-all think Henry mought of did it?" Gobbler demanded, astonished.

"Nan—debt—ambition," Cal replied. "Maybe you won't understand that, but you will later. But your skirts are not clean yet, Brisco. I'm going to ask you some questions—and be careful that you answer truthfully and fully."

Gobbler nodded, his eyes dumbly upon the inspector.

"Where were you when Ben Stroud was shot?"

"I war at Henry Pliler's store."

"Are you sure?"

"In course, I am!"

"Do you not, as a rule, stay with Dave Hawkins, in his cabin, when stopping overnight in Deer Lick?"

"Yeah. But that night," he shot a glance of apprehension in Nan's direction, "we-all had a leetle game of kyards, an' I wa'n't at Dave's. Nan don't lak for me to gamble—"

"Never mind that," Cal admonished. "Who played in the game?"

"Well, at fust thar was Henry Pliler, Dave Hawkins, Tom Barbee, an' me. We war playin' in Henry's room at the back of his store."

11

GREEN INK AND PURPLE

CAL CONSIDERED THAT with knitted brows. Then: "You said 'at fust.' Who joined you later?"

"Nobody. Henry drapped out. Long about ten o'clock, an' that left us three playin'."

"Oh, I see! And where did Henry 'drap' to?"

"He said th' light hurt his eyes, 'count of his head aching, so he went over to Dave's cabin. Said for us to play on, an' he'd make th' rest of th' night out at Dave's."

"And the rest of you played on—until when?"

Gobbler cleared his throat, eyes on something outside the door, and, apparently, not hearing Cal's question. The inspector glanced outside, saw nothing, and spoke again.

"I want your attention, Brisco!" he said sternly. "What's the matter with you, anyway?"

Gobbler brought his eyes back to Cal's with visible effort.

"Whut war that las' question?" he asked. "I war a thinkin' about somethin' an' didn't onderstand."

Cal looked at him long and keenly, then put the question again.

"How long did you fellows play?"

"Ontil we heered th' shot which kilt Ben," was the answer.

"Humph! I guess if what you say is true—and it can, of course, be either proved or disproved—it lets you out of the case. Narrows down now to Jim Hilliard and Pliler. Now, what happened to distract your attention a moment ago?"

"I reckon it wa'n't nothin' much," was the answer. "Only, when I went in Henry's room that night I set my rifle gun in a corner beside hisn. When I heered th' shot which kilt Ben, I lep up and went for my gun. My gun war thar, all right, but it war th' onliest one which was. Henry's war gone. Maybe that don't mean nothin'—an' maybe it do. I didn't place no importance on it, ontil you-all kind of p'inted me to'ards Henry. Then I happens to remember about it."

"You are sure Henry's rifle was there when you put yours in the corner?" Cal asked, eyes searching the face of the old trapper.

"Absolutely. Henry's gun war thar when I went in, an' it war gone when I tuck mine up," was the positive statement.

"Did any one else come in or go out of the room after you put your rifle down?"

"Nobody. Jest Henry."

"Then it is absolutely certain that Henry Pliler took his rifle with him when he went out to Dave's cabin," Cal said. "Now, would there be anything unusual in that?"

"Well, yeah," was the answer. "Henry always packs a short gun in his pocket. Whut would he want with his rifle, lessen he war goin' deer or b'ar huntin'?"

Cal nodded slowly.

"Or man-hunting," he supplemented.

Gobbler started, but said nothing.

"Now, Nan," said Cal, turning suddenly toward the girl, "what has Jim to say for himself? Is he coming in?"

The girl got up, a startled look in her eyes. "I—he—why, Mr. Inspector," she stammered, "whut makes you-all ask me—"

"Never mind, Nan," Cal broke in. "I know you have been in touch with Hilliard. If I'd wanted him very badly I could have got him by following you. Speak up. What is he going to do? Unless he acts, and acts quickly, and in the way an innocent man should—I'm going after him, and when my men go after a man they get him! Tell me, what is Jim Hilliard going to do?"

For an instant Nan hesitated, but the look in Cal's eyes warned her that he was in deadly earnest.

"He's comin' to Deer Lick, this afternoon!" she broke out suddenly. "That's all I'm goin' to tell you. He'll be there about sundown—an' he won't need nobody, even rangers, to protect him from a mob! He'll have all the protection he needs!"

Nan turned and, before Cal could intercept her, dashed out the back door. Like a deer she fled into the timber.

Calhoun, accompanied by Gobbler, returned to Deer Lick at noon.

"You stay around where I can get hold of you, Gobbler," Cal ordered when they separated at the door of the inspector's cabin.

"Shore," Gobbler agreed, and proceeded to Banks's saloon.

"Now, Murdock," said Cal, immediately upon entering headquarters, "what have you dug up?"

Murdock's face was rather crestfallen, and Cal knew that things had not fallen out well.

"We've combed the town, and there isn't a pair of trousers in the whole place from which those woolen threads could have come," Murdock answered. "Jeans, corduroy, denim, and brown duck," he went on, "are here in plenty, but pants of the peculiar gray-green color we want are not here."

Cal nodded slowly. "They are of a texture little known in the swamp," he commented. "Still, they have been here, because we found the evidence on the tree. Did you search Pliler's place?"

"Thoroughly. No trousers, or coat, remotely resembling what we are looking for."

"What about boots?"

"Pliler's are there. We searched his bedroom. Boots there, in good shape—heels and all."

"Did you investigate those other ex-lovers of Nan Brisco's?" Cal asked.

"We did. All innocent of possessing gray-green, woolen trousers or incriminating boots. It's my opinion that the chap who wore those trousers and those boots is not in the town."

"You may be right," Cal replied thoughtfully.

"We found something in Henry Pliler's room that might or might not be important," Murdock went on, drawing two papers from his pocket. "These things wouldn't have attracted me, only they evidently were quite recently associated with Ben Stroud, and Stroud's signature is suspiciously fresh on one of them."

He laid the papers before Cal.

"Hum! One is a chattel mortgage in which Pliler tied up everything he owns, stock, store building and all, in Stroud's favor," he commented. "I've heard about this mortgage before. Until I heard about it, and certain other matters, I had no more reason to suspect Henry than to suspect any of the other fellows who might like to put a quietus on Hilliard, because of Nan Brisco. Now—well, let us see what we have here."

He turned the document over, and his eyes fell on a written release which had been scribbled on the margin of the sheet. It was correct and regular in phrasing, written in a hand clearly not that of Stroud, whose signature appeared at the bottom.

"Written in green ink, quite fresh, and purporting to be signed by Ben," Cal commented. "Now for the other paper."

He spread it open on his knee and looked long at it. Finally he read it aloud:

"HENRY PLILER:

"Your mortgage and note are long overdue. I've got to have the money. This fur war has been a drain, and I need cash. You pay up, and do it before the week is out, or I will take possession of your stuff and sell it out.

"BEN STROUD.

"Ben was right on top of Henry, judging from this note," Cal commented. "Written in purple ink. Signature on the note and the one on the release are close enough in resemblance to warrant us in believing them to have been written by the same hand. The ink, now—did you look into that?"

"I did," Murdock replied. "The note was evidently written in Stroud's store. There is a bottle of purple ink on the desk there—one bottle, and no more of any kind in the building. Henry Pliler has a bottle of green ink on his desk—and no other."

"Then Stroud must have signed the release in Henry's store—wait!"

Cal's eyes were intent upon the sheet of paper containing the note written by Stroud. In the center of the page, slightly above the text, appeared a green blot. Rather, it was a half blot; circular on the right side and straight on the left—much the same as a circle cut in half and the left half taken away.

The mortgage next came under Cal's eyes, and his face lit up suddenly.

The missing half of the blot was on the mortgage, just below the signature.

Taking the two papers, Cal laid the note over the lower half of the mortgage, brought the sheet containing the mortgage down slowly until the two half blots became one!

"There you are!" he cried exultantly. "Pliler, or some one, had the papers in this position—laboriously, but cleverly, copying Stroud's signature, and a blot fell on the two sheets, where they lapped. Look, Murdock, can't you see the difference in the genuine signature and the bogus?"

"I can now," Murdock declared. "But it is good enough to fool most anybody! Stroud didn't go to Henry's place and execute that release. Henry did the executing himself."

"Exactly."

The door opened, and Henry Pliler came into the room.

12

COME A-RIDING

"YOU—YOU, WHUT YOU been searchin' my place for?" Pliler snarled.

The man's face was mottled with anger and his speech choked with rage.

"Somebody been searching your store, Henry?" Cal asked calmly. "Sit down, compose yourself, and tell us about it."

"You know it, damn you!" Pliler charged. "Dave told me all about it, atter I got back frum down th' bayou. Yore men come an' searched th' store an' my room in th' back. Tuck some papers away, too. I want them papers—an' I want 'em damned quick!"

Cal nodded to Murdock, and the next instant Pliler found himself forced into a chair. A tug at his waistband, and his pistol slid into Cal's hand.

"Bite, now, Henry," the inspector grinned. "Your fangs are drawn!"

Pliler's blue lips spouted profanity. The two rangers listened quietly until, from sheer exhaustion, he subsided.

"Now," said Cal, "I'll explain that searching. You were not alone in it. We searched half a dozen other places, including all the dry goods places. We found a lot of things—including these two documents. You'll have to explain them—but that will come later. In the meantime, will you behave, or shall we put irons on you?"

"You ain't got no right, by God!" Pliler shouted. "You can't put handcuffs on me!"

"Maybe we can't—but we will," Cal told him tersely. "Get out of here, and stay out, if you don't want us to do it. Furthermore, if you are caught with a gun, short or long, in your possession again while we are here, you'll go up for it. That goes as it lays! Lead him to the door, Murdock!"

The big ranger yanked Pliler out of the chair, rushed him to the door and thrust him into the street. Then he faced Calhoun.

"He's dangerous," he said. "Why not lock him up?"

"Let's consider Henry first," Cal replied. "Have we got anything on him? That forgery? Well, yes. It can be proved. But that's all."

"Didn't he kill Stroud?" came the amazed query.

"Let us see if we can make a case against him. Stroud holds his note and mortgage, covering all he owns, and is pressing payment. Henry can't, or won't, pay. Can't, probably. He hates Stroud. Henry is ambitious—covets influence and prestige, but has to play second fiddle to Stroud and Hilliard. Then Stroud kills Hilliard, and he's playing second only to one.

"He won't be long, however, because Jim Hilliard will surely come back and kill the slayer of his father. Jim comes, and Henry hears him say that he won't harm Stroud if the latter killed old Lee in fair battle. Henry knows Lee fell trying to get Ben. Therefore Jim will not rid him of the man he hates and envies.

"Now, Henry wants to marry Nan Brisco, and he thinks that Jim Hilliard is the only obstacle to his desire. So he takes his rifle, shoots Ben. Of course, everybody will take it for granted that Jim Hilliard did it. Probably Jim will be lynched, and the matter closed. Stroud will be out of the way, and so will Jim. I think I know how Henry figured to get hold of that mortgage and forge Stroud's signature. I'll know for certain in a few minutes.

"Then I show up, and Henry begins to realize that the law might take a hand in the game. He goes ahead, however, safe in the belief that Jim Hilliard will have to pay the penalty for the crime he himself committed.

"Now, if what I have adduced proves to be true, we have a case against Henry—but one we'll have a devil of a time proving. Come. We'll see if we can't add a few more links."

Cal led the way directly to the undertaker's store.

"Who helped you bring Stroud's body here?" he asked Benjy Ford.

"Thar was Fred Names, Ellis Fisher, Joe Brunt, an' Hen Pliler," the old man answered.

"Did anybody help you prepare Ben for burial?"

"Yeah. Hen Pliler did."

"So. Did Stroud have—let's see what articles he had in his pockets. You have them yet, of course?"

"Shore."

The old man went to his desk, and opened a drawer. Among other things there was a big leather wallet. This Cal took up and examined.

"Full of papers—mortgages, notes, and the like," he commented to Murdock. "Did he make a practice of carrying business documents with him?" he asked Ford.

"Whar else would he carry 'em?" the old man demanded. "Leave 'em in his desk fur a fire to come along an' destroy, maybe?"

"I'd think he'd keep them in a safe," Cal suggested.

"Thar ain't no sich thing here," was the reply. "Don't reckon thar's airy iron box of any kind, ceptin' th' leetle one at th' post office."

"Let's go," Cal said leading the way out. "We've learned something. Pliler could—probably did—extract his mortgage from Ben's wallet, while he was helping prepare him for burial. Helped for that very purpose, no doubt. The chain is getting stronger."

They were on the walk, when Cal spoke, and Murdock stopped abruptly.

"That's all very well," he said, "but we're forgetting something."

"What?"

"A certain boot-heel, and a pair of gray-green trousers!"

Cal's face suddenly fell.

"Damn that boot, and those trousers!" he exclaimed irritably. "But for them, I'd pinch Pliler this minute! As it is—" he paused.

"Well," Murdock bade him. "Go on. As it is—what?"

But Cal's eyes were directed up the street to something moving toward the village from the Crampton road. A great cloud of dust made it difficult to distinguish objects, but in the swirl the inspector made out men on horseback, then, a bit later, a long line of covered wagons, drawn by mules. The entire cavalcade headed down the village street in the direction of the bank of L'Anguile Bayou.

Citizens poured forth into the street, exchanging

comments with one another. Surprise and mystification marked the faces of all.

Suddenly Calhoun grasped Murdock's arm.

"That fellow in the lead—on the roan horse!" he exclaimed. "If it ain't Jim Hilliard—then I don't know split beans from coffee!"

13

PELTS ARE TOO HIGH

THE DUSTY TRAIN moved slowly down the street, and presently Cal was able to form an estimate of the number of wagons in it.

"Thirty wagons!" he exclaimed. "Filled with men, women, children, and household goods! Homesteaders—by the Eternal! Settlers! And Jim Hilliard riding at the head!"

Murdock grasped his arm fiercely, and shouted above the din:

"Better call all the boys, Cal! Yonder's our man—Jim Hilliard! He's wearing gray-green trousers tucked into the tops of his boots! I told you the man that climbed that tree wasn't in Deer Lick!"

Cal looked closely at the man in front of the cavalcade, almost opposite him then. It was as Murdock had said. He wore trousers of the peculiar color which matched the threads of wool in his pocket.

Cal looked—but he took no action. He waited. Presently Hilliard drew his horse up, and the train of wagons came to a stand. Horsemen rode up to Jim, all grim-faced men, armed and alert. The noise of dogs barking, children crying and men and women calling to and fro, was all but deafening. Finally Jim, aided by his fellows, restored a measure of silence. Then he spoke—and all the town of Deer Lick was there to hear.

"Men!" he cried. "When I ran away from Deer Lick, a few nights ago, I did not do so because I was guilty of that damnable murder! I ran because I knew the temper of you all—knew what you would do when you thought I had murdered Ben Stroud in cold blood. I admit that everything pointed to me as being the murderer. There would have been no chance for me had I fallen into your hands that night. So I ran—to come back again as you see."

Silence had come upon them all. Cal glanced around and saw the pale face of Henry Pliler half a dozen paces back of him. His eyes, full of hate, were on the horseman's face. Jim went on talking:

"A year ago I left Deer Lick," he reminded them. "Everybody was told that I had gone to Memphis seeking a job. That was only partly true. I had gone to Memphis seeking—but not seeking a job. This is the true state of affairs:

"Father came to me one night, a year ago, and said these words to me:

" 'Jim, the day of the trapper and the fur buyer is almost gone. This country is going to be settled by farmers, and farmers here will spell the end of fur animals. Boy, turn your attention to the land. If you want to have something for yourself, and do something big and worth while for the swamp country, take up a homestead and try to interest others in doing so. There's the hill country, back in Tennessee, where you were born.

" 'A lot of poor devils are trying to coax a living out of those red clay hills and mountains, when they could be living here in this paradise. One or two farmers couldn't make a go of it in this section, because the swampers would drive them out. But a colony of them could. Think it over.'

"I did think it over—and I acted. I went back to my old home, talked to my old neighbors, and the result is before you. Every man of us has homesteaded land in and around Deer Lick. We have come to settle on it.

"A week before I got the news of my father's death, my friends here set out for their Promised Land. They would have to travel slowly. It was my intention to come on by train and reach here a day or two in advance of them. Then the news came. I hurried home. You all know what happened the night I got back.

"I ran away to join my friends, the homesteaders. I knew that we would be strong enough to prevent violence against me when I got back. Now here we are."

The little knot of horsemen drew closer about Jim, eyes searching among the crowd, alert to detect the first sign of hostility.

Hilliard continued:

"A few days before I heard about father being killed, I received a letter from him. I'm going to read it—then you will understand why I did not come back here with murder in my heart toward Ben Stroud."

He drew a letter from his pocket, and read:

DEAR JIM:

The price of pelts is too high. I'm not referring to the war between Stroud and me. That's over and done with—almost. What I mean is this:

A million acres of the finest land in the United States, and in the L'Anguile Bottoms, are producing nothing but hides. That's what I mean, Jim. The country is paying the potential productiveness of those acres for a few pelts!

It's too high a price—and lots of folks are beginning to realize it. The government is. The natives have held the swamp selfishly, in order to carry on shiftless habits of life. They are drones—and the hide buyer is simply a sort of king-drone. Remember my advice to you: turn your attention to the land. Make corn and cotton grow where the river grass and flags now are. You can help, and I believe you will.

One last word: I am going out soon—within a few days, at longest—to settle my business with Stroud. He has broke me. If I'd broke him he'd go for me. I know that. If Ben gets me, he will do it fairly, and if it falls out that he does, you must not take up the quarrel. There is none between you and Ben. Feuds are wrong—they involve too many and last too long. The fight has been between Stroud and me. Let it end with us.

Silence followed the reading of the letter, though Cal saw many a grizzled old man surreptitiously wipe his eyes.

"Do you think that, in the face of that letter, I would come back here to kill Ben Stroud? No. I came to find out whether or not my father had fallen fairly—and learned that he had. That's all, men—except that my friends and I mean to settle on farms and till the soil. Father was right. The price of pelts is too high!"

"Hold on, there!" cried Bullhead Brown, as Jim lifted his horse's reins preparatory to moving on. "You ain't brung no proof that you didn't kill Ben Stroud. What air you-all goin' to do, you rangers, leave him git away?"

Cal stepped to Jim's side.

"How about that oak tree you climbed—the one back of Stroud's store, and from which you could get a fine view of him standing in the door?" he asked quietly.

Hilliard stared at him in amazement. "How did you know I climbed that tree?" he demanded.

"I know it, and that's sufficient," Cal replied. "Why don't you tell all there is to tell?"

"I meant to go straight to you with the rest of my story," Jim replied. "But if you want it here in public—all right!"

Jim dismounted, and a number of his companions did so, too. The crowd pressed in—and Cal noted that his men were stationed here and there among them.

"I couldn't sleep, that night I came home—and little wonder," Hilliard said. "I was sitting in the doorway of my room in the back of the store. Don't know what attracted my attention that way, but my eyes were on the door of Dave Hawkins's cabin when a jet of flame burst from it, followed instantly by the report of a rifle.

"I leaped up, and then I saw what had happened to Stroud. Saw him crumple up in your arms, Mr. Calhoun.

"It didn't take me long to figure out what would happen to me, since I would undoubtedly be accused of the killing. No matter who did it, I wouldn't be alive to prove it, ten minutes after the mob got headed for me. I ran. Ran out the back door, and toward the timber. I had to cross back of a big weed patch in order to gain shelter—and I ran into a man. A man who was making tracks from a point in a direct line from Hawkins's cabin.

"We collided, there was a muttered oath—then the moon came from behind a cloud, and I recognized the man. At the moment of impact, he dropped a rifle which he had been carrying. He ran on and left it. I picked it up. Then I ran until I came to the woods.

"There I paused. I knew, or thought I knew, who had done the shooting. I was certain he had not recognized me. Maybe after a little I could venture back, find you, Mr. Calhoun, and tell what I had seen.

"I felt certain that the killer would remain here, because he would think I wouldn't dare show my face in Deer Lick again. And if I did he would have nothing to fear, since I would have already been tried and convicted in the minds of the citizens—as well as the rangers.

"So I climbed up that tree in order to be hidden from the mob when it searched. I sat up there awhile, then concluded to give up the idea of going back. I'd be safer after I joined my friends. So I climbed down, losing a boot-heel when I did so, and set out for the camp of the home-steaders. That's all, I guess."

14

THE LAST KING-DRONE

"EXCEPT THE NAME of the man you saw," said Calhoun.

"It was Henry Pliler!"

"That's a lie—a damned lie!" yelled Pliler, who stood near. "You can't prove no such thing!"

"I kept the rifle," Jim answered simply. "Just like it was when I found it—the exploded shell in the chamber. It's yours, Pliler, Everybody will recognize it!"

He drew the gun from his saddle-boot, and held it up.

"In course, it's my gun!" Pliler exclaimed. "But it's been missin' for more than a week back! It war stole outen my room, an' I laid low about it, figgerin' to ketch th' thief with it! Jim Hilliard got holt of it some way, kilt Ben, now he's tryin' to put th' rope which belongs around his neck, around mine instead!"

"That's Henry's rifle!" Gobbler Brisco shouted. "An' th' night Ben war kilt it was a settin' in th' corner of his room— as Tom Barbee will swar to, an' so will I! Henry lef' th' store about two hours afore Ben was shot—an' he tuck th' rifle with him! Whut Henry says about somebody stealin' it, is a p'int blank lic!"

Cal turned toward Pliler. It was time for action.

One of the horses from which a homesteader had

dismounted, stood near the merchant. In one leap he was astride the animal, and had sent him plunging into the crowd. A moment, and he was into the road and going like the wind.

Cal, without a word, leaped to the back of Hilliard's horse, and set off at a dead lope.

The horse in front was a good one—but Cal's was better. When Pliler gained the timber line, Cal was on his heels.

"Stop!" the inspector called. "You can't get away, Pliler! Stop—or I'll drop you!"

For answer, Pliler turned in his saddle and, whipping out a revolver, fired at Cal. The bullet missed the ranger—but struck his mount squarely in the forehead. The horse quivered, dropped to his knees, attempted to rise again, then dropped back dead.

But Cal had not fallen with him. Realizing what had happened, he leaped from the saddle, swung his six-gun over a crooked elbow—and sent Henry Pliler tumbling face down into the dirt of the road.

When the inspector reached him, Pliler was dead.

Jim Hilliard and his homesteaders made good on their land—holding it in spite of all the natives could do. In that they had the support of Calhoun and his rangers, which, in fine, means that they had the government behind them. **THE UNITED STATES** Land Office also had the idea that the price of pelts was much too high.

THE SWAMP ANGEL

*He Was as Elusive as an Autumn Wind,
and There Were Hundreds Beholden to
Him for Their Food and Clothing*

1

SINKING OF THE *LINDA LEE*

AT EXACTLY FIVE minutes after nine o'clock in the evening, Kansas City, Fort Scott & Memphis Train Number Two, carrying two passenger coaches, a baggage car, and a combination express and mail car, arrived on the west bank of the Mississippi River, opposite Memphis. She was on time to the minute.

A brakeman ran ahead, turned a switch, signaled the engineer with his lantern, and the train ran off the main line onto a "Y." When the circuit of the Y was completed, the train had reversed herself—the engine heading west instead of east. Again the brakeman signaled, and the engineer began backing down a mile-long incline to the bank of the river.

At the foot of the inclined track a ferryboat lay at anchor. Its function was to transport trains from one bank of the river to the other. In the year 1890, there were few bridges across the Mississippi, and there was none at this particular point.

The train came to a stop at the river's edge, then moved on again until the two rear coaches were safely bestowed side by side, in a tunnel-like passage in the boat's center. Then the brakeman pulled a pin, separated the balance of

Cal was gathered closely in the embrace of powerful arms—

the train from that part aboard the ferry, and immediately thereafter the little transport puffed away with its burden.

Thirty minutes later the ferry, having delivered the two coaches to an engine crew on the Memphis side, returned to its Arkansas moorings. The trip did not usually require so long a time, but on this evening the river was running high, the current swift, and progress was slow.

The ferryboat's crew of "roughnecks," four tough-looking white men of assorted sizes and varying ages, leaped ashore, made the ferry fast, then stood with watchful eyes upon the cars backing slowly aboard. The two remaining coaches—the baggage, and combination mail and express cars—were safely deposited in the tunnel.

"Good night, skipper!" the engineer yelled from his cab. His responsibility ceased then and there; the train would leave Memphis under the guidance of another driver, with a fresh engine.

"See you next trip, Mounds," the lank ferryboat captain bawled in return. "Cast off there, you ague-ridden, splay-footed, wall-eyed rum suckers! What you paid for? To

—as the figure in the water struck toward the Pigeon

stand on th' bank till yore feet take root in th' sand? Cast off, damn you—"

There followed an eruption of profanity which would have chilled the marrow in the bones of one not accustomed to the ways of the river in general—and boat captains in particular. The "ground-hogs" went leisurely about the work of casting off. They knew the captain—knew that it was just his little way.

The pilot jerked a bell-rope, the engineer backed slowly into the current, and the boat felt its way slowly into the pall of darkness that clothed the giant river.

On the Tennessee shore the conductor of Train Number Two stood on the levee, watch in hand, and scowled darkly at the ferrymaster, who had charge of the work of the little transport.

"The *Linda Lee* is taking her time getting the rest of my train across!" he growled. "We were on time at the Junction—now we are fifteen minutes behind schedule! Why don't the transport company junk the old tub, and get a boat that can get up and move?"

The ferrymaster made no reply. None was expected. The two men were very good friends, and understood each other. The *Linda Lee* was, it may be said here, a very good boat; plenty fast enough for the purpose she served.

Ten more minutes passed, while the conductor fussed and fumed, watch held under the rays of his lantern. Then the ferrymaster suddenly came to life.

"By George, Jim!" he exclaimed to the trainman. "The *Linda* must be making the crossing with her lights out! That's strange—not even a riding light! Captain Blount wouldn't do that, I'm sure! Must be something wrong!"

"They've left the Arkansas side," the conductor declared. "I heard her whistle off. Say, Turner, what could happen to her? She's a good, sound old hull, ain't she?"

"Of course!" was the response. "I can't understand why she has her lights out! That's what gets me! There might be something wrong with them, of course. Kerosene played out. But that is extremely unlikely. We'll wait a few minutes longer—"

"We won't do any such thing!" snapped the conductor. "Two cars of my train are on that transport—and I'm going to look after 'em!"

Five minutes thereafter, Captain Turner, the ferrymaster, and Conductor Jim Seeds, were pulling for the Arkansas side in a skiff, eyes anxiously searching the dark surface of the water for hint or sign of the *Linda Lee*. They reached the far bank, went ashore and stood there looking blankly into each other's eyes.

They had seen nothing of the *Linda* while crossing—and she was not at her moorings against the shore.

"Hal-l-o-o-o! Bender! Come down here quick!"

Bender, signal man for the transport company, descended from his room at the top of the signal tower, and ran hastily down to the river.

"The *Linda!*" he cried, in answer to Captain Turner's question. "She cleared from this side, carrying the last two cars of Train Number Two, forty-five minutes ago! Hasn't she made Memphis yet?"

"Sunk!" Seeds declared. "Sunk, right before our eyes!"

Turner shook his head. "No," he declared. "There's nothing in the river to sink her—no snags, or the like. There were no other boats running at the time of her crossing, and no chance, therefore, of a collision. Besides, counting the mail messenger, baggageman, expressman and your brakeman, there were twelve men aboard. Twelve men in all! Surely some of them, if not all, could have taken to the small boats and made it to shore, in case of accident! There's no wind, and the river, while swift, is smooth enough. The *Linda* did not sink out yonder."

He pointed to the river, which could be heard sweeping on its course, though darkness completely veiled it.

An hour later, two dozen skiffs, a tug and two small steamers were busily searching the Mississippi for trace of the missing transport. Dawn broke, and not a soul had sighted her.

All day long the search continued, while the telegraph stirred the river district into unwonted activity. Rewards were offered for news of the transport, her crew, or any member thereof. Men along the shore below Memphis and as far south as the news had gone, watched the muddy river, knowing that if the *Linda* had really sunk and carried her crew down with her, bodies would sooner or later be found floating in the eddies.

Thus passed two more days, during which not the slightest clew to the *Linda's* fate came to life. She had put off from her landing on the Arkansas shore, headed for her Tennessee wharf, directly across the river. She had failed to dock. Dragging had not located her.

What had become of her?

The final verdict of a majority of those most interested, officers of the transport company, the railway and express companies, was that the *Linda Lee* had sunk in midriver—sunk suddenly and without sufficient warning to enable her crew to take to their boats and escape.

Such sinkings had occurred before, it was pointed out. Besides, the river was running almost bank full, and was a mile wide at the point of the transport's crossing. The current was swift, and no man, be he ever so fine a swimmer, could have reached shore in that flood, hampered by his clothing.

A ferryboat, two train coaches, and twelve men—all sucked down by the muddy Mississippi within a few moments' time!

Such was the popular verdict.

2

A DARING DEED

THE POST OFFICE Department, while not openly skeptical, nevertheless desired the sinking of the *Linda Lee* looked into—thoroughly. If she lay at the bottom of the river, that fact must be established beyond possibility of doubt. If she was not on the bottom of the river—then where was she?

Emphatically, the Post Office Department desired to know what had become of its mail car, messenger—and over a hundred thousand dollars' worth of registered mail.

Jack Calhoun, inspector of United States Rangers, sat at a table in his headquarters at Hulet's Point, in northeast Arkansas, listening with grave face and attentive ear, while the telegraph instrument beside him clicked off the story of the *Linda Lee,* Hubbard Wheeler, ranger chief, was sending from his headquarters at Oak Donnick.

The instrument ceased its clicking for a moment, then resumed. Wheeler, having acquainted Calhoun with such particulars as were in his possession, was sending his orders. They were few. Soon the instrument became mute again.

Calhoun placed a finger on the key, repeated the orders given him, received Wheeler's "O.K.," then got up and prepared for a journey. An hour later he was traveling down

Bayou L'Anguile in his bateau, driving it forward as rapidly as current and paddle could send it. His first objective lay thirty miles distant—Helena, on the west bank of the Mississippi.

Shortly after daylight on the fourth morning subsequent to the loss of the *Linda Lee,* Ferrymaster, Captain Lance Turner, raised his red-lidded, harassed eyes from staring out the window of his office at the Mississippi's swiftly rolling tide, and found a man standing in the doorway.

Turner had never seen the man before, but he instantly recognized the uniform he wore. The stranger was a United States Ranger by his dress. A tall man, nearing the age of thirty, he was. The skin of his face was a smooth bronze, indicating much exposure to wind, sun and rain, while what might be seen of his closely cropped hair had that sun-bleached tone common to men who dwell in the open. The eyes were deepset, and blue-gray in color—steady, wide-open eyes, they were.

The stranger smiled, exposing a wide mouth full of strong, even white teeth—a smile that banished the native homeliness of his countenance.

"My name is Calhoun, Captain Turner," the ranger said, his voice drawling the words. "I'm here to pester you a bit, and the sooner the pestering begins the sooner it will be over. Orders, you know."

Turner sighed, then laughed. The young chap had a likable way about him, and the tired captain, who had done little but answer questions since the *Linda* disappeared, motioned his caller inside.

"Ask," he said briefly. "I'll answer—if I can."

"When did you last see the *Linda?*" Calhoun queried, filling his pipe, and going directly to the point.

"When she left this side on her return trip after the balance of Train Number Two—at half past nine o'clock," was the answer.

"Could you follow her lights, with your eyes, while she made the crossing? If not, at about what distance were they no longer visible?"

"They were visible all the way, and after she docked," was the reply. "Except when there was a storm blowing and the river was running waves. At such times her lights would appear and disappear at intervals. When very stormy, she was never visible after she docked."

"Was there a storm blowing the night she disappeared?" Calhoun asked.

"No. The river, while high and swift, was placid enough."

"Did you see her lights after she docked?"

"It's this way, Mr. Calhoun," Turner explained. "I have been so accustomed to seeing the *Linda* at her work I never paid much attention to her except while she was over here. That night I stood talking to Jim Seeds, with no thought of danger to the *Linda* in mind, and I may or may not have marked her lying there on the Arkansas shore. Frankly, I can't be positive. However, she did get over, and her lights were burning—the signalman vouches for that."

"I am satisfied that she had her lights going while docked on the other side that night, captain," Cal said quietly. "What I am trying to establish is this:

"If the *Linda Lee* had begun her return trip with her lights going—headlight, riding-lights and all—then suddenly put them out, would not that circumstance have attracted your attention? Remember, the night was not stormy, there were no high waves, and the lights undoubtedly were visible from where you were standing. I am certain, captain, that you were subconsciously aware of the *Linda* and her lights all the while you were conversing with Conductor Seeds—is not that so?"

Turner nodded. "Most likely I was," he agreed.

"Now," Calhoun went on, "had she started across to this side, her lights glowing, you would have noted that fact, even though your interest happened at the time to be centered elsewhere, I take it?"

Again Turner agreed.

"Seeds, I understand, stood with his lantern in the crook of his arm, and his watch in hand," Cal continued. "He was on time when he came over with the first two cars, and quite naturally did not want to fall behind his schedule. He called your attention, did he not, to the circumstance of the *Linda's* slowness?"

"He did—very impatiently," was the answer.

"The natural thing for you to do, then, would be to cast a glance toward the Arkansas side in search of the *Linda*. Did you do so?"

"Unquestionably."

"Did you see her lights?"

"I'm certain I did not."

"Thought it strange, didn't you?"

"Yes. But there was a chance that something had happened to the lights. They might have been neglected, and run out of kerosene. That, at any rate, was in my mind. It was past the time for the *Linda* to show up, and I naturally cast about for the reason."

"Ever know the *Linda's* lights to fail before?" Cal asked.
"No."

"Would not Captain Blount have put back immediately, rather than chance a crossing during high-water, had his lights suddenly gone bad on him?"

"I—I think he would—yes," was the hesitating answer. "Blount was reliable, most of the time. Sometimes he drank a bit—but I don't think he had been drinking that night," he ended hastily.

Cal eyed the ferrymaster closely for a moment, then continued his interrogations.

"Let us say, captain, that the *Linda's* lights went bad while she lay against the Arkansas shore," he proposed. "Blount could have procured kerosene there, could he not?"

"Yes. It is likely, though, that he had a tank of oil aboard."

"He would never have started across without filling and lighting those lamps, would he? I think we may assume not. Now, did you ever observe a kerosene lamp when its wick was all but drained of oil? No doubt you have. It gives ample notice of its state, does it not? Sputters, smokes, casts off a strong odor. Even a small table lamp will burn along for five or ten minutes, dimly and protestingly, after the oil has been sucked from the bowl. You know that, do you not?"

"I suppose so—yes."

"Let us suppose, continuing, that the *Linda's* lights were out while she lay docked," Cal went on, bending forward, his pipe dead and forgotten. "Your signalman could not have failed to mark that, and so report. He says they were burning clearly while the boat lay along shore—that was his statement, I believe? Yes? All right. Since her lights were burning clearly when she lay at her Arkansas dock, they would have continued to burn after a fashion—sufficient for you to observe them—until she was well past the middle of the river, granting that the oil in them played out. Do you agree to that?"

"I must," Turner replied. "It's clear reasoning, and can't be denied. Not that I wish to deny it, of course. Go on, Mr. Calhoun."

"Bender, the signalman, reported the *Linda* away from her dock on time to the minute, her stern lights, at least, burning. He could see them. As to the forward lights, headlight, and so forth, he cannot be certain. It is, then, established that the transport left her dock on time, her stern lights going as usual. Now—who attends to the filling of those lights?"

"The mate attends to it every morning, supervising it, of course. The work is actually done by a deck hand."

"Do you recall whether he looked after the lights on the morning in question?"

"I—well, I'm sure he did," Turner declared. "It is part of my job to see that all such things are done, and had he failed I should have observed the omission. Yes, Mr. Calhoun, he undoubtedly had those lamps filled."

"How long should they burn on one filling?"

"Easily through the entire night," was the answer.

"All right—the *Linda's* lights were not dark because of insufficient kerosene. That brings us back to this: You do not recall seeing her lights while she was, presumably, crossing. You are, as a matter of fact, always conscious of the *Linda* and her lights, no matter where she is, because she is your charge and you are always somewhat anxious about her. That right?"

"Absolutely."

"Had she left the Arkansas side, her lights going, then suddenly gone dark about the middle of the channel—what then? Could that have happened without you being aware of it?"

"I am certain it couldn't," was the emphatic reply.

Calhoun sat back in his chair with a sigh of relief.

"It has taken quite awhile to dig it out, captain," he said quietly, "but we have, I think, established the fact that the *Linda Lee* left her Arkansas mooring with her stern lights going, but with her headlight and all forward lights dark. We know that if the stern lights were burning, all her lights were in condition to do so. We know, also, that those forward lights were dark for a purpose."

"What purpose?" gasped the ferrymaster, leaning forward.

Calhoun arose, stretched himself, then answered:

"Robbery," he said shortly. "The *Linda Lee* was stolen from her mooring, Captain Turner. To hold that she could have sunk in midchannel—where there would be enough water to cover her stacks—and do so without attracting the attention of any one, to say nothing of the fact that her skipper, mate, and deck hands undoubtedly were at their stations on deck while crossing and should long ago have been afloat on the surface if drowned, is little short of foolish.

"No! An organized gang of thieves—the most daring, considering what they have just done, that I have ever heard of—stole the *Linda Lee*. They stole her for sake of the express funds and the registered mail she carried—one hundred and fifty thousand dollars cash. That is my belief. If true, it is susceptible of proof—and my job is to prove it."

Turner leaped to his feet, his face ghastly. "But—but it just couldn't happen!" he cried, terror in his voice. "It just couldn't have happened!"

Calhoun, in the act pf taking leave, replied:

"Yet it did happen," he said gravely. "You have followed the course of reasoning by which I reached my conclusion. Think it over. There are other particulars which I shall require of you later. At the moment I have other things to do."

He was gone, leaving the ferrymaster staring after him, a look of slowly dawning belief upon his features.

3

"THE SWAMP ANGEL"

CAPTAIN TURNER DID think over what Calhoun's examination had developed. He also talked. The newspapers, eager for sensational news played up the new theory strongly. Those persons—there were many—who had been on the fence as to theories in regard to the *Linda's* disappearance, tumbled to Cal's side to a man. Viewed in the light which the ranger had turned upon the problem, it became very clear to almost every one that the transport had not sunk in midchannel.

There was renewed activity on the part of the officers, and private citizens who, hoping to earn the large rewards offered by the various interests represented, devoted their time to sleuthing.

Calhoun was suddenly in demand—very much so. But he was not to be found. Captain Turner received a second visit from him on the night of the first interview. Many questions were asked and answered, and when the inspector departed the ferrymaster had given up everything he knew about the case—and a lot he had not theretofore suspected himself possessed of. But Calhoun divulged nothing about himself—where he might be found, while in Memphis, or what his next move would be.

In view of the later theory concerning the *Linda Lee*—
that she had been stolen in the most daring manner ever
heard of—the people asked themselves and each other
the question:

"Who is responsible? What master criminal planned
and carried out such a stupendous piece of deviltry?"

With the exception of a few dissenters, the opinion of
the public was unanimous:

"The Swamp Angel!"

No doubt about it. Who so cunning, daring, ruthless?
The newspapers agreed, and printed a brief summary of
the crimes generally attributed to that vague personality
known as the Swamp Angel. Ask any man who the Swamp
Angel was, and his reply would run something like this:

"I don't know. Nobody knows—except, of course, those
to whom he chooses to reveal himself. He is, however, a
master criminal. Of that there is no doubt. The head of an
organization of thieves who dwell in the fastnesses of the
swamp country, and who concern themselves only with
major operations. Village banks, railway trains, paymasters who carry funds to the remotely located saw-mills—
such as that. They never fail to carry out their plans, and
they never leave a trace denoting where they came from,
or whence they go. The Swamp Angel is, in fine, the
super-criminal of his day. That is all any one knows—or is
likely ever to know."

According to the newspapers, a criminal possessed of far
more than ordinary intelligence, a penchant for organization, and an insatiable appetite for plunder, had saddled
himself upon the region. His depredations had begun
some two years prior to the *Linda's* mishap—and they

had covered every fertile field the country afforded. Train robbery was a hobby of his, the plundering of banks in small villages near the confines of the Sunken Lands, his pastime. In train robbery, the following method was invariably followed:

Obstructions such as no locomotive engineer would dare attempt to run, would be placed on the track, a red lantern atop of them. When the train came to a stop it would be surrounded by such a formidable number of men, all idea of resistance would immediately vanish. Each bandit would be masked, no one standing out more than another—making it impossible to do more than guess at who the leader was. If the robbery went through without a hitch, the masked band would fade away into the night. If trouble arose in the way of resistance, he who caused it would be shot down, the plundering would go forward—and, in some cases, the entire train would be set on fire.

The bank robberies invariably occurred at night. A large party of masked and armed men would descend upon a given town, take the cashier from his bed, force him to open the vault—in most cases only an old-fashioned safe large enough for the bank's needs—and ride away to the swamp with the funds. In the event the bank cashier proved unavailable, entrance would be forced, and dynamite used on the safe.

Paymasters, carrying pay roll funds into the saw-mill districts, were robbed—and invariably killed.

Such crimes had been so numerous during the past two years, they no longer created astonishment in the minds of the people—and all of them were laid at the Swamp Angel's door.

Then came the theft of the *Linda Lee*—by far the most daring thing he had done.

"Get the Swamp Angel!"

The people demanded it, and the order went out officially from States, counties and towns in the river district.

Get the Swamp Angel? Could it be done? Many thought not—perhaps a majority were of that opinion. He was as elusive as the breeze that stirred the muddy waters of the Mississippi in autumn. How get him?

Had he not won the loyalty and support of the natives of the Great Swamp, by his lavish bounty? Were there not hundreds of persons beholden to him for the food they ate and the clothing they wore? And for other favors, too—such as this:

Charlie Bedford, a native of the Coon Island district, wanted for murder, had ventured out of hiding and found himself in jail at Harrisburg, county seat of Poinsette. His guilt was so plain even he could not deny it. He would undoubtedly hang, come the fall term of court.

Did he?

He did not—for the simple reason that when the fall term of court came round, Charlie Bedford was not there to be tried. Long before the first day of November, when court was due to convene, a band of masked men—fifty in number, it was estimated—rode to the jail in Harrisburg, slew the jailer and his deputy, who resisted, and carried Bedford away.

Granting that he could be located and trapped, could such a master criminal be taken out of the swamp? Would not the natives swarm to his assistance, liberate him, and drive his would-be captors out?

So two questions arose, after it was definitely settled that the Swamp Angel had stolen the *Linda Lee:*

Could the Swamp Angel be identified and captured? Could he be taken out of his stronghold and made to answer with his life for the many lives he had taken?

4

STIFF ORDERS

JACK CALHOUN, SEATED beside a table in the low cabin of the *Clipper*—smallest, dingiest and most unattractive steam launch afloat on the waters of the Mississippi, pondered those two questions and answered "Yes" to both of them.

The "yes" was expressed mentally—perhaps not consciously at all, but the nature of the task which absorbed the ranger was in itself an answer in the affirmative.

On a small table, bracketed to the starboard wall of the tiny cabin, lay a large sheet of tracing paper. Its creases indicated that it had been folded many times—probably to fit a coat pocket of its owner. At the moment, however, the map—for such it was—lay spread out before Calhoun, its compiler. The ranger studied it intently.

Tom Murdock, Inspector Calhoun's favorite aid, sat on a locker a few feet away from his chief, silent, eyes following the tracing of Cal's long forefinger.

"Found out," Calhoun jerked out in fragments for his aid's benefit, "that *Linda* had been in dry-dock eight months ago. Hull in perfect condition. Nothing wrong with the boat at all. Couldn't just fall apart and sink, as some folks seem to believe. No floating log could have stove her in, that's certain. Even had such been the case, she couldn't possibly have received injury enough to sink her on the spot—and drown all hands. Damn foolishness, that. She didn't sink. Two passenger coaches, even weight, side by side on parallel tracks aboard. Therefore she couldn't have listed suddenly to either side, thereby sinking. Nothing like that could have occurred. I made sure of that."

Murdock made no comment during the long pause which followed. After a bit Calhoun resumed speaking:

"Captain Lance Turner, ferrymaster, did the hiring and firing for the transport company. He hired Captain Blount, and Stamford, the mate. Also Pilot Brady and Engineer Brickett. Four deck hands, too—Joiner, Vance, Devlin, Newby. Hired 'em all. Says Blount, Stamford, Brady and Brickett all had regular papers. Blount, hired a year ago, came to him from the Lee Line—all regular, I learned. Brady, the pilot, came from the Twin City Navigation Company, three months ago. He's regular, too. Telegraphed Twin City people. He seems O.K. But—Brickett and Stamford, engineer and mate, who came two months ago, had forged papers, and lied about their former employment. I learned that, too. Both supposed to come from privately owned boats in the White River trade. Telegraph divulged those boats never had them aboard—their owners and skippers know nothing about them."

Cal bent over his map, becoming silent again.

"What about the deck hands?" Murdock ventured finally.

"Deck hands. Deck hands, you ask?" said Cal, looking up. "They don't have to carry papers or give references. They don't count, you know. White men who follow roustabouting on Mississippi River steamboats—well, they are picked up as wanted, and fired when no longer needed.

"Walter Brokamp, mail messenger, carried a forty-five. Government issue, Number 188165. Keep that in mind, Tom. Arthur Meadors, express messenger, was also armed with a forty-five. Company gave me the number, 166421. Got it? May lead to something. If Peter Larkin, the baggageman, and Jeff Claxton, the brakeman, were armed, I have been unable to establish it as a fact.

"The *Linda,* carrying capacity load as she did, could make fifteen miles an hour downstream. Not above ten upstream."

The inspector paused, let the point of his pencil dwell upon a tiny cross on the map, beside which appeared the name "Memphis," then he drew an irregular circle, using Memphis as a more or less central point. The upper part of the circle was somewhat closer to the central point than the lower.

"Here we are, Tom," he said, motioning Murdock to his side. "The line of the circle above Memphis embraces the farthest limit to which the *Linda* could have traveled in five hours' time. The line of the lower part of the circle marks the limit she could have gone in a like time. Why allow five hours for running time after she disappeared? Let us see.

"The *Linda* left the Mississippi by way of a tributary creek, bayou, or whatnot, sufficiently deep enough and wide enough to float her. Such is my opinion. She proceeded up such creek or bayou until she reached a lake of sufficient depth in which to sink her. I'll tell you why I know that later. Now, as to the running time allowed:

"Five hours—she disappeared shortly after nine

o'clock—would give her until two o'clock in the morning in which to travel. It becomes daylight at four, at this
season and in this locality. She would not dare be upon the
Mississippi after dawn. Allow two hours in which to run
up the bayou into the lake, scuttle and sink the boat. Not
enough time, you will say—and you are probably right.
However, I am allowing plenty of time for the run up or
down the river, and have embraced in the circle every bayou
and lake she could have reached, suited to her require-
ments, in that time.

"The bayous and lakes she could have used are not
many—two above Memphis, and one below. The one
below, Swan Lake, we can dismiss as a possibility. Plenty of
depth to cover the *Linda*, once her smokestacks were down,
and Wolf Creek is wide and deep enough to float her. There
is this, however, against Swan Lake: There are three private
fishing and hunting clubs located on its shores, and the
surrounding country is not wild enough—the place, in
fine, lacks the necessary isolation.

"That leaves only Gar Lake, reached by way of Buckhorn Bayou, and Panther Lake, reached by Little Panther
Creek. Both are remote from anything savoring of civilization; both have sufficient depth. Gar Lake has no fishing
club buildings on its banks, but Panther has one—owned
by a number of St. Louis sportsmen, but neglected these
three years past. The one is thirty miles above Memphis,
the other thirty-five."

Calhoun ceased speaking, folded his map, restored it
to his pocket, and waited sufficiently for any questions
Murdock might wish to ask.

"Which of the lakes gets your vote, Cal?" the ranger

inquired, after a moment. "I am somewhat acquainted with the country around Gar Lake—and I'll say it is the wildest, most nearly impassable section of swamp I know of. Hell itself might be located there, and nobody be the wiser. And, by George, speaking of hell naturally raises the thought of fire—and that seems to furnish a flaw in your reasoning. Hate to find it, inspector—but it's there. Want to hear what it is?"

Cal nodded. "I know what it is already," he said with a grin. "Some other lake, a shallow one—and there are plenty—could have been used, and the *Linda* might have been burned instead of sunk. There are two reasons why that theory is not a sound one: First, the boat and the train cars would make a mighty blaze, and it would require considerable time for the fire to consume them. The blaze would undoubtedly attract attention, granting any one happened to be in the vicinity—a chance hunter, fisherman or the like. Second, bits of charred board from the burning wreck would, in all likelihood, float out to the Mississippi by way of the creek—thus furnishing a possible clue. No, Tom, take my word for it, the *Linda Lee,* her cargo of train cars—and, most likely, some of the human beings who were aboard—lie beneath water. That is the only logical way in which she could be hidden. It's up to us to find the spot—the Government has ordered it."

"I beg your pardon, inspector," said Murdock contritely "I might have known—but no matter! When do we start?"

"Who is now aboard?"

"Ted Stone, Joe Ballard and Blackie, and the men from Oak Donnick," was the answer. "A full crew, has the *Clip-*

per—most disreputable boat on the river, and, incidentally, the fastest little devil afloat. What are your orders?"

Calhoun did not reply. His head was bent in a listening attitude.

High, shrill voices on the dock, coming near, caught Murdock's ear also.

"Newsboys yelling 'Extra!'" he exclaimed, stepping to the foredeck. "I'll get one."

When he returned, a copy of *The News,* damp from the press, in hand, his face was more serious than Cal had ever before seen it.

"What's gone wrong?" he asked casually.

"Enough!" exclaimed the aid. "This extra carries the news of the finding of a floater below Greenville, Mississippi, during the past night. Identified as the corpse of Walter Brokamp, the missing mail clerk. No wounds. Evidently drowned. That isn't all, either. From among some bits of drift, just above Greenville, a painted board was picked up—the name board from the pilot house of the *Linda Lee.* No mistaking it, of course, since the name is there in big letters. Lastly, a stove-in skiff has been found aground on Ramsay's Island—only forty miles from here—and it, too, bears the *Linda's* name!"

"Well?"

Calhoun's face did not change its customary calm expression, nor was there the least trace of concern in his voice when he put the brief query.

"Well!" Murdock almost shouted, waving the copy of *The News* frantically. "Don't you see what these discoveries do to your theory about a lake, and the *Linda Lee* resting on the bottom of it? Don't you see that this news blows your robbery theory plumb to nothing? The *Linda,* says *The News,* undoubtedly sank that night—from accident. The drowned body the name board, and the stove-in skiff—*The News* talking, understand—establishes her fate beyond doubt! This scribe takes a punch at you, to wind up with.

"He says that no one need feel ashamed of going wrong on the Swamp Angel theory, since so able and favorably known a sleuth-hound, who shall be nameless, but who is high in the Ranger organization on the Arkansas side, was himself so badly in the fog! Think of it—damn it—'so badly in the fog!'"

The speaker threw the offending extra upon the floor and sat down in deep disgust. He was recalled a moment later by the cool voice of Calhoun.

"You asked for orders, a few minutes ago, Tom," the inspector said. "Here they are: Cast off, and run without loss of time to the mouth of Buckhorn Bayou—thirty miles up river. Anchor there, until further instructed!"

Murdock stared incredulously.

"You—you still stick to your theory?" he demanded in amazement.

Calhoun nodded, while the fine lines about his wide mouth visibly tightened. "I do," he replied. "I am more certain of it now than ever,"

Murdock spun around on his heel, reached for the wall ladder which gave into the pilot house atop the cabin, and mounted swiftly out of sight.

Five minutes later the *Clipper* was plowing her way up the Mississippi, on the first leg of her journey into the lake region—after the Swamp Angel.

5

THE LAUNCH ON PANTHER LAKE

THE *CLIPPER*, PUT in commission by a well known business man of Helena, and ostensibly his boat, was in reality the property of the Government, assigned to ranger service. The craft was, as already stated, not good to look upon. To make up for that it had many excellent hidden qualities. Speed was one. A light draught, enabling her to cruise the creeks and bayous of the swamp lands, was another. Her crew was composed of experts in their particular duties, which is an invaluable asset to any watercraft. Lastly, she had many lockers and compartments not visible to the casual eye—and those lockers and compartments were important.

When the launch reached her destination at the mouth of Buckhorn Bayou, she lay at anchor only long enough for Calhoun to make sure that the presumably deserted log cabins on the south bank—there were four, formerly occupied by fur traders and trappers, but now almost in ruins—were actually vacant, and that they had not been recently occupied. Then, all seemingly well in that quarter, the launch proceeded to Gar Lake.

For ten miles the route followed the meanderings of a very crooked bayou in which there was scarcely any current. The low, marshy shores were heavy with virgin timber, grown up with brush and young trees, and choked with watergrass and like vegetation. It required skill and a vast amount of patience to navigate such a tangled course. Murdock, who piloted the *Clipper*, had both, and within two hours after leaving the Mississippi his craft floated on the placid waters of the lake.

Gar Lake measured a bit over three miles in circumference, and was almost circular in formation. The *Clipper* steamed slowly along its shores, stopped for an inspection of a hunter's camp of three cabins which stood in the timber on the north bank, then completed the circle. Not a soul was to be seen, nor was there the least bit of evidence indicating recent human habitation.

Putting across to that part of the shore upon which the hunting camp stood, Calhoun landed Ted Stone and four men, then transferred certain stores of provisions from the *Clipper* to the cabins. Two small skiffs then were unlashed from the boat's pilot deck and launched for the use of the Gar Lake party.

"You should be able to complete the first part of your task here, Stone, within three days at the most," Calhoun said at parting. "You know your instructions, so there is no need going over them. Use your own head as well. Keep together, and always have at least one man on guard—no matter what you are doing. That is all."

The *Clipper* rethreaded the maze of Buckhorn Bayou and, hugging the Arkansas shore, continued up the Mississippi. No habitations of any kind appeared on the banks of Little Panther Creek, at its mouth, and the *Clipper* went directly inland. Save that it was five miles longer, the route was almost an exact counterpart of the serpentlike wind-ings of Buckhorn. There were no cabins on its shore.

Panther Lake was egg-shape in formation, and was nearly three times as large as Gar Lake. A number of small islands—mere mudbanks, tree-clothed and covered with undergrowth—stood up from the surface. The *Clipper* steered directly to one of the islands, probably of five acres in extent, which lay almost opposite the entrance to the lake, then circled it slowly until the entire body of water unfolded before it.

Calhoun, glass focused, scanned the north shore, where a large house, built of unbarked logs, stood sentineled by a number of fine oaks. Other and smaller cabins flanked it on both sides, and a boardwalk extended from the front veranda down to a small wharf.

Anchored near the wharf, her twin stacks sending up only the faintest suspicion of smoke, floated a long, snow-white launch. The afternoon sun glinted and sparkled upon her metal, and Cal, with half an eye, saw that the craft was spotless and tidy, from bow to stern.

"Those St. Louis sportsmen," Murdock suggested, lowering his glass. "That beauty belongs to somebody with money to burn! Can you make out her name board?"

"The *Pigeon*," Cal replied, after shifting his glass until he found the name. "Lay alongside her," was the brief order.

Until the dingy little launch was standing well over toward the *Pigeon* not a sign of life was visible aboard the latter. Then, just as Cal was about to hail her, the texas door opened and a squat man in a uniform of spotless white stepped out.

"Lay well to sta'board!" he called in a deep voice. "We've

got a line ashore, and swing with the wind. A hundred feet will clear you!"

Murdock, at the wheel, followed directions, and presently the *Clipper* stood above her anchor in twenty feet of water.

"What's your business here?" called the man on the *Pigeon's* foredeck.

"I believe that's a question we have a better right to ask than you," Calhoun called in return. "We are a fishing party, and have leased rights to this place—including the buildings. What are you doing here?"

The man on the foredeck was silent, apparently considering Calhoun's words. Then he called: "Wait a minute!" and disappeared inside the texas, returning almost immediately.

"You are wrong about having rights here!" he shouted. "We are the only persons privileged to use the lake and clubhouse. Advise you to get out!"

"That'll bear discussing!" Cal said in return. "We are about to board you. Then we'll settle matters!"

Joe Ballard, with Blackie Winters manning the oars, steered the *Clipper's* smallboat about, and Cal stepped in.

"No need to come aboard!" the squat man cried. "We know our rights, and that's all there is to it!"

Cal made no reply. Standing up in the boat, dressed in worn corduroy britches, scuffed high boots, flannel shirt and weather-soiled felt hat, he looked anything but prepossessing. His companions were no better. They might easily have been taken for a party of professional fishermen, such as they claimed to be. The small boat bumped against the starboard side of the *Pigeon,* and Cal and his mates stepped aboard. Up the companionway to the boiler-deck they climbed—to be confronted by the squat man in uniform, a scowl upon his face.

"State your case quickly!" he snapped. "We've no time to fool away with such as you! You claim rights here, and I know that claim is without foundation—so you may expect no courtesy or consideration from me!"

"Well, now," drawled Cal, "it might be that, as dispensers of courtesy and consideration, we are just as niggardly as you be. We ain't exactly asking for such, as it happens. All we want is to know why you city fellows come in here and take possession of our rights—even to occupying our clubhouse. Our leased one, I mean. That's what we want to know—and what we aim to find out!"

The man of the *Pigeon,* besides being squat, was heavily built, possessed a round, heavy face, snub nose, black eyes and a flowing mustache. It was easy to see that he was out of his element in the wilds. He looked the soiled Cal over from head to foot, making not the least effort to hide his disgust at the contact, then asked:

"Have you got anything to show that you and your party hold a lease on the fishing rights of this place?" he demanded.

Cal grinned. "Have you?" he asked.

"Yes. Should any one vested with the authority to do so, demand to see the papers, they will be shown. They are not, however, open for inspection on the demand of any chance caller," was the sneering reply.

Cal's eyelids narrowed. "I take it you are one of the hired hands aboard this craft," he said with studied impudence. "Suppose you trot out the boss of the outfit, and let him

have a say? I'm boss of my gang, and I ain't used to discussing business with no underlings. Trot out the big gun. He's
the one to settle with me!"

The squat man's face was a study. From red it went to
white, then to red again—finally settling upon purple for
a lasting color.

"If you are not off this boat, and out of this lake in the
next fifteen minutes—" he began, only to be interrupted.

6

A COTTON KING

THE TEXAS DOOR swung open and a man appeared. Advancing no farther than the sill, he leaned against the jamb, surveyed the group on the foredeck with cool eyes, then spoke—his voice soft and pleasing:

"What's the trouble, Andrews?" he asked, addressing the squat man. "These gentlemen appear to be in error concerning some fishing rights—am I correct?"

"They pretend to be!" was the reply. "But I have my doubts! Look them over, sir—"

"Sir! Ha!" Cal broke in. "You are the hired hand, after all! It takes me to pick 'em!" he cried, turning to his mates, a smirk upon his face. "I knew he wasn't the big gun on this palace! Knew it the very minute I laid eyes on him." He turned in explanation to the man in the door.

He—that man leaning nonchalantly in the doorway—was worth studying. About five feet and eleven inches tall, his figure was slender without being in the least delicate or effeminate. On the contrary, there was that in his pose which suggested a coiled, steel spring. His face, almost too fine in color for a man, had an unmistakable look of high breeding: a well formed, delicate nose, thin lips, and an imperious quality in the look of the sky-blue eyes, bore further testimony. As to dress, he was immaculate in white duck. Cal rudely looked his fill. Presently the man in the doorway smiled and spoke:

"Captain Andrews is not exactly a 'hired hand,' my friend," he corrected pleasantly. "He is, in fact, the skipper of the *Pigeon*. Suppose now, you lay your grievance before me, and let us see what can be done about it."

"I'll surely do that thing, Mr.—er, Mr.—"

It was a broad hint, and one that provoked a chuckle from the man addressed.

"I am Roth Linguard," he said simply, "planter of cotton, with a place in Mississippi County, above here. If you've been much in that district, you may have heard of my place."

Astonishment smote Calhoun, but never by the flicker of so much as an eyelash did he betray his state. Roth Linguard—wealthy planter, sportsman—genteel idler! Certainly he had heard of the man. Who had not, in the district centering about Memphis? The Linguard mansion was invariably pointed out to visitors to the city—a show place. Linguard, whose father, reputed to be of Danish extraction, and, like the son, showing it in his appearance, had amassed a fortune in cotton, during his day. Roth Linguard was not a waster, it appeared, but used his inherited wealth as a means to gain more—and he had been successful. So, at least, repute had it.

"Never been up to your place, Mr. Linguard, sir," Cal said, respect in his voice, "but I surely have heard of you. I'm right sorry for this disturbance, but we got a lease on the fishing rights at Gar Lake, which we got from the

Arkana Land and Lumber Company that holds the timber rights—"

Linguard laughed quietly, and a look of relief passed over his face.

"My dear sir," he said, "you have indeed made an error—but, fortunately, one easily cleared up. This is Panther Lake, not Gar. That lake lies five or six miles below here, and is reached by way of Buckhorn Bayou. Somebody surely misdirected you."

Cal stared blankly at the speaker, then at the triumphantly glaring Andrews, then at his companions, the last named looking rather sheepish. Finally his eyes came back to Linguard.

"Are—are you-all sure about this being Panther, instead of Gar Lake?" he asked dubiously.

"Absolutely," was the assured answer. "Gar has no clubhouse—just a few cabins, and is not as large as this body by two-thirds. Just a mistake, as I was certain we should learn the moment I looked at your honest face and those of your worthy men. Sorry, but—"

"Oh," Cal exclaimed, "we're the ones to be sorry! Why, we've been plumb damned fools! But, like I say, when folks goes to runnin' waters they ain't never run before, they're like to make mistakes! Well, we'll make up for ours, and right now!"

He turned toward the smallboat anchored alongside, his companions following sheepishly.

"Wait!" called Linguard, gesturing them back. "We should have a bit to drink on this, just to show there's no hard feelings!"

Cal turned a grinning face toward the speaker, licking a dry tongue against dry lips.

"You surely are mighty fine to us, Mr. Linguard!" he praised. "And there ain't nothing little, or high-and-mighty about you, neither! We'll take a little noggin with you, and thank you!"

A black man silently made his appearance from the texas, bearing bottle and glasses on a tray.

"Good luck to your fishing!" Linguard proposed, holding his glass in a delicate-looking hand.

"And here's luck to you, sir—no matter what you do!" was Cal's response, as he downed his mellow brandy.

Linguard stood against the rail, smiling at them as they pulled away.

7

PLAYING A LONE HAND

NOT A WORD passed between Cal and his men during the return to the *Clipper*.

"What now?" Murdock asked when they were once more aboard the launch.

"Pull out," the inspector ordered. "Run slowly. Be ready to stand by for a landing when well hidden in the creek."

While the *Clipper* was being brought slowly about, awkwardly, as though her handlers were novices, Calhoun was digging kit, rifle and blanket out of a locker. Peterson and Spence occupied themselves in unlashing and righting a small dugout which lay on the after deck, beside the engine room.

The *Clipper* dropped the lake astern, ran the first long turn of the creek, then put in as close to the north shore as it could with safety, and stood by, her reversed engine holding her steady against the current.

Peterson and Spence launched the dugout, and Calhoun tossed his outfit aboard, then stepped in and took up a paddle.

"Tie up at the mouth of Little Panther," he told Murdock, repeating orders theretofore given, for the benefit of the assembled crew. "If you do not receive word from me within two days, run into Panther Lake and have a showdown with Linguard—or whoever you find there. That's all."

The *Clipper* resumed her way, and Calhoun shot his shell under a clump of brush which shaded the creek on the north shore. Completely hidden, from both water and shore, he lay back in the boat, closed his eyes and gave himself to thought.

Two years previous to that day, he had been present in Marked Tree when the man thereafter called the Swamp Angel received his christening. A newspaper reporter from Memphis, on the scene of a robbery and murder laid to the hands of the Angel and his band, had done the christening.

After listening to numerous stories lauding the generosity of the bandit, he had grinned and said:

"If those things are true, then this section is to be congratulated upon having acquired a very desirable citizen! By all means find him—and pin a medal on his breast! What a pity the outside public has so distorted a view of him and his—er, beneficent operations! A sort of ministering angel—a swamp angel, and quite naturally one with soiled wings—who has adopted the poor of the whole region, it appears! What a pity there are not more like him!"

Ironic, that speech, but because of it the bandit was thenceforward called Swamp Angel. Hence the "Angel's" sobriquet did not arise from the gratitude of the natives, but originated in the sarcasm of a newspaper reporter.

Taken to task for his scoffing, by a bystander who cited many instances bearing testimony to the lavishness of the bandit, the reporter had been content to say:

"You hear a lot about this thief's kindness to the natives

of the hinterlands. That he feeds and clothes them, and even rescues them from jail when their misdeeds find them out—with the sheriff's aid. The same thing has been said about every notorious outlaw who ever succeeded in capturing the popular fancy of his time—from Robin Hood down to Jesse James. The same will be said of all such who come afterward.

"Why? Because it is in part the truth. When a bandit distributes the proceeds of his deviltry with bounteous hand, he does so, not because he possesses a sympathetic and generous nature, but because he has a shrewd and self-centered mind. Take the Swamp Angel, admitting him for the sake of argument. It is commonly believed that he can never be taken out of the swamps, should any one succeed in locating and trapping him, because he has bound the natives to him with ties of gratitude. They constitute a bulwark against invasion of his lair, and capture of his person. There you have the only reason why a bandit bestows charity."

Calhoun found himself in hearty agreement with the reporter's viewpoint. The Swamp Angel would prove difficult to capture and difficult to take to prison, should any one set out for that purpose.

But—had Calhoun such an end in view? He had not committed himself to any one as holding the belief that the Swamp Angel had perpetrated the *Linda Lee* outrage. The public had leaped to that conclusion of its own accord.

"The public may be right," Cal thought. "That most able of crooks may have planned and executed the theft. But I am not looking for any such person," he argued. "My job is to find out what happened to the *Linda* and her crew, and bring in those responsible for the crime. If this Swamp Angel person is at the bottom of it, then I want him. I want Captain Blount, too—else positive proof that he died that night in defense of his charge. Likewise the other members of the crew.

"Brokamp, if that *News* story is to be relied on, is already accounted for, and it is reasonable to assume that none of the train crew had a hand in the thing. I am as certain as it is possible to be of anything not yet fully established that the *Linda* is on the bottom of Panther or Gar Lake. I'll know all about Gar Lake within a few days, and if we draw a blank there, then the field is narrowed down to Panther.

"As to Panther—this Linguard is a poser. Wouldn't be surprised to learn that he owns the lake and the neighboring timber land, and that his presence here is just a coincidence. Still, he'll bear looking over. He's on the spot—one of the spots, at any rate—where reason tells me to look for the wreck of the *Linda*—and that's a sufficient cause for investigating him."

The sun dropped behind the westward wall of trees, and shadows began to come into the swamp land. Cal dug up some cold food, ate supper, then got ready to go ashore. When darkness came at last he slipped silently away across the waste in the direction of the north shore of Panther Lake.

A young moon made light enough to travel by, provided care was used, and after an hour's time Calhoun reached a point where the lights of the Panther Lake clubhouse were visible. The windows of the lower floor were all aglow.

Not a spark was visible on the water, where the *Pigeon* presumably lay at anchor.

It is probable that the wilderness boasted no man who could excel Jack Calhoun in woodmanship. With as little noise as a moccasined Indian he could traverse the most intricate tangle of trees, vines and underbrush. His own shadow was scarcely less noisy, as he glided from tree to tree, than he.

To gain a point of vantage much nearer than he had at first was to Calhoun an easy matter. He moved on, and came at length into the fringe of trees which shadowed the clubhouse itself. There he paused, listening.

Laughter sounded inside, seeming to come from the room close to which the inspector stood. The lower half of the window directly opposite was masked by a sash-curtain, the upper portion was bare.

Calhoun mounted silently until he sat upon the first branch of the tree he had chosen, and looked into the room.

Linguard and Andrews, with three other men—all well dressed and seemingly of the planter's station in life—sat at cards. Liquor bottles were in evidence, and from the snatches of conversation wafted to his ears through the open window, Calhoun judged that the talk was of the game and the game alone.

For half an hour he remained in the tree, then began to descend—only to halt midway, then climb noiselessly back to the limb again.

A shadowy form had stolen from around a corner of the house and, with cat-like tread, gained the window of the room in which the card players sat. A moment and he was nothing but a huddled shadow beneath the sill.

8

THE FIGHT

FIFTEEN MINUTES PASSED, during which the man beneath the window was as motionless as was Calhoun in the tree. The party in the clubhouse grew noisier, and the clicking of poker chips could be distinctly heard.

Suddenly Cal's eyes were drawn to the shadows which marked the north fringe of timber. Something had moved in that direction, and a twig had snapped. He was not in any measure prepared, however, for what followed immediately.

The man beneath the window arose and glided toward the front of the building and, in the twinkling of an eye, the clearing about the club was alive with moving figures. They came from the woodland and from the lake, moving silently, and all armed.

What struck Calhoun particularly was this:

Every man of that apparition-like crew was masked.

A circle was quickly formed about the building, then from in front came a command in a voice so deep, harsh and savage, as to cause Calhoun to start violently.

Where had he heard such a voice before? His mind groped into the past, but came back to the present instantly. Things were happening.

"Open!" came the repeated command. "Open—or we'll blow you all into the lake!"

Calhoun, observing through the window, saw the card players leap to their feet—saw weapons drawn—then the lights of the entire lower floor were suddenly extinguished.

"Who are you, and what do you want?"

The speaker was Linguard, and his voice was calm and clear.

"He asks what we want?" came the deep voice again. "Show him!"

With a splintery crash the front door fell in. From Cal's side of the house a group charged the windows, forced them with the butts of their rifles, and leaped inside.

The roar of a heavy caliber revolver, followed by a crashing volley, drowned all other sounds. As suddenly as a hail-storm descends, a storm of bullets poured into the club building. There were yells and groans, and loud oaths. Those inside fired in return, as Cal could see through the window. Above all other sounds, however, the voice of the leader of the attackers rose in command.

Suddenly a window in the upper story opened, a man appeared on the sill, grasped it with his hands, lowered his body through and dropped to the ground. Without the loss of an instant he was on his feet again and running for the lake.

Calhoun dropped noiselessly from the tree and darted away on the trail of the escaping man. He reached the wharf in time to see a dark figure dive into the water, then come up and strike off toward where the white bulk of the *Pigeon* showed mistily.

Casting aside the rifle, to which he had clung, Cal was

on the point of diving also when a heavy tread behind caused him to turn swiftly—to be gathered closely in the embrace of powerful arms.

"No you don't!" boomed in Cal's ear—the voice which had set Cal's mind groping into the past. "You don't get off so easily! Mr. Roth Lin—"

Calhoun acted. With a lithe twist of his powerful body he slipped from those tightening arms, brought the heel of a heavy boot hard against the speaker's shin, striking upward for his chin with his right at the same time. There was a groan, an oath, and the sound of a body falling heavily to the ground.

Cal reached for the mask which shrouded features he longed to see, yanked it away and stared down upon the twitching face. The face of a man in the middle forties, marked with deep lines, tanned to the color of autumn leaves. A cruel mouth, beaklike nose, high, broad brow topped with a shock of gray hair. But the feature which drew Cal's eyes most attentively and held them was this:

The right side of the man's face was pock marked and disfigured by a deep and hideous scar which began in the hair above the temple and extended downward almost to the point of the chin.

Cal's lips formed words though he did not give them utterance. "Almost—but not quite!" he thought. "I know, if only I can remember! Got him!" he exclaimed, triumphantly.

The man on the ground sat up, and Cal, who had not been delayed for more than a pair of minutes at longest, dove into the water.

He was but a short time behind the first who took the

plunge, climbing to the lower deck of the *Pigeon* almost on his heels. Toward the engine-room the man ran, gained it and passed through. Then Calhoun saw his purpose.

A skiff rode lightly in the water, barely discernible in the shadows.

The fleeing man leaped in, cut the rope painter, seized a paddle and pushed off.

Then Cal leaped also.

"Pass me an oar, Linguard," he said quietly. "Two can make better speed than one!"

From the shore came the sound of rifles in action, and bullets rained around the *Pigeon*. The bull-like voice of the man Cal had struck down was raised high in angry roars of command.

The astonished man in the stern of the skiff, after a moment's petrified hesitation, came to life and shoved a spare paddle along toward Cal. The latter caught it up and thrust it deep into the water.

"Put all you've got into it!" the inspector ordered. "We've got to make cover behind yonder island—and make it as quick as ever we can!"

9

AN INVISIBLE FOE

THE SKIFF SHOT into the moonlit space beyond the *Pigeon's* berth, and lead sizzled in the water about it—sang in the air, clipped off bits of wood from the gunwale nearest the shore.

Neither man spoke, each bending all his energies toward getting out of the danger zone. In a very brief space of time—much less than it seemed to them—the island was gained and the skiff, for the moment, safe.

"They'll be on our heels!" Cal panted, resting a moment from his exertions. "Are you hit?"

"No!" came the answer.

"Let's move, then!"

"Where?"

"Into Little Panther, of course!" Cal exclaimed. "Where else would we have a chance of safety?"

"I'm ready," Linguard told him. "Whenever you are."

"Change places with me!" Cal ordered, getting up from the bow seat and motioning Linguard out of the stern.

"I—what is the idea for that?" the latter asked in surprise.

"Never mind the reason!" Cal snapped. "Perhaps it's because I'm better with a steering oar—perhaps it's because I don't want you at my back. In any case, get into the bow!"

Linguard hesitated, peering through the moonlit veil between them.

"I know your voice—" he began.

Pop! Pop! Pop!

A boat rounded the upper end of the island, manned by three men, two paddling, and the one in the bow opening up at close range with a revolver.

Calhoun's gun was in his hand in a flash, and the next instant the marksman in the pursuing boat pitched overside—a bullet in his head.

"In the bow!"

Cal swung on Linguard—and there was no longer any delay. The Dane, careful not to swamp the small craft, slid into the place Cal had vacated, and the inspector, bending low in order to afford as small a target as possible for the aim of those in the skiff behind, dropped into the stern seat, seized a paddle and headed toward the mouth of the creek.

Some one else was shooting from the pursuing skiff now, but the distance between pursuer and pursued had increased and the light was poor. Cal turned in his seat and sent two shots into the boat. They had the effect of slowing the other craft down, and, it seemed, cooling the ardor of those who manned it.

Little Panther was reached, the first bend traversed, and Cal shot the skiff under the brush where his dugout lay.

"Into the dugout!" he ordered Linguard. "It's faster—and we need something with speed!"

Linguard transhipped without comment. Leaving the skiff to drift at will, Cal shot his light shell downstream, making greater speed than he had before, and greater, he felt certain, than any one behind him could make.

Mile after mile fell behind; Linguard, in the bow, proving himself a first-rate hand with an oar.

"I place you now!" exclaimed the latter, who had not spoken since the dugout had taken the place of the skiff. He ceased paddling, and turned toward Cal. "You are the fisherman who boarded the *Pigeon* to-day! How came you to be on the scene to-night?"

"You'll find it more profitable to use that paddle," Cal retorted, "than to question me! Get going!"

Linguard, without another word, returned to his work.

An hour later the dugout shot into the Mississippi, headed downstream in answer to Cal's paddle, and dropped gently against the *Clipper*, which, showing only docklights, lay snug against the shore.

Spence challenged them, received Calhoun's answer, and lent a hand at the painter.

"Right ahead into the texas, Linguard," Cal ordered, when both had disembarked. "You won't find anything approaching the *Pigeon*, as far as luxury goes, but I daresay you'll be able to make out with what we have. Right ahead!"

Under the cabin light Linguard appeared curious, but undisturbed. Cal, scrutinizing him closely, realized that the man possessed a cold nerve and superb self-control.

"Sit down, Linguard," he directed. "You desire to ask a few questions—and you may. First, however, I will give certain orders to my skipper."

Murdock made a sleepy entrance at that juncture, came wide-awake with a start at sight of Linguard, then drew himself up in strict attention.

"Send two men up Little Panther in a boat, Mr. Murdock," Cal ordered. "A mile will do. They are to report the approach of any one by land or water. Get steam up, and hold yourself in readiness to slip your bank line on short notice."

Murdock disappeared into the quarters at the rear.

"Now, Linguard, what do you desire mostly to know?" Cal asked.

Linguard brought his eyes to a level with Calhoun's and, holding them there, replied:

"Who you, and your party, are—besides being fishermen?"

"We are United States Rangers on Government service in the Sunken Land country. I doubt not that you have heard of the organization, and its work. My name is Calhoun, and I am, as you have probably surmised, in charge of this party. Anything further?"

"Yes," Linguard replied. "I'd like some dry clothing, and then a cigar, pipe, or whatever you happen to have to spare. Perhaps I'll ask you, then, what you were doing in the club grounds to-night."

The Dane's tones were devoid of anything suggesting uneasiness. He had the air of one who was for awhile forced to endure the society of men inferior to himself. His request for clothing and something to smoke savored of a command.

His wants were attended to, then:

"A small drink of something like I gave you this afternoon would not be amiss," he suggested. "I'll confess I'd like it. Suppose you set a bottle out—"

"None aboard," Cal told him shortly. "We manage to get along without it. Anything more?"

Linguard waved away the question of liquid refreshments with a nonchalant movement of a delicate hand. "One other question," he said. "Why were you spying about the clubhouse?"

To get a line on you, Linguard—the real you," was the answer.

"Did, er—did you get it, my friend?" Coolly.

"Perhaps. Any more questions to ask?"

Linguard gave him a long, steady look, then shook his head.

"Not just now," he replied. "I yield to you."

"And I haven't a single question to put!"

Calhoun shot that statement over suddenly, then watched its effect on the Dane.

"Ah," he commented, grinning, after Linguard had betrayed the tension he was really in by the faintest suspicion of a start, "that surprises you, I see! Well, turn about is fair play. You had your turn this afternoon, there at Panther Lake. We start out on a search for the Swamp Angel—and find Roth Linguard, the wealthy planter-sportsman-clubman and what-not, instead."

Linguard got slowly to his feet, his eyes, the lids of which had suddenly narrowed to slits, never wavering from those of the lank man whose gaze seemed to bore into his.

"You use my name in connection with that of the criminal, the Swamp Angel, my friend," he said gently, separating his words with the briefest of pauses. "Why? You do not suspect me of being he, surely?"

"I do not suspect you of being the Swamp Angel, Linguard," Cal said slowly, "for the simple reason that the Swamp Angel does not exist!"

10

HIS BACK TO THE WALL

LONG SILENCE GREETED Calhoun's amazing statement. Linguard's lids came wide apart for a brief moment, during which Calhoun saw the pupils of his eyes enlarge then swiftly contract. No other indication of surprise was evident.

"Are you joking?" the Dane asked.

"Not at all. Allow me to explain. The Swamp Angel is multiple. *He,* therefore, does not exist. *They* exist."

"Ah, you play with words!"

"Call it so if you wish," said Cal pleasantly. "Some three years ago a remarkably intelligent crook escaped from the penitentiary at Little Rock, where he was being held for Eastern authorities. The local jail was not considered strong enough to hold him, even for the period of a few days—such was his prowess. Truly, a formidable man. Forger, counterfeiter, then murderer—such is his record in the East. Even the penitentiary failed to hold him, for he succeeded in escaping—after knifing two of his guards. Both died from their wounds.

"A week after his escape, he fell again into the hands of the law. A United States deputy marshal caught him at Helena, just as he was in the act of boarding a steamboat bound down river. Kindred, the deputy, was assigned to the job of returning the criminal to Little Rock, along with another deputy. Nobody knows the right of what happened, save the crook himself. Before the train had covered half the distance to the capital, the few passengers in the smoker, where Kindred had his prisoner, were startled by the roar of a gun, then a second report, followed almost instantly by a crash of glass—as the prisoner flung himself headlong through a window.

"Much may be surmised concerning that escape, however. The handcuffs and leg irons which had bound the prisoner were found on the floor of the car. He had slipped them off with seeming ease. Kindred's revolver was missing, and it is likely that the prisoner snatched it from its holster.

"Kindred and his buddy, Lane, both died in their seats. So, as I said, surmise is all we have.

"One thing, though, was learned about the fleeing criminal, which was thought at the time would lead to his speedy apprehension," Cal went on to say. "A man, answering his description, appeared one night at the home of a country doctor—two miles from the nearest village. The right side of his face was in a terrible state—a ragged cut extended from beneath the hair above the temple, clear to the point of the chin. Glass might have caused the wound, according to the doctor's later statement. At the point of a gun the doctor was forced to dress the wound, feed the man, saddle a horse for him—then lie down and submit to being bound. His wife was treated in a like manner.

"Since that moment, Lynch Bullard—to use the name under which he was committed to the penitentiary at Little

Rock, and which is thought to be the one he began life with—vanished completely. At least, no one has owned to seeing him since."

Calhoun ceased speaking, fished out a pipe and pouch, and thumbed a charge of tobacco into the bowl. Apparently he had no more to say.

"Very interesting," Linguard commented, concealing—perhaps accentuating—a yawn with the spread fingers of a hand. "I read the newspapers, of course, so the Bullard matter is not exactly news to me."

Cal applied a match to the tobacco, puffed a time or two, then spoke.

"Sorry if you happen to be sleepy, Linguard," he said. "Afraid we're not due to shut our eyes to-night. What I have said about Bullard has a bearing on another matter—important to you and to me.

"Shortly after Bullard's last escape, the public having presumably ticketed him as gone forever, the authorities on this side of the river became aware that a master criminal was loose in the swamp lands. A man with a penchant for organization, possessed of great resourcefulness, and an insatiable greed for plunder. Public fancy was caught by that nickname, 'Swamp Angel,' bestowed by the newspaper reporter, and thereafter the Swamp Angel became a very real person. So real, in fact, that every crime of major proportions happening in the swamp country thereafter was attributed to him.

"But there is a limit to the activities of a single man, and the Swamp Angel would have to be super-human to have committed all the outrages blamed upon him. He did many, of course, but not all.

"That brings me to the plural nature of the person under discussion. Imitators. That is the answer. No doubt Bullard is the original Swamp Angel—'A' let us call him. Inspired by his success, B comes into the swamp country, and C and D and so on. Their depredations are popularly attributed to A.

"When the *Linda* was believed to have been stolen, the public acclaimed the Swamp Angel as the thief, the one and only person who had the shrewdness and the daring to commit the crime. Later that same public repudiated its opinion, and returned to the theory that the *Linda* sank. She sank, all right, but in the waters of either Gar or Panther Lake. Which body of water holds her wreckage will speedily be determined.

"Now you are astonished, Linguard—and, if your expression counts for anything, incredulous. To proceed:

"If the public becomes convinced that the *Linda* was stolen—as the public will be soon—the Swamp Angel will come into the limelight again. No doubt of it. But the public will be wrong. The Swamp Angel did not steal the *Linda*—that is to say, Bullard, the original, did not."

"You seem very sure of yourself," Linguard commented. "I fail to understand why you should be so. Have you definite knowledge of this Bullard's whereabouts that night, and that he could have had no part in the theft?"

"No, as to Bullard," Calhoun answered. "Here is my answer—my reason for acquitting Bullard of blame: The thing was too crassly amateurish."

This time there was no mistaking the effect of his words on the Dane. Cal chuckled and motioned him back into his seat, from which he had started.

"In the first place, there are so few places where the *Linda* could be hidden—so few, that is, within her reach. The Swamp Angel—Bullard, that is—would merely have plundered the express safe, the mail, and cut the throats of those aboard. He would have disdained to attempt to hide the evidence of his crime. He is all business, that fellow—and does not run to the spectacular.

"Secondly: Had Bullard run the *Linda* into a lake and sunk her, that would have ended the matter, so far as he was concerned. Let the public guess. Let it blame who it would. He would not have held onto Brokamp, keeping him alive for the purpose, and then send his drowned corpse floating down the river, along with the *Linda's* name-board and a stove-in skiff, also saved for the purpose, in order to lead the public to believe the transport had sunk, rather than that it had been stolen. No. Bullard would not have done that. Whatever else he is, he certainly is not an amateur at crime.

"That final touch—so lacking in criminal technique—convinced me of two things: That the *Linda* had been stolen and sunk, and that Bullard had had no hand in it.

"Acting on the theory, I, by a process of elimination, singled out two lakes in which the *Linda* could have been sunk. At Gar Lake I found no one. At Panther Lake—I found you.

"How long had you been at Panther Lake, Linguard, when I saw you there?"

Cal shot the question over, leaning across the table and boring the Dane with his eyes—eyes that seemed to look clear to the back of the mind.

Linguard's glance never wavered, and he answered with undisturbed calm.

"Sorry to blow up the possibilities of Panther Lake, my friend," he said, "but the *Pigeon* reached the place two days before the *Linda* disappeared, and has not since been away. No boat of any kind has been in the lake, save our own, during our stay. The *Linda* is elsewhere, if your theory is true. She could not possibly be in the mud of Panther Lake, with none of us the wiser."

Cal nodded slowly. "You are right," he agreed. "She could not be at the bottom of Panther Lake with none of you the wiser. Now, one question, and I'm through—for the moment:

"Have you any explanation to offer concerning the attack upon the clubhouse tonight?"

"Good heavens, man!" the Dane exclaimed. "What other explanation could there be than that of robbery? It is obvious! We, the members of my party and myself, are known to be men of considerable means. What more natural than that one of your swamp angels should conceive the notion of plundering us? I made no comment concerning it, to you, thinking none was needed. However far astray that peculiar bent of yours may lead you in other directions, the attack on the clubhouse to-night had but one object—and that object was plunder!"

Again Cal nodded agreement. "I believe you," he said simply. "Plunder."

"Thank you," Linguard said with a smile.

Cal grew thoughtful, seemed to forget the Dane. The latter stirred, and cleared his throat.

"Wherever women are, Linguard—women of your

station in life—diamonds, pearls, emeralds and like valuable baubles are usually to be found," Cal began, raising his eyes to the Dane's; "they take their jewels even into the wilds—hunting and fishing clubs, for instance. For, what is such an outing to them? Just another opportunity to display their charms—and no blame to them. Jewels are desired, and therefore taken. How many women were in your party?"

"Why—none," was the answer, slightly drawn out. "It was strictly a stag affair."

"I thought so—knew it, in fact. There were no women—and any fisherman will tell you that it is yet too early in the season for bass to bite. What object had your stag party?"

"An outing—cards, and the like," Linguard replied.

"An outing—cards, wine, but no women. And the outing was rather a protracted one. Now, Linguard, had there been women and, therefore, much jewelry at the clubhouse, then I could understand why Bullard would attack and plunder it. Otherwise not. He doesn't go after anything but big stuff—more than a party of sportsmen would be likely to have upon them in the wilderness. What do you suppose the Swamp Angel was after?"

Linguard had no answer. He merely stared at Cal for a moment, then said:

"You have the fact that he, or some one, did attack the club, and you agree that it was done for sake of plunder—"

"Yes!" Cal snapped. "Plunder from the *Linda Lee!* Plunder which he was blamed for taking, but did not! Plunder which he did take, however, *from those who got it in the first place!*"

11

RUNNING DARK

LINGUARD, WITH A snarl of rage, leaped to his feet, his right hand clenched and pounding the table before him.

"In effect," he shouted, his calm a thing of the past, "you accuse me of being the amateur who stole the *Linda Lee!*"

"I have not done so," Cal returned.

"It is the same thing!"

"Is it? Well, perhaps so. Sit down," Calhoun bade him. "Let me make it clear to you why I suspect you, and when that suspicion was born."

Linguard dropped into his chair, attempted to rally his mental forces and assume his old-time self-possession, failed, and merely glared from cold eyes.

"I suspected you when I learned that there were no women in your outing party," Cal resumed. "Men of your kind do not go away on pleasure bent, and for a protracted stay, and leave the women out. Bass are not biting—it is not yet their season. Why the outing on the lake?

"That was not enough, you will say, to arouse suspicion against a man of your standing, reputed possessions. True. It was enough only to cause me to give thought to you— and to investigate you.

"But, when Bullard attacked you—"

"How do you know he did?" snapped the Dane. "What proof have you that Bullard did it?"

"The proof of my own eyes and ears," Cal replied. "You see, I looked Bullard over at Helena, before Kindred took him away. Heard that big voice of his, too. When he roared out the command to open the clubhouse door, his voice stirred my memory. Later, on the dock, while you were in the water, I had a look under his mask while he lay insensible on the ground. The man was Bullard, and no mis—"

"You had him in your hands, insensible, and let him slip?" There was incredulity in Linguard's voice.

Cal nodded. "What else was I to do?" he asked. "Could I have carried him away bodily—swimming the lake with him on my back? Could I have remained on the dock, clinging to him, and defeated the efforts of his men to rescue him? Hardly. Besides, I was not after Bullard, at that moment. I was after an imitator—one who was about to elude me.

"So, you see, it was Bullard's determined attack upon you which cinched my belief that you are guilty. Bullard does not make mistakes—at least, he has not so far. He attacked you because he knew beyond doubt that you had the plunder from the *Linda Lee*. He has it now, I have no doubt. I am not, understand, asking you to confess. I shall not need an admission from you. To-morrow morning I shall search among the dead in the clubhouse—there will be many, never fear—and I have no doubt those members of the *Linda's* crew planted aboard her for the purpose of betraying her, will be among them. Some of them, at least.

"Furthermore, I have dynamite enough on board the *Clipper* to lower the surface of Panther Lake, by exploding it at the mouth of the creek. The lake is much higher than the bed of Little Panther, due to much mud and silt deposited there. The obstruction removed—you see the point, do you not? If the *Linda* is on the bottom of the lake, that fact will be determined—and you have admitted being on the lake since two days before the transport disappeared. No boat but your own has been in those waters, you affirm. Do you see your position, Linguard? A denial such as that is equivalent to an admission of guilt, should the *Linda* be where I think she is."

Linguard's face went white. His lips moved, but no sound came from them. Suddenly his right hand shot toward his hip—to be checked before it reached the butt of his revolver, while his wide eyes stared into the muzzle of Calhoun's forty-five.

"Sit down!" came the stern order. "Keep your hands on the table!"

Linguard did as he was told, and Murdock, who had been a silent listener since sending the boat up Little Panther, calmly removed the gun.

He isn't toting anything more, inspector," said the aid, after running a deft hand over the Dane's body.

"Good! Now, Linguard—"

"You'll sweat for this!" Linguard blazed. "You can't make a thing like this stick! A man of my standing, my known wealth—"

Cal held up a hand for silence—and got it.

"I will be surprised if it does not transpire that your wealth is all a myth," he said—" that your cotton exchange operations have not netted you a loss, instead of the gains you are reputed to have made. As to your good standing, you have probably forfeited it—in secret. However, the draining of the lake will—"

The texas door swung open, and Spence darted inside.

"Inspector," he said, his voice ringing with excitement in spite of obvious effort to subdue it, "I have to report the *Pigeon* on the way down Little Panther, running dark. She is now about two miles away!"

12

A LONG CHANCE

THE EXCITEMENT OCCASIONED by Spence's announcement was instantly manifest, but in different ways.

Linguard's face, pale before, went dead white, and his glance flashed to Calhoun's face. Murdock got up slowly, his face impassive, the nervous twitching of his fingers alone indicating emotion. Calhoun, who had moved his head slightly in order to observe Spence when he entered, turned again toward the Dane, his eyes resembling twin chunks of winter ice.

"How many men were aboard the *Pigeon* when you went ashore last night? Don't trouble to lie, because that could avail you nothing now. How many?"

Linguard, nervy though he unquestionably was, shivered slightly under the cold scrutiny of his inquisitor. Up to that moment Calhoun's manner had been pleasant, though stern—humane, withal. The passing of an instant had changed him completely. Linguard, unable to sustain the shock of those glinting eyes, dropped the lids over his own.

"One," he answered, his voice denoting almost unbearable strain.

"Who?"

"A deck hand. One watchman seemed enough."

"How many were in the house with you?"

"Four, not counting Mose, the negro."

"Four. I saw them through the window," Calhoun told him. "Now—in what part of the house had you hidden the survivors of the *Linda's* crew? Answer! Time is precious, and I have none to waste on you! If you are guilty, there is no way in which you can evade punishment now—that ought to be clear. Answer!"

Linguard palpably struggled with himself. The ticking of Calhoun's watch was distinctly audible in the cabin. Then, with startling suddenness, Linguard's nerve cracked, and, leaping to his feet, he shouted:

"Curse you! You are not a human being—you are a devil, a fiend! You want the truth! All right, I'm done—thanks to you! Stamford and Prickett, with Devlin and Newby, the four men planted aboard the *Linda,* were on board the *Pigeon* when I saw them last. There's a secret compartment—a place where they could hide, if necessary! Now, damn you, don't ask me anything more! I've stood all I can from you! Let up—"

"Take him away," Cal ordered, a look of contempt visible for an instant upon his face. "He's done."

Two rangers seized the Dane, reduced to a mere limp semblance of his former self, and hustled him out of the cabin.

Cal turned to Murdock, jerking out crisp orders.

"Stand away and below the creek. Tell Spence to get his men posted. Let the *Pigeon* choose her course, up or down, then run alongside—close enough to hail. That's all."

Murdock leaped away, and Calhoun, going to a locked

compartment forward, opened a wide door and revealed a small brass cannon, mounted and ready to be rolled onto the foredeck. At that moment Flahive and Riddle, two more of the crew, came in.

"If ordered, you will run the gun onto the foredeck and disable the *Pigeon* by pouring your fire into her engine room. On no account must you rake her decks—unless by my command."

The two gunners nodded and Cal withdrew to the foredeck. The sound of the *Pigeon's* engine was now plainly audible. The *Clipper* was dropping away from shore, and down the current, to take up a position covering the mouth of Little Panther. Spence ran up to Calhoun and thrust a magazine rifle into his hand.

Calhoun took the arm and stood leaning upon it, eyes intent upon the approaching *Pigeon*, faintly discernible through the timber. But his mind was concerned, not with the boat's nearness and the battle in prospect, but with sudden doubt as to who constituted her crew.

Had Linguard spoken the truth? Had his nerve really broken to such an extent as to render him desperate? Or had he a card up his sleeve—a card which was now about to be exposed?

Cal had little time in which to think, for the *Pigeon*, now that her bow was clear of the creek, suddenly increased her speed, while her pilot swung her head down the river.

Calhoun had eight men aboard, with only four who could be spared for combat—four, exclusive of himself. If Linguard had spoken the truth, they were enough, and to spare. But—if Linguard had lied—

13

"TILL ONE OF US SINKS"

"AHOY! ON BOARD the *Pigeon!*" Calhoun's voice, strengthened and amplified by the trumpet, rang out high and clear above the *chug-chug-chug* of the engines, and the surge of running water.

The *Pigeon*, all lights ablaze the minute she entered the river—a circumstance that surprised even the inspector—slackened speed instantly, and a voice answered through the darkness:

"The *Pigeon*, out of Memphis, Andrews commanding! Who are you?"

Without doubt, it was Captain Andrews answering. Calhoun had a distinct recollection of that unpleasant voice. How came he aboard? Had Bullard allowed some of the men penned in the clubhouse to escape, and had Andrews managed to gain the boat, rout out the men aboard and escape to the river?

For an instant Cal hesitated, then resolved to openly avow himself.

"The *Clipper*, United States Ranger service!" he shouted through his trumpet. "Calhoun commanding!"

A brief silence ensued, then:

"What is wanted?" came the voice of Andrews again.

"Who is your owner?" Cal called.

Again silence. Apparently Andrews was consulting some one before answering.

"Roth Linguard, owner!" Andrews shouted.

"Is he aboard?"

After a brief space, the answer came:

"Yes!"

"You lie!" was Calhoun's prompt reply. "Hold on your present course, and don't attempt to put in to shore until you reach the port of Memphis! Don't launch any small-boats! You, and your crew and passengers, are under arrest—in the name of the Government!"

No answer came from the *Pigeon*. Cal waited, noting that the *Clipper* had crept up within easy rifle range of the big launch while he talked with Andrews. Murdock knew his business—that was certain!

Suddenly a bell jangled in the engine room of *Pigeon*, there was a loud hiss of escaping steam—and the launch seemed to leap ahead on her course. Her boiler-doors were thrown open, the blaze of her fires illuminating the river in a wide circle about her. The stokers were giving her all the wood she would take. The *Pigeon*, patently, meant to run for it, and was getting up a full head of steam.

The *Clipper's* safety-valves were already popping. She was ready for a race. Once again Calhoun summoned Andrews to surrender.

"We'll overhaul you—and we won't be gentle about it!" he called. "Proceed at slow speed, or we'll fire!"

"Fire, and be damned to you!" came a bull-like roar from the *Pigeon's* upperdeck. "Overtake us, if you can! The boat hasn't been made that can clip this pigeon's wings! Full speed ahead, you there in the pilothouse—show that dirty tramp out there your heels!"

Calhoun turned to the mouthpiece of a speaking-tube which communicated with Murdock, at the wheel:

"Linguard lied!" he called up, his voice tense. "Brickett and his mates probably were in the clubhouse, and died with the rest! Bullard—the Swamp Angel—is aboard the *Pigeon!* He's probably running for the Gulf! Made his, and using Linguard's boat for his get-away—knowing the Dane can't squeal! It's Bullard we're about to lock horns with—Bullard, and the Lord knows how many of his crew!"

"Orders?" Murdock's voice came down the tube.

"Full speed ahead!" Cal snapped. "Hang to her heels until we reach the first bend—Newsome's Bend—then overhaul her, standing a rifle-shot off her port! Hold her there—until the *Pigeon* goes ashore, or—" he hesitated a second, then finished grimly— "or we go to the bottom!"

Murdock's reply was heard in the engine room—a loud jangling of the pilot's bell.

14

ONE DOWN

THE *CLIPPER* SHOT ahead, cleaving a course after the manner of a lean pike, the disturbed water splashing over her bow and drenching her foredeck, covering Calhoun with spray.

Calhoun opened the texas door, shouted a command to the two men beside the gun, then mounted to the pilot-deck and took a position forward in the shadow of the wheelhouse.

The *Pigeon's* wake soon became a wide swath of churning water, and the throbbing of her engine was like the pulse-beat of something alive. Her engineer, throwing caution to the winds, was crowding steam beyond the safety point.

"She's got speed!" the inspector muttered to himself. "And men to man her! It'll be nip and tuck between us!"

From the twin stacks of the flying *Pigeon* arose two streams of fire, and bits of burning wood trailed behind her for a space.

"They've put their blower on!" Murdock shouted from the wheel-house. "Forced-draft! See those burning chunks?"

"Newsome's Bend is just ahead!" Cal shouted. "Can we do it?"

"Yes!" Murdock answered, and reached for his bell, at the same time shouting down his speaking-tube: "More speed, O'Neil! Give 'er hell, if she busts wide open! If you've got steam, let's have it now!"

Calhoun was conscious that the *Clipper's* deck, just beneath him and over the boilers, was hot to his feet, penetrating the soles of his boots. The launch seemed to leave the water and hurtle through the air, as, in obedience to Murdock's plea, O'Neil eased his throttle wide. Chunks of flaming wood now spouted from the *Clipper's* stacks. O'Neil was forcing her draft, too. The mad jangle of Murdock's bell rang out from the engine room, and the pilot's stentorian voice added to the din, as he called down his tube:

"Give 'er hell, O'Neil! We're gaining! More steam! Crowd 'er, boy, crowd 'er!"

O'Neil promptly responded, though how he coaxed another ounce of pressure into the cylinders must forever remain a mystery. Cal only knew, by the sudden lurch of the deck beneath him, that he had. The *Clipper* ceased to be a hull of wood, and steel, it almost seemed, and became as a live thing, running free and of its own accord, its teeth bared, tongue lolling, eager for its prey!

The distance between the two boats began to diminish. Slowly, but with unfailing steadiness, the dingy little launch was crawling up on her snow-white sister. Murdock gave his wheel two spokes to port, the launch nosed off the course she had been following, swung to and sped on.

"Once more, O'Neil!" Murdoch's command was a plea. "Just a half-hole more, old man! We've got to have it—got to! Damn it, man—that's the boy! Give 'er hell!"

The *Clipper*, now carrying every ounce of steam she could—the safety point long since exceeded—shot on, the muddy water boiling about her, drenching her lower decks and casting spray into the face of Calhoun, who stood upon her top.

The smell of scorching paint came pungently to the inspector's nostrils, and the next instant he had torn the cover from a water-barrel, caught up a bucket, and was drenching the deck where the twin stacks came through. The dry pine was all ablaze, for the *Clipper's* stacks were red with heat!

Having extinguished the incipient blaze, Cal flung the bucket aside, cast a glance in the direction of the *Pigeon*, saw that the *Clipper* was in the act of running alongside about two hundred feet to port, then sprang down the companionway to the lower deck.

Flahive and Riddle, crouching beside the little brass cannon—now braced and ready for action—cast an inquiring glance at their commander.

"When I give the word—"

Cal broke off, and turned toward the texas door.

Linguard, white as a sheet, stood there, his eyes seeming to burn like live coals.

"Take these damned things off!" he shouted, holding out his hands and exposing the manacles which had been put upon him. "Take 'em off!" he begged. "Give me a gun, and a chance! You'll need me—and I swear to stay with you till the end! Give me a chance—to—die out here, rather than—"

His voice trailed off, but Calhoun had no need to hear. In the eyes of Linguard's mind was a scaffold, and a rope—

and a hushed and solemn, but justly vengeful crowd! He wanted to die out there!

"Get back!" Cal bade him sternly. "There isn't a man on these decks who'd honor you by fighting in company with you! Get back—liar! What did you hope to gain? Did you think the Swamp Angel would blow us to hell-and-gone, and you'd have a chance for a get-away? Get back, and if you put your head out that door again—you'll be shot on sight!"

The Dane, shrinking before the fury in Calhoun's face and eyes, disappeared into the texas, and the inspector turned his attention to the boat ahead. The *Clipper* now lay alongside, an easy rifleshot away.

"Bring her to, lads!" Cal ordered. "Get her paddlewheel, or put one into her engine-room. Fire when you are ready!"

There was silence for a short space, while Flahive bent anxiously to his sights. Suddenly he leaped back, raised his hand—

B-o-o-o-m-m-m-m!

It seemed as though the *Clipper's* every timber, from her keel to the pilot-house roof, must have been shaken loose. The little boat staggered drunkenly, then righted herself with a lurch and sped on. Deafened by the roar of the cannon, Calhoun dropped to his knees on the fore-deck, peering beneath the pall of smoke which wreathed the *Clipper* round.

"A hit!" he yelled. "Smack into the engine-room! Give 'er another, men! The wheel this time, the wheel!"

The *Pigeon*, realizing her inability to show her heels to her dogged little pursuer, suddenly slackened speed, else the shots from the *Clipper's* gun had damaged her seriously.

Little points of light began to show along her cabin-deck guard, followed by faint explosions which were all but smothered by the noise of the engines. Bullets spattered around the *Clipper's* bow.

"They're going to give battle!" Calhoun announced. "Ready with that gun?"

Another roar and burst of flame and smoke. Again the little launch staggered on her course. Cal, peering beneath the smoke, gave a yell of triumph.

"Carried it clean away!" he shouted. "She's as helpless as though she lay ashore!"

The *Pigeon*, minus her wheel, was wallowing helplessly toward the channel. The lines of her decks, on their port sides, were now blazing with streams of fire. Shot after shot was poured into the *Clipper*.

"Take cover!" Cal shouted.

Flahive darted into the texas and returned, dragging a shield of heavy boards covered with boiler-plate, assisted by Riddle. Protected from the fire from the *Pigeon*, they crouched beside their gun.

"Get ready to clear that boiler deck!" Cal ordered, taking the pilot deck companionway at a bound. "Murdock!" he shouted.

"Here!"

"The *Pigeon* is drifting out toward the channel! Get between her and the shore! Watch out for landing parties— and ram 'em!"

The *Clipper* swung about, circled the helpless *Pigeon*, and got to shoreward of her. There she hung.

"Ahoy! On board the *Clipper!*"

Above the din the voice of the Swamp Angel soared.

"Aboard the *Pigeon!*" he replied.

"What are your terms?" came the question.

"Unconditional surrender!" was the instant reply.

"I'll send the swag over in a boat," came the proposal. "In return you will allow one boat to land! Otherwise we'll fight until hell freezes!"

"Go to it!" shouted Calhoun. "And look alive—for we're coming aboard!"

A loud laugh greeted his words, and bullets fairly rained against the *Clipper's* sides.

"Clear the decks!" Cal ordered.

The cannon roared, and the woodwork beneath the boiler deck of the *Pigeon,* amidships, became a ragged, gaping hole. Shouts of anger, pain and fear carried to the ears of the attackers.

"Now get one into her boiler-room," came the command.

While the little piece on the foredeck was being swabbed out and reloaded, the men who constituted Calhoun's rifle crew poured a deadly fire into the floundering launch, raking her decks fore and aft.

B-o-o-o-m-m-m-m!

Again the cannon spouted flame, and this time with most decisive results.

The *Pigeon* was seen to stagger in her every quarter, then to begin settling forward. There was a wild yell from the stokers as they dashed from the pit before the boiler doors and leaped overside.

"She's sinking!" Cal called to his men. "Watch for small-boats!"

Two skiffs rattled down the *Pigeon's* sides, and were

quickly filled with men. Calhoun, watching closely, found the man he sought in the forward boat.

"Bullard is in the bow of the first boat," he called to Murdock. "Get that one! If the other gets away, let it! We want Bullard!"

Murdock swung the *Clipper's* bow onto the skiff Cal had pointed out, and the little launch swept toward it.

"Come aboard, Bullard!" Calhoun called. "You're whipped!"

"Never!" snarled Bullard. "You've won—but you haven't got me yet!"

He leaped to his feet, fired his revolver in the direction whence Cal's voice had come, then plunged over the skiff's side in the direction of the near-by shore.

Calhoun's gun roared once. When Bullard, the Swamp Angel, struck the water he was dead.

15

THE RECKONING

ANDREWS HAD BEEN a traitor all along. He was, in fine, the one who kept Bullard informed concerning Linguard's movements, and was responsible for the attack on the club-house at Panther Lake.

He was executed the following fall. So was Linguard.

Panther Lake, with the aid of dynamite, gave up the wreck of the *Linda Lee,* and the bodies of Captain Blount, Pilot Brady, and the three trainmen theretofore unaccounted for. Joiner, Vance, Devlin, and Newby, the four deck hands who had been planted aboard the transport by Linguard and Andrews, were found later, when the club-house was searched.

Stamford, the mate, and Brickett, the engineer, were apprehended within a few days after their leader was taken. Andrews supplied the information which led to them. It was from Stamford, who confessed before the rope claimed him, that the truth about what occurred on board the *Linda* that fatal night was learned.

Stamford and Brickett had formerly served Linguard on board his launch, the *Pigeon,* and when Linguard, in desperate need of large sums of money, and inspired by the example of the Swamp Angel, conceived the idea of stealing and robbing the transport, he contrived to place the mate and engineer aboard her. Captain Turner was entirely innocent, having been taken in by false papers forged by Andrews and which purported to be genuine service records of the rivermen. Being aboard the *Linda*, it was an easy matter for Stamford, as mate, to engage the four deck hands sent him later by Linguard.

On the night of the crime, the *Linda Lee* was in the hands of Stamford and his companions before he reached mid-stream on the return with the remainder of Number Two's train. Devlin, a deck hand, slew Pilot Brady at the wheel, using a blackjack, since the report of firearms might have been heard ashore. Devlin, it appears, was something more than a deck hand—he was a first-rate pilot as well. He took charge of the wheel after Brady fell. Captain Blount was attacked in his cabin by Vance and Joiner, and stabbed to death.

Those members of the boat's crew not in the scheme disposed of, there remained only the four trainmen. Claxton, the brakeman, was killed by Newby, who engaged him in conversation until he got a chance to use his knife.

Stamford, himself, entered the express car and shot the man in charge, stuck up the mail messenger, who was later bound and reserved for questioning by Linguard, who thought thereby to get valuable information about the movement of registered mail. His subsequent fate has already been described. From the end door of the mail car into the baggage car is only a step, and, having brought his business in the first coach to a successful termination, the mate entered the baggage car and slew the baggage man without a word of warning.

It was wholesale murder—and what made the thing even more revolting was the fact that each murder had been deliberately planned and provided for.

Once the boat was wholly in the hands of her captors, she was run upriver to Little Panther Creek and there scuttled, as Jack Calhoun had surmised.

One very interesting matter was cleared up as an incident to the capture of Linguard and the killing of Bullard.

Bullard, the Eastern crook, proved to be the one and only "Swamp Angel." That is to say, it was he upon whom the nickname was conferred in the beginning. Having escaped from the officers who were returning him to Little Rock, he made his way into the swamps, found congenial spirits also hiding there, organized them and made himself their master.

Most of the big crimes committed in the section subsequent to Bullard's arrival in the swamps, were the work of his brain and hands. Being unusually shrewd, he conceived the idea of binding the natives, among whom his lot had been cast, by ties of gratitude, thereby safeguarding himself against betrayal and, in the event of discovery and attack in the swamp, insuring their aid in repelling the attackers.

Calhoun and the crew of the *Clipper* succeeded in getting a line aboard the *Pigeon*, the night of her capture, and towing the wreck into shallow water, where she sank only up to her freight deck.

The loot from the *Linda Lee* was found aboard the small-boat in which Bullard attempted to escape to shore, and on his person. A vast amount of other loot, in the form of currency and jewels, was later recovered through information of various members of the gang.

Calhoun had reckoned correctly when he concluded that the Swamp Angel, seeing his chance to get clear of a section rapidly becoming too hot for him, was intending to reach the gulf on Linguard's boat. Having made ample provision for himself, out of the rich booty he had acquired during his swamp land depredations, Bullard was ready to retire and live in luxury thereafter.

But—he was the victim of an oversight: He had reckoned without the *Clipper,* Calhoun and his crew.

THE NEGATIVE CLEW

*Calhoun Searches for an Outlander Who, With
Miles of Bottomless Mire in Which to Bury
His Victims, Burns Their Wagons Instead*

1

"RAZORBACK" BENSON, WEARY from tramping the tangled aisles of a primitive woodland, skirted the south-ern end of Bottomless Bog and followed a dim trail which lay along its eastern edge. As he walked, he bent his lank, skinny frame and peered here and there through such openings as the shrouding underbrush offered, as though searching for something. At intervals, leaning against a tree or reposing on a fallen log, he would raise his powerful voice in a high, far-carrying wail:

"Wh-o-o-o-o-e-e-e-e! Wh-o-o-o-o-e-e-e-e! Purg! Purg! Wh-o-o-o-o-e-e-e-e! Purg!"

One unused to hearing such a sound would have taken refuge when it first fell upon his ears, or at least have avoided the locality whence the vocalizing emanated. Surely no one in possession of his senses would wander about the deep woods, shouting in such manner!

Then another thought would probably take hold upon the uninitiated:

"Perhaps some poor fellow is lost!"

The wise, were such within sound of Razorback's cries, would know that the native was merely out on his hog-range, "whooping 'em up."

"I kain't skursely find no hawgs a-tall!" Benson grumbled, sitting down on a stump and contemplating the dense

"Found it!" he shouted. "All buried under the woodpile!"

foliage on the east—the rankly growing trees and bigleaf plants which clothed the bosom of Bottomless Bog. Out there, huge, trackless, masked from the eyes of men, as well as forbidden to their feet, lay two thousand acres of slimy muck—black, sticky, bottomless. "It don't stand to reason," he argued, shivering slightly as he continued to gloom at the waste, "that they done gone an' got into th' bog. Hoss-critters might. I knows; but no hawg ain't no sech a dum fool! Reckon, now, whut done come of that passel of grunters?"

No answer, of an enlightening character such as Razor-back sought, came to him from the morass. The damp, chill breeze which blew across the face of the place at all times, was freighted with the croaking of frogs, the cries of brants and fisherbirds, and the eerie strains of a mud-crane's plaint.

The Sunken Lands of Northern Arkansas contained no other spot quite so blackly forbidding as Bottomless

Bog. Two thousand acres, almost in a square, in the heart
of the forest—two thousand acres wherein nothing save
fish, fowl, and reptile might live. A mile from its western
marge, the St. Francis River clove its course, and between
it and the river the soil was wet and worthless.

On the east, in the direction of the Mississippi River
which lay forty miles away, the ground was higher, and,
here and there, native swampers dwelt in stilt-cabins,
the latter set in tiny clearings on the banks of slough and
bayou. Ten miles north of the bog, where the St. Francis
forked, creating from its eastern channel what was locally
known as Ten Mile Slough, Buck Island began. It stretched
a ten-mile length due north, and was, at its widest, some
five miles across.

Razorback's brooding mind took note of Buck Island,
and his tongue began wagging again. Men accustomed to
the solitude of primitive places often commune with themselves. The hog-caller had never known anything different
from the setting he then was in—nor had his father and
grandfather.

In other words, Ephraim Benson—called Razorback
because of a real or a fancied resemblance to the long, lean
swine peculiar to the region thereabouts—was a bred-in-
the-bone native of the Sunken Lands.

"I ain't never lost no hawgs, ontel them settlers come
in an' cluttered up th' country," he told himself, a note of
deep injury in his voice. "I got a good notion to go right
up to Buck Island, walk into Cleve Trask's gineral sto', an'
tell him, an' all th' rest of th' dang furriners which happens
to be thar, whut I think of 'em—a passel of hawg thieves,
blast 'em!"

He got to his feet slowly, straightening each joint separately, and devoted a few minutes' time to cursing his rheumatism.

"It's you, you infernal breed-place fur snakes, an' frawgs, an' sech," he shouted, shaking a fist impotently in the direction of Bottomless Bog, "an' others lak you, which damps th' country up an' spreads th' rheumatiz into th' bones of decent folks! Sometimes I reckons to move plumb away frum sech a country!"

It was an idle threat. Rheumatism, or no rheumatism, Razorback, being swamp-born and raised, would have found existence outside intolerable. He sensed that, without knowing why.

"Wh-o-o-o-o-e-e-e-e! Wh-o-o-o-o-e-e-e-e-e-e! Purg! Purg! Dang you, you hazel-splittin', sprout-eatin', mud-grabbin', contrairy, brush-hidin' devils—"

He stopped abruptly in what seemed likely to prove a record-breaking flight-of-adjectives, to stare owlishly at a large black fowl which rose from the limb of a dead tree near by, to take its flight leisurely deeper into the timber. Another followed, and still another.

"Buzzards!"

Just the one word. Then he stood in an attitude of deep reflection, scratching his stubble of beard, which was just beginning to show the gray that fifty years of life had brought him. His face, brown and lined, and marked by the greenish tint of constantly present malaria, had a whimsical cast, despite the deeply solemn expression it habitually portrayed. Perhaps the twinkle far back in the deep-set blue eyes lent it such. One looking upon the man for the first time would not have hesitated to ask directions of him, nor to follow his guidance in all trust.

Yet, to tell the truth about Razorback Benson, he was all but shunned by his widely spaced neighbors—shunned because they, each and every one, looked upon him with something akin to contempt. In their own vernacular: "He's tre'chrus as a cotton-mouth!"

Whatever Razorback might think about his neighbors in his idle time, his mind was, on this occasion, wholly devoted to the flight he had just witnessed—and the nature of the birds which flew.

"Buzzards, huh? Well, now, wharever you sees buzzards thar's buzzard-bait around somewhars clost. You kin lay to that. An' buzzard-bait is cyarn which has been a long time dead. Lak th' hide an' entrills of a hawg, maybe, which a thief would naturally leave behind. Some of my hawgs, I'll be bound! Them'd be buzzard-bait!"

Forgetting his rheumatism, Razorback plunged into the timber and strode rapidly eastward—arousing buzzards to flight at frequent intervals.

"Havin' a reg'lar festibul, ain't you—damn you!" he yelled at the scavengers as they flew. "An' offen my hawgs, I'm bound!"

Razorback's reasoning was quite good, but he was soon to learn that his conclusion was wrong. Something far more ghastly and gruesome was in the deep woods beside Bottomless Bog that day—something which drew the buzzards in droves to a feast quite different from the "hawg-hide an' entrills" of the native's vision.

Upon the trampled grass of a small clearing, screened from view by trees and underbrush until Benson broke his way through, lay the buzzard-bait which had drawn the scavengers down from the air. Razorback's face became a shade greener than was its wont, and he leaned weakly against a tree, wide eyes taking in the scene slowly, but with entire comprehension.

In the center of the cleared spot was a large heap of ashes among which bits of metal lay—the metal parts of a roadwagon, to be exact. Ten feet from the ashheap were the skeletons of two horses but lately dead, and denuded of nearly all flesh by the buzzards. The harness with which they had been clothed had also been burned, as the metal bits clearly showed.

But the native had seen something else—something which drew his horror-stricken eyes and held them.

The wolves and jackals, too, had been at work. From shallow graves, which had patently been covered with logs at the time of interment, the bodies of two human beings had been exhumed. From the fragments of clothing visible, Benson easily determined that the corpses of a man and a woman were before his eyes.

With sickening certainty, he recognized them—the man and the woman. Only a week had passed since he had seen them alive. Now—

2

HE WHEELED AND was gone. Possessed of unusually long legs, the native could cover the ground rapidly when he chose, and he was then in a humor to run—run as he had never before. An hour later he reached his cabin beside the river, miles below the foot of Bottomless Swamp, where he leaped into a dugout with only a shouted word or two to his daughter who kept house for him, and headed downstream for Oak Donnick—headquarters of Hub Wheeler and his rangers.

With the third or fourth stroke of his paddle, however, came a stunning thought into Razorback's mind. He sat inert for a moment while the little shell drifted under the impetus his erstwhile eagerness had given it, then he back-paddled, swung around and headed to shore. When he stepped onto land again and bent over to make the painter fast, his body was in a cold sweat and his hands trembled.

"Lawd!" he ejaculated, casting a fearful glance toward the trim figure of a young woman who was coming down the path toward him, "I'm glad I didn't say nothin' to Emmy!"

"What's th' matter, pappy?" Emmy Benson asked, pausing at the water's edge and eying her father curiously. "You was in a turrible swivet, a minute ago, now you looks lak you ain't hardly able to drag one foot behin' th' other! Had a chill, or somethin'?"

"Yeah!" Razorback gulped. "A ch-chill, Emmy—a reg'lar shaker! Reckon I needs a drap of whisky an' kwinine, to straighten me up!"

He hurried to the cabin, dosed himself generously, then retired to the wood pile in the edge of the clearing—not to cut wood, but to think.

"They'd accuse me shore—" he assured himself miserably, nervously fingering the handle of his axe. "Splint Robbins an' Sloughfoot Snyder war both settin' in thar dugouts on th' river when them folks driv up to my cabin an' axed me to show 'em th' road 'round Bottomless. Heered 'em say they'd pay me to guide 'em into th' trail to Buck Island—an' worse an' more of it, they seed me go away with 'em!

"Now, after a week has done passed, I finds them same folks dead in th' swamp, right on th' aidge of Bottomless, not more than half a quarter frum th' road. No matter if I does hurry an' tell th' law about it—I'm th' last pusson seed with 'em, an', (thanks to my neighbors which don't lak me because I works, raises hawgs, an' tries to make a crop—an', moreover, don't feel so pizen mean to'ads th', furriners—I got a bad reputation, anyhow!

"Thank th' Lawd I tuck a secon' thought, an' didn't run to Wheeler an' tell him! Another week, an' thar won't be no trace of them—them corpses. I'm goin' to keep my trap shet about it!"

He fell to cutting wood in a fury, and that night slept not at all. When morning dawned he was restless, had no appetite—and his eyes, in spite of the effort of his will, continually sought the heavens beyond Bottomless Bog, where, in imagination, he could pick out myriad small specks circling, circling, ever circling—

The scavengers of the air!

"THIS NATIVE, RAZORBACK, I believe they call him, piloted Roger Blackwell and his wife part of the way—that much is positive."

Deck Lundsford, sheriff of Poinsette County, fanned himself with his wide-brimmed hat while he rested before Headquarters House on Oak Donnick, and talked to Hubbard Wheeler, chief of the rangers.

"Yes," seconded Rafe Hillman, a settler from Buck Island. "Mr. Robbins and Mr. Snyder are here and can speak for themselves." He paused, indicating two natives who were in the background beyond the circle formed by Lundsford and his half dozen deputies. "They saw Roger that day, and saw Benson when he walked off into the timber ahead of their covered wagon, his rifle on his shoulder. They have so stated, and will also testify."

Wheeler nodded. "So I have already heard," he replied.

"Here's where we stand," Lundsford continued. "We have it from Mr. Hillman here, a step-brother of the murdered man's, that the latter was expected to reach the settlement on Buck Island some time in the fore part of last week. He was on the lookout for them. They failed to show up, in spite of the fact that a letter reached Hillman at Marked Tree, stating that Blackwell and his wife had started overland for the swamp country. They journeyed from Kentucky, where many of the Buck Island settlers hail from, and intended to make their home here.

"Now, Hillman inquired at Marked Tree, learned that

a man and woman answering the description of his step-brother and wife had stopped in town, asked direction to Buck Island, bought some provisions, and gone on. The time of their presence in Marked Tree coincided with the time they should have reached there, barring accidents. Splint Robbins happened to be in the store where Hillman made his inquiry, and told him about seeing such a man and woman at Razorback's cabin on Tuesday of last week.

"Then it developed that Razorback had piloted them into the woods beyond Bottomless. They failed to reach Buck Island—only ten miles away after they reached the Bog Road."

Wheeler merely nodded, and waited for Lundsford to speak further.

"Hillman tells me that Blackwell carried money—not much, it is true, but several hundred dollars," the sheriff went on to say. "He owned a small place in Kentucky, sold it. How much do you reckon he carried, Hillman?"

"Not above five hundred dollars, I'd judge," the settler replied. "Roger, like myself, was a poor man. He couldn't have had more."

"Hum! Now, there was no trace of the money to be found on the scene of the crime," Lundsford went on triumphantly. "Who ever shot those poor travelers through the head, killed their team and burned their wagon and belongings, did it for robbery—and succeeded! I think that much may be taken for granted."

"It certainly would seem so," Wheeler agreed. "What steps have you taken, so far?"

"Not many," Lundsford answered. "Acting on the knowl-edge that the travelers had reached Bottomless Bog and the final ten mile stretch of their journey, we searched the forest for sign of them. Some of our party, observing buzzards circling in the air, penetrated to the clearing in which the bodies lay. We had the corpses taken to the settlement at Buck Island. We are about to take further and more important steps, however," the sheriff continued. "Steps which, we feel certain, will take us right to the inhuman beast who fired the slugs into two human and two brute victims. It's this way:

"In the soft earth of the clearing, near the edge, we found the foot-prints of a man—a man who wore gaiters with broad toes and a straight last. Gaiters such as ninety-nine out of every one hundred swampers wear. The prints were clear-cut—unmistakable, and that proves a native was on the spot. What native? It strikes me that the answer is not far to seek!"

Lundsford sat back, having divulged that latest development.

"And what do you want of me?" the ranger chief inquired quietly.

Lundsford cleared his throat. "Well, you know, Wheeler, that you chaps have been running the law in this section, mostly, where the settlers are concerned," he answered. "Calhoun, particularly, has helped us out considerably. I thought maybe you'd like to send a man along with us when we examine Razorback, and—well, that's why we stopped here."

"I'm just about to set out for Hell Hole," a quiet voice broke in, and a tall, sandy-headed young man who had been sitting on the door log of Headquarters House, stepped forward. "If the chief wishes, I will stop off at Benson's cabin and be of what service I can."

The tall young man was Jack Calhoun, chief inspector of United States Rangers, and while speaking he gave Hub Wheeler a significant glance which went unnoticed by the others.

"Very well, Calhoun," Wheeler consented. "You will accompany Sheriff Lundsford and his party, and remain as long as he desires it."

The chief rose. He was a busy man, and the conference was over.

Calhoun tossed his kit into a dugout, placed his rifle lengthwise on the rack, and followed the sheriff's party up the St. Francis. Two hours after embarking they stepped ashore at Razorback Benson's cabin—a lonely appearing log shack among the trees.

Emmy, her face expressing surprise and uneasiness, stood on the door log, but Razorback was nowhere in sight. When the party assembled before the cabin the girl spoke.

"Pappy ain't been feelin' well lately," she explained. "He's layin' down."

3

"SO—HE AIN'T BEEN feeling well lately, eh?" Lundsford winked broadly at Calhoun. "Well, tell him to step out here and let us see if we can't fix up something that'll help his case! Step lively, now!"

The girl—she was not yet out of her teens, and was decidedly pretty—looked frightened, and her eyes roved from one face to another in the crowd; finally they rested upon Calhoun, one she knew more intimately than the others present, with the exception of the two natives.

"I—I don't rightly unde'stan' this-all, Mr. Calhoun!" she exclaimed, clasping her hands nervously in front of her. "Pappy's sick! Whut does these men want with him?"

"I'm sorry, Miss Benson," Cal said, "but your father will have to come out, else some of us—Mr. Lundsford and myself, at least—will be compelled to go in after him. There is no harm intended, I assure you, but our business is important." He raised his voice and called: "Come out, Benson!"

Razorback appeared in the door. He walked slowly, and any one who doubted the genuineness of his claim to illness had only to look at his face to be convinced. The man was haggard, and his eyes had the light of fever in them.

"Whut kin I do for you-all, gentl'mens?" he asked quaveringly.

"You can answer some questions!" Lundsford snapped. "Come on out! It would be too crowded in the cabin, and it's cooler out here!"

Razorback walked into the yard, and Emmy, Cal assisting, brought chairs out of doors.

"Did you act as guide for a man named Roger Blackwell, about ten days ago—last Tuesday a week, to be exact?" Lundsford asked when all were seated.

"Yes," Benson answered.

"How far did you accompany him?"

"Ontel I made shore they could find thar way to whar they war goin'," the native replied. "I left 'em on th' Bog road, about th' middle of it—th' Bog, I mean."

Lundsford nodded. "That accords with our best belief," he said. "Now, what were the travelers doing when you last saw them?"

"They war drivin' along th' road to'ads Buck Island," Benson replied.

"What did you do when you left them driving along the road?"

"I come straight back home."

Lundsford looked down at the native's feet, clad in home-knit socks only.

"Bring out your pap's shoes," he said, turning to Emmy. "Bring every pair he's got."

"I ain't got but jest one pair," Razorback told him plaintively. "Go and fetch 'em, Emmy."

The girl brought the gaiters, and Lundsford, after consulting some figures in a notebook, took a tape measure from his pocket, and carefully measured the soles.

"Ha!" he exclaimed, dropping the shoes. "You came

straight home, did you? Well, that sure is odd! Now you listen, while I tell you what you really did do!"

Razorback, shaking with fear, sat limply in his chair, his eyes wandering from face to face of the gathering. Calhoun glanced at the daughter, and found that, instead of fear being depicted upon her features, the flush of anger dyed her brow.

"Mr. Sheriff!" the swamp girl exclaimed, stepping to her father's side. "Pappy is sick, an' you ain't got no right to talk mean to him! He ain't done nothin' deservin' of it, an' if thar was any real men here they would see fairness done! At least, you can come straight out an' say whut it is you air accusin' him of!"

In his heart Calhoun applauded the spirit of the girl, but he showed nothing of that upon his face. He waited for Lundsford's reply. When it came it startled even Cal.

"I'm accusing him of murder, that's what!" Lundsford shouted, standing suddenly, and pointing a long finger almost in the cowering Razorback's face. "A double murder! I'm saying, and expect to prove, that he suspected Roger Blackwell had money, being a settler coming into a new country he would naturally carry considerable money with him!

"Benson guided them into the road beside Bottomless Bog, the most isolated spot in the whole swamp country, and there shot them dead. He robbed them, burned the wagon, buried the bodies, safely, as he thought, with logs piled on top of the graves!

"The buzzards would pick the horses clean, and the weeds would soon grow-up over the ash heap! That's what he figured—but he didn't figure it right! You wanted me to

come right out and say what I was accusing your pap of—
well, I've done it! Now what you got to say, young woman?"

"Oh, my God!"

That was all the swamp girl could say. Her eyes, distended
with horror, sought her father's face, then they flitted to
Calhoun—and rested there.

"Yes! He did just that!" Lundsford went on. "Yesterday we found tracks in the clearing near the bodies, and
those tracks were made by your father! Figures don't lie!"
He turned to Razorback. "Well, what you got to say for
yourself?"

"Wait a minute!"

It was Calhoun speaking. Lundsford turned upon him,
his upper lip curling scornfully.

"Reckon the county can handle this, Calhoun!" he
barked. "It's a dead open and shut case—"

"You asked for me," Cal reminded him. "And you knew
when you did so that I'd not stand like a dummy and let
you run the show to suit yourself—particularly when I
can, with a few words, wipe those footprints clean out of
the case. You are being misled, and I'm going to show—"

"Hell!" Lundsford bawled angrily. "Didn't you just see
me measure them shoes? And don't the measurements jibe
to a gnat's heel?"

Cal nodded. "True enough," he agreed. "I'm not quarrel-
ing with your deductions in that matter. I will go farther
and say that in all probability Razorback made the tracks—
but he made them long after the killing took place."

For all that Cal's words were spoken quietly, they had
almost the effect of a bombshell dropped in the center of
the circle.

"Wait!" Cal commanded, holding up his hand and silencing the questioners who were shooting at him from all directions. "Think this over:

"You found footprints in the marsh, and you found them ten days after the day we are forced to assume the killing occurred. Don't you—any of you—know your swamps better than that? Don't you know that those prints you saw could not have been many hours old—let alone days? I know the character of the soil adjacent to Bottomless Bog. It is wet and loamy—not a particle of clay in it. Footprints in such soil never lay long aground. Any swampman will verify that."

He turned, while silence reigned, to the only swampers there—Splint and Sloughfoot. Both nodded agreement.

"Calhoun has got th' right of it," Splint declared.

"Them air th' facts," Sloughfoot agreed, nodding sagely.

The figure in the chair straightened, and, as though he had in truth found a friend among a host of enemies, Benson took courage. He essayed to speak.

"Shut up!" Lundsford snarled. "Your time to talk will come—down at the county-seat! Now, Calhoun, what difference does it make whether Benson made the tracks ten days ago, after he done the killing, or only yesterday? What does that prove?"

"It proves that you are going ahead too hastily," Cal answered quietly. "You are rushing things, and a man's life, or liberty, is at stake. Why not calm down, and get at this thing quietly? I'm sure there's more to it than you think, and I'd say make haste slowly."

"But—"

"There isn't any 'but' about it," Cal interrupted. "You

affirmed that those tracks you found were made by the murderer when he killed Blackwell and his wife. I show that it is impossible that those tracks could have laid aground, clearcut and perfect, for ten days in such soil. You are proved wrong in one of your hypotheses, why not in some others?"

"If you think you can do better," came scathingly from the sheriff, "why go to it!"

"I shall," Cal retorted. He turned to Razorback. "Where did you spend yesterday?" he inquired.

"I war huntin' my hawgs, which I turns loose to feed on th' mast in th' swamps, Mr. Calhoun," was the reply.

"What part of the swamp were you in?"

"I was all over this part of it, fust an' last, but I was up along th' east aidge of Bottomless, if that's whut you-all air gittin' at."

"What attracted you to the spot where the murder was done?"

There was silence. Everybody seemed astonished—everybody, that is, except the man most concerned.

"It war th' buzzards," he answered. "Look here, Mr. Calhoun, I'm goin' to tell all I knows about this thing—an," he exclaimed, getting to his feet, his voice rising, "I would of done it yistiddy, if it hadn't been fur that feller thar, Lundsford, whut calls hisself a sheriff! I started down-river to tell you rangers, but I thought about Lundsford and I come back! All he ever looks fur is somebody he can fit to a crime! That satisfies him, an' spares him a heap of trouble! He don't keer whether a man's guilty—"

"Never mind all that!" Cal spoke sharply. "You are talking to me, now, and you can leave Lundsford out of it."

"Let him talk!" the sheriff gritted, glaring at Razorback. "He can say what he pleases! I've got the evidence, and he can't get out of it! He'll talk on the other side of his mouth, when his trial—"

"I'll ask you to keep quiet, too, Lundsford!" Cal broke in, "This is supposed to be an investigation into a murder, and not a rag-chewing match!"

The sheriff subsided, and the ranger again addressed Razorback.

"Now," he bade him, "go on and tell us all about it."

4

———

THE NATIVE DESCRIBED what had passed on the previous day. How the buzzards, frightened away from their
feast, attracted him to the place of crime, and his actions
subsequent thereto.

"I was afeered to take chances on th' sheriff gittin' holt of
me," he finished. "I knowed it could be proved that I war
with them just afore th' time they must of been kilt—an'
that'd be enough fur him to hang a man on! Hangin' me
would make him poplar in th' swamps!"

"Stuff and nonsense!" Lundsford exploded. "Are you
being taken in by all that, Cal?"

"I believe that Razorback went to the murder clearing
yesterday, just as he says," Cal replied calmly. "His tracks
prove that. I am not saying that he did not commit the
crime, understand. I do say, however, that the fact of his
acting as guide for them on the day they probably met
death, is not sufficient to warrant you in accusing him
of killing the man and woman. He is a rather promising
suspect—that is all."

"Here's something else to make him more 'promising,'"
Lundsford remarked sarcastically. "These bullets!"

He fished two lead slugs out of a vest pocket, and
extended them toward Cal. The ranger took them.

"Shot from an old-time Sharps," he remarked, after a

moment's examination. "A type now almost extinct, even in the swamps."

"Yes!" Lundsford exulted. "We got 'em from the skulls of the horses! What kind of rifle do you shoot?" he demanded, turning upon Razorback.

"One of them Sharps," was the answer.

"Well, what now, Mr. Ranger?" the sheriff asked triumphantly.

Calhoun pointed silently to Splint Robbins, indicating the gun which lay across his lap. "Splint also shoots a Sharps—and he also knew that there were strangers on the Bog Road," he said. "Why not he, as well as Benson?"

"Looky here, Mr. Calhoun!" exclaimed Splint getting to his feet. "Don't you-all go accusin' me of—"

"Keep your shirt on, Splint," Cal advised. "When we want anything from you we'll call you by name!"

Splint subsided, muttering.

"Now, as to those Sharps rifles," Cal resumed, "I suppose there are not more than half a dozen in the whole of the swamp country—relics of a bygone era they are, nevertheless, highly valued by some of the older natives. Don't suppose anybody but a native would cling to one. Any of you folks in the Buck Island Settlement own such a gun?" He asked the question suddenly of Rafe Hillman.

"The settlers shoot nothing but the latest magazine rifles," was the cold response. "That is why we are superior to these folks you call natives. We have better methods, better tools, better arms—"

"This meeting was not called for the purpose of comparing the merits of outlander and native," Cal interrupted severely. "You have answered my question—and, should I ask you another, you will confine yourself to a direct reply, and nothing more."

Any one knowing Calhoun would have instantly recognized the fact that something had got "under his collar." His eyes glinted coldly, and there was ice in his voice.

"If Razorback owned the only rifle of the pattern used by the murderer," he said, turning to Lundsford, "your case would be complete. In view of the fact that he was last seen with the victims, and that he did carry such an arm, makes things look dark for him. Add that he was foolish enough not to report the crime the moment he discovered it, and the case grows still blacker. But, circumstantial evidence is, in my opinion, inadequate when it is a man's life which is in the balance. If Razorback is guilty, then there should be direct evidence to that effect. Let us see.

"What conversation took place between you and the travelers when they drove up to your place?" he asked Razorback.

"Well, th' man hollered 'Hello!' I war on th' river bank, talkin' with Splint an' Sloughfoot, an' I went up to see what war wanted. Th' man axed me if I war Mr. Ephraim Benson, an' I told him yes. Then he turned to the woman and told her that this was th' place they war lookin' fur. Th' next thing he done war to ax me if I'd show 'em how to git to th' Buck Island road, an' offered to pay—"

"Ha!" Lundsford broke in. "That's it! When he paid Benson, he took out too much money, an' Benson couldn't resist the tempta—"

"He didn't pay me nothin'!" declared Razorback indignantly. "Think I'd let a man pay me fur helpin' him find his way in my own country? You might, Mr. Sheriff—but I war raised to know better!"

"Stop it!" Cal snapped. "Now, Razorback, are you sure that Blackwell asked if you were Mr. Ephraim Benson?"

"In co'se!" the native declared. "Them war his words!"

Splint Robbins nodded affirmatively.

"Razorback air tellin' th' facts," Sloughfoot corroborated.

"All right. I guess I have no more questions to ask?" Cal said. "What are you going to do, Lundsford?"

"Speaking of the money the settler had," the sheriff replied, "has given me an idea. I'm going to search Razorback's cabin. Say, you," he demanded, turning to the native, "how much money have you got on these premises?"

"I ain't got above forty dollars in this whole world!" Razorback answered, "let alone on th' premises!"

"Where is it?"

The native took out a worn wallet, extracted four ten-dollar bills and a few silver coins and passed the whole thing to the sheriff.

"That's all the money there is on this place?" the latter demanded.

"All," was the laconic reply.

"All right! Now, men, search the cabin, and give it a good going over!"

Cal sat in his chair, taking no part in the search. Ten minutes sufficed to complete it, and Lundsford was standing in the doorway, a glum look upon his face, when a shout from behind the cabin caused him to start eagerly. The next moment a deputy darted round the house, waving what appeared to be a bundle of rags in his hand.

"Found it!" he shouted. "Found a wad of bills and a

watch, all buried under the wood pile! Reckon this ought to be that 'direct' evidence Calhoun wants!"

Lundsford's jubilant voice announced, a few moments later, the total of the sum found.

"Four hundred dollars in big bills!" he shouted. "And Rafe Hillman says the watch belonged to Blackwell! Well, Calhoun, what you got to say to that?"

"Looks bad—for somebody," was the quiet reply.

"Yeah!" vindictively. "And that somebody is going down to the county seat with me! Git your belongings, Benson! Hat, coat, and whatever else you want to take along! Watch him, men!"

There was little need of watching Razorback. He appeared too stunned over the revelation of his wood pile, even to move.

"Mr. Calhoun!" he began piteously, only to be motioned into silence by the ranger, who stood up.

"Take him along, Lundsford," Cal said. "You are bound to, of course. But let me point out a few things before you proceed further:

"You have clues in plenty which indicate the identity of the murderer. Razorback was the last man known to have been with the victims; he carried a Sharps rifle; his footprints were found on the spot, admitted by him to have been made under the circumstances related—suspicious, I grant. Last, the dead man's watch is found on his premises—and a large sum of money is also discovered in a hidden spot. That, after Benson has declared that he possessed only about forty dollars in cash. Clews? Evidence? Yes—plenty.

"Now, all those clews are positive ones. They point

unmistakably to Benson. They are positive, too, because they are of a material character—tangible.

"Lundsford, your clews are the kind any well-trained officer can be counted on to find—the little things which point, or seem to point, to the criminal. A sleuth always hunts for the tiny thread—the seemingly unimportant lead which will guide him right. And—in looking for those little, positive clews, he sometimes fails to see the big, negative ones.

"Just as there are sounds too finely drawn for human ears to hear, and existing things too small for human eyes to see, there are other things—clews, for instance—too big for some of us to note. Negative clews are sometimes of the latter character. Now, if you are so minded, take Razorback along."

"Oh, Mr. Calhoun!" Emmy cried, supplicatingly. "You don't believe Pappy kilt them folks! I knows you don't! Please don't let him take him away!"

Cal turned to the girl. "Emmy," he said gently, "you believe your father is innocent, do you not?"

"Indeed I do!"

"Then why worry? There is only one thing which can keep him from you, and that is the proof of his guilt. If he did not commit the crime, then there not only is no such proof existent, but it stands to reason the proof which really does exist will lead directly to the man who did commit the deed. So, as I have already asked—why worry?"

The girl, sensing that Cal was with her father and herself, took courage. Within a few minutes she had packed a worn bag for the prisoner, and had tearfully bidden him good-by.

At the river, Lundsford turned to Cal.

"About them fine-drawn sounds, and them negative clews which nobody but you smart rangers can see—to hell with such bosh!"

Cal, sitting on a log beside the weeping Emmy, watched the sheriff and his party drop away down river toward the distant county seat.

"Well, Emmy," he said, getting up from the log, "we shall now learn whether or not that negative clew I spoke of deserves to be consigned to hell, as Mr. Lundsford seems to think. Keep your courage up, and remember that, if innocent, your pap will not suffer harm."

"I'm trustin' to you-all, Mr. Calhoun!" the girl cried, as Cal pushed off and headed up the river. "Pappy didn't do it—and I'm trustin' you to give him back to me!"

5

TWO DAYS AFTER Razorback Benson's arrest, Lundsford returned to the settlement at Buck Island, bringing
the coroner with him. A jury was impaneled, and it, after
a perfunctory survey of the evidence, returned a verdict
naming Benson as the slayer.

The inquest was held at the cabin of Rafe Hillman,
which stood on a knoll, surrounded by the one-hundred
and sixty acres he had homesteaded. The bodies of the slain
man and woman, both in the same homemade coffin, were
in the cabin, and permission was asked and received, by
Hillman, for interment some distance from the dwelling,
under a large white-oak tree.

"The funeral will take place to-morrow afternoon," Hillman replied to those who asked. "I should like as many of
you neighbors to be present as care to come."

Assisted by friends, he dug a grave, thereafter erecting a
picket fence around the spot.

Calhoun, who had not been in evidence in or near Buck
Island since Emmy saw him heading his boat toward his
headquarters at Hell Hole, appeared at Hillman's cabin
while the inquest was in progress. He was, however, an idle
spectator, saying nothing during the proceeding.

Lundsford eyed him uneasily. He well knew that when
Calhoun was quietest he was thinking deepest, and he was

not at all surprised when the ranger accosted him after the verdict had been rendered.

"Stick around, Lundsford," Cal bade him. "Maybe something will happen tomorrow that you would be sorry to miss. I'm not certain that it will be to-morrow, but I can promise you something to think about within a day or two at latest."

Lundsford grew thoughtful. "Hum. Well, I can't very well get back to the county-seat to-night," he said. "And, that being so, I'll stay on and be present at this little party of yours—or is it to be a party?"

Cal grinned good-naturedly. "No," he replied. "It's to be a funeral!"

"Huh?" demanded Lundsford, startled. "A funeral? There's going to be one, of course, the Blackwells are to be buried—"

"That's the one," Cal interrupted. "Be there—will you? And, in the meantime, here's a bit of information received at Headquarters House over two weeks ago:

"Hez Thorpe, the old swamper who peddles honey down at Marked Tree, reported the theft of a rifle from his cabin on Caney Fork, while he was in the woods after bees. Remember what I said about the scarcity of Sharps in the country, and how those who owned them cherished them? Well, Thorpe's rifle is a Sharps. He wants it back—naturally. Anything significant in that, to your mind?"

"Hez ought to put a lock on his door," Lundsford replied. "Then his goods and chattels would be safe during his absence."

"Ever hear of one swamper stealing from another—robbing his cabin?"

"Can't say I ever did," Lundsford acknowledged.

"And you still do not see anything significant in the theft of Thorpe's Sharps rifle?" Cal's tones expressed astonishment.

"If you are hinting that somebody used that stolen Sharps to kill Blackwell and his wife with, I'll say that we've got the killer and the rifle along with him," Lundsford retorted, nettled.

"Maybe. Now, here's a question I want to ask, and I'm really trying to give you a chance to see this Blackwell murder in a different light. One which will reflect credit upon you. Here's the question:

"If you knew, beyond doubt, that no swamper was guilty of that crime, who among those not native to the country, and who were in position to plan and execute the crime, would you suspect?"

"Why—why, I don't know," Lundsford answered, patently puzzled. "What the hell are you getting at, anyhow, Cal?"

"I'm not getting at anything," Cal replied. "I'm only trying to. But you are absolutely proof against—well, we'll pass that along. Here is another point which should give you material for thought:

"Blackwell drove up to Razorback's cabin and inquired for *Ephraim* Benson. Think that over, and be here to-morrow for the funeral."

Cal left the sheriff standing on the river bank, an unhappy frame of mind evidenced by the scowl upon his face.

That scowl had not entirely disappeared when, at two o'clock the following day, the sheriff accompanied the crowd of settlers and natives to the little knoll under the tree which was to furnish the murdered couple with a last resting place. Calhoun evidently had nothing up his sleeve, he thought, for the inspector had not put in an appearance during the day.

Just before the time came to lower the rude coffin into the grave, Calhoun, accompanied by Tom Murdock and two more rangers, appeared—and from that moment on things happened.

"I am sorry to interrupt," the inspector said, stepping forward and halting the men who were about to lower the box. "But those bodies may not be buried until certain important matters are cleared up."

There was a mutter of resentment on the part of the settlers, and Rafe Hillman, his face red with anger, loudly protested.

"I claim the right to bury my dead without interference!" he shouted, appealing to Lundsford. "These rangers have no right here!"

Lundsford shook his head slowly. "You are wrong, Hillman," he said. "The rangers have the right, because they take it. Better shut up, and let Calhoun have his way. He'll have it anyhow."

"Listen!" Cal's stern command attracted all eyes to him, and stilled the protesting tongues. "I am about to acquaint you with the results of certain inquiries and investigations conducted by my men and myself. And I am going to begin by making a statement:

"Razorback Benson did not kill Roger Blackwell and his wife!"

He paused while that sank in, then resumed:

"I shall go further, and say that no native swamp man is guilty—and I shall, later, make it clear to all of you why that is so. It was that certainty which directed my investigations away from Razorback and his kind, and in the proper channel.

"In the first place, Roger Blackwell drove up to Razorback's cabin and inquired for *Ephraim* Benson. What does that argue? It clearly establishes the fact that Benson was not chosen by Blackwell in a haphazard manner, picking him for a guide by mere chance. It unmistakably proves that he had been directed to Benson.

"Now, who in the swamps or in Marked Tree would have directed him to *Ephraim* Benson? How many of you natives gathered here are aware that Benson's name is Ephraim? Few, I'll warrant—and those few are to be found only among the older folk. Any native who directed Blackwell would have told him to ask for *Razorback* Benson—not *Ephraim!*"

A queer look came over Lundsford's face, and he turned hastily to see how the others present were receiving Cal's words. He saw agreement upon the faces of most of them.

"The truth is, Blackwell was instructed *by letter* to inquire for a certain guide—and that letter-writer learned the name of the man he wished to act in such capacity. He learned his real name, and wrote it down.

"Now, the sheriff, as well as myself and others present here, were informed that Roger Blackwell was a poor man, and that he could not have possessed more than four or five hundred dollars in money at the time of his death. Inquiry by telegraph to Blackwell's former home in Kentucky, elicited the information that he had inherited property from his own mother—he was, you understand, Rafe Hillman's stepbrother—and that he had deferred his journey here for the sole purpose of selling that property—otherwise he would have made the trip with his stepbrother and the rest of the settlers gathered on the island.

"It is, then, established, that Blackwell carried considerable money with him—he had over five thousand dollars when he left Kentucky. Yet, only four hundred was found under the wood pile at Razorback's cabin! What became of the rest?

"I think I can show you that presently.

"Now, Lundsford, you considered all the positive clews—those affirming Razorback's guilt—but you failed even to see the negative, and the negative was, of course, in Razorback's favor. It was also in the favor of every other swamper in the Sunken Lands."

6

"**WELL, WHY DON'T** you spit it out?" the sheriff demanded. "You've harped on that negative thing long enough!"

"So I shall," Cal told him. "You overlooked the real clew in the case, Lundsford—it was a big one, too. It covers two thousand acres. It is, in fine, Bottomless Bog!"

Profound silence greeted the statement. Folks looked at each other as if to say:

"Is the man insane? What is he talking about, anyhow?"

Cal sensed that. He laughed. "I'm not crazy, folks!" he said. "Listen:

"I can see Razorback Benson shooting down his victims, there beside Bottomless. I can see him robbing them, and preparing to dispose of the evidence of his crime. But there," Cal suddenly thundered, "I cease to see Benson, and vision another in his place!

"I see another who digs graves and buries the dead bodies—buries them for the wolves and jackals to dig up again! A swamp man would have known better! I see him burn a wagon, and its contents, and then leave the scene stealthily, flattering himself that he had arranged the details of a crime such as a native would have committed!

"Let us go back to Razorback. Let us assume that he committed the crime, and desired to hide the evidence. How would he have proceeded? I shall tell you:

"He would have placed the bodies inside the wagon, fastened the reins to the dashboard—and lashed the horses into Bottomless Bog, where horses, wagon, bodies and all would have sunk beneath the mire, never to appear again!

"That is what Razorback would have done! That is what any other swamper would have done! With a great, secretive graveyard such as Bottomless Bog, right at hand, would any one who knew that bog have wasted time burning wagons and burying bodies? I say no!

"But, an outlander, who knew little or nothing about the bog, and who desired to arrange evidence pointing to some one else, would have acted just as he did in the Blackwell case.

"He would have learned what kind of rifle Razorback, the man he had chosen to bear the blame, habitually used. He would—and did—learn where another such rifle could be had, and then he would have stolen that rifle. Stealing from cabins is an easy matter in the swamp, for no one locks his door. Swamp men do not steal from swamp men. Later, after the deed, it would be an easy matter to plant evidence under a wood pile at the far edge of a clearing, and then insidiously steer searchers to the spot. All that was done.

"Since no swamper did it, who did, then? Well, who had knowledge of the exact time Blackwell should arrive here? Who knew that he would carry a large amount of money? Who was in communication with him, and thus able to direct his movements after he entered the swamp so as to insure his arrival in the isolated forest under the guidance of the man he had framed?

"It is well known that Razorback Benson is a solitary

man; one who does not enjoy the full confidence and liking of his fellow swampers. He is industrious, and has never joined hands with his own kind in the effort to prevent settlers from entering the Sunken Lands. It is not to be wondered at that he should be at outs with his neighbors. Now it happens that all this had a bearing upon the case in hand. Razorback would be an easy victim; his fellow swampers would not flock to his aid, framing alibis for him. He could, moreover, be taken out of the swamps without a murmur in his defense.

"The real murderer in this case picked a friendless man for his goat!

"Who?

"Only one man in this section could have had all the information needed for the planning and perpetrating of the crime. That man is the stepbrother, Rafe Hillman!"

"You lie, damn you!" Hillman shrieked. "You haven't a thing to go by but your cursed theories—"

"Haven't I?" Cal queried. "Maybe I have more than that. Your cabin has been searched, thoroughly, and you have been closely watched. No trace of the five thousand dollars has been found. I think, though, I can now find it. You insisted upon burying the bodies in your own ground— here beneath this tree—instead of sending them back to Kentucky, or over to the Ridge, the usual burying ground— where they would be safe from high water at flood time. Let us see why you did that."

Murdock stepped forward, wrenched the lid from the coffin, thrust a hand down beneath the quilt with which the box had been lined—and produced a roll of bills.

"You meant to dig this up later—at your convenience—"

"Look, out!" Lundsford shouted, starting forward.

But Calhoun had acted before the words were hardly out of the sheriff's mouth. He had seen Hillman's right hand go for a hidden gun—and his own crashed down upon the murderer's head, felling him across the mound of fresh earth beside the grave.

BIG TIMBER

"So You are Afraid of Mosquitoes," Said
Cal. "Of the Kind That Stung Barwick—
the Kind That Means Death"

1

ON KIMBALL'S POINT

"RED RIVER" BRADY, in the pilot house of the Lee Line packet, the *Gray Eagle,* squinted hard through the starboard window at the man on Kimball's Point—a man who staggered out upon the crumbling earth of the slender wedge, beckoning frantically. An instant later he snatched up a pair of binoculars and leveled them shoreward.

Kimball's Point thrust itself out into the Mississippi in the form of a V, and was well grown over by big trees, with scarcely any undergrowth. Back of the point the forest crowded green and dense, stretching away for thirty miles inland to the shores of the St. Francis. No human being lived on the Point, nor was there a settlement within a dozen miles of the place in any direction.

Yet a man stood there, wavering upon his feet, as Red River could plainly see with the aid of glasses, and signaled to be taken aboard. Small steamboats made a practice of sending a skiff after chance passengers who hailed them between landings, but such large craft as the *Gray Eagle* disdained to do so. Yet, there was something about the forlorn figure then beckoning that held the pilot's attention.

A slender man, not above medium height, dressed in

"store" clothes—albeit muddy and tattered—and, more-over, seemingly in dire distress, was what the glasses revealed.

Red River made his decision. He signaled the skipper's cabin, and, when that individual responded, called down the tube:

"There's a man on Kimball's Point, cap'n," he said, "and there's something unusual about him—seems in distress. I think he has some sort of injury. Seems scared, too. Signaling us like it might be a matter of vital importance. What are your orders, sir?"

Red River Brady was an old timer, an excellent pilot, and a man of good judgment. Captain Blades did not, there-fore, hesitate to give the order to stand by, and then send a boat ashore.

Lafe Barker, nicknamed "Blueblazes," mate of the *Gray Eagle*, put out in the steamer's lighter, accompanied by two oarsmen, while Brady backed and filled to hold his position off the Point. The *Gray Eagle* stood not more than one hundred yards out at the moment. Curious passengers, most of them bound down river to Memphis, lined the rails and watched the progress of the landing party.

Red River, holding his glasses on the man on shore, observed him casting frequent glances over his shoulder toward the heavy forest-growth a hundred yards away; then, as the lighter neared its landing, he crumpled to his knees, got up with great difficulty, and leaned heavily against a tree.

"Plumb exhausted!" the pilot muttered. "Scared, too! Now I wonder what is up? Something, surely, to make a man take to the woods in this isolated spot, running

He threw his arms above his head and crashed upon his face

himself half to death, and then flag down a big boat like mine. Well, we'll know all about it in a few minutes, I guess."

That Red River was wrong in the supposition that they "would know all about it in a few minutes" need be no reproach to him. The man on the Point desired to be taken aboard the *Gray Eagle,* and was waiting. Blueblazes and his boat-crew were even then against the shore, and the prospective passenger was walking unsteadily toward them, casting frequent glances back toward the deep timber.

It did indeed look as though there was little left to do, save ship the man and transport him across the hundred yards of muddy water which lay between the Point and the *Gray Eagle.* The passengers along the guards shared Red River's belief that curiosity would soon be appeased.

The deep tones of Blueblazes's bull-like voice floated back to the ears of the pilot, and the latter knew that the mate was urging the slowly approaching passenger to hasten. It costs money to hold a big boat such as the *Gray Eagle* in midstream.

P-i-i-n-n-n-g-g-g-g!

A bullet crossed the steamer's bows, droning its way spitefully far out into the water, and a faint report from somewhere back of the tree-line followed instantly. Red River, startled, got to his feet. Holding the wheel with one powerful hand, he scanned the shore with his glasses.

A tiny puff of smoke in the edge of the heavy timber a hundred yards beyond the Point was his reward.

The man on shore, with apparent effort, gathered his energy and sprinted for the lighter.

Pop!

Just the faintest sound from the timber. Again Red River's glasses showed him a puff of smoke. There was no whine of bullets across the *Eagle's* bows this time, however.

The man on shore stopped ten feet from the lighter, whirled around as though he meant to return whence he came, trembled as if a chill had seized him, threw his arms above his head, and, with a cry that chilled the blood in the veins of those who heard it, crashed upon his face, writhed frightfully for a moment, then lay still.

No bullet had whined across the *Gray Eagle's* bow that second time, because it had found a mark in the strange man's heart.

2

BULLETS FROM THE BRUSH

THOSE OF THE passengers who realized that a tragedy had been enacted on the Point, right under their eyes, stood motionless with astonishment and horror at the suddenness of it all.

Red River, realizing that a man had been slain by a cowardly shot from the brush, devoted his attention to the spot whence the spurt of smoke had come. Breathlessly he searched the foliage, hoping for a glimpse of the assassin. No one showed, however. All was still over there.

Barker, the mate, hesitated for an instant after the running man had fallen—held, no doubt, by surprise. Then he whipped out a gun and leaped ashore. There was nothing for him to shoot at, though, since the marksman in the brush, had he been visible, was well beyond revolver range. The mate ran toward the prostrate man, shouting for one of the oarsmen to follow.

The stranger had grown still. Death had calmed him. Barker, followed by the man he had summoned, neared his position, and Red River trained his glasses on the group.

Pop!

Again that faint explosion—and Blueblazes Barker

pitched forward across the body of the man he sought to rescue.

Quick as a flash the pilot switched his binoculars toward the place where he had twice caught sight of smoke. Again he found it—a tiny puff only. It was in precisely the same spot as before.

Windom, the oarsman, who had followed the mate ashore, dropped to the ground and crawled into the protection of a tree, crouching there in a shiver of fear.

"Orders!" Red River yelled down his speaking tube.

"Hold your position," Captain Blades commanded tersely.

The pilot continued jockeying his craft, holding approximately the same position he had occupied from the beginning. Grasping the binoculars with his left hand, he continued to search the tree line for sight of the man in the brush—the man whose bullets had slain two.

On the boiler deck the captain and his officers were giving orders.

"Clear away from the rails!" Blades commanded. "Go to your staterooms, all of you, and do not show yourselves at the ports!"

Within five minutes the decks were clear of all save those who had a right to be there. Then Red River's tube whistle sounded shrilly.

"How close can you run to the Point?" Blades wanted to know.

"I can lay the *Eagle* against it!" the pilot replied. "Plenty of water there!"

"Lay alongshore, then!"

Red River seized the bell cord and sent his orders

jangling down below. The *Gray Eagle* ceased her jockying, her head swung about, and she bore slowly but certainly on shore.

On the boiler deck stood Captain Blades, the second mate, and the chief clerk, all armed with rifles.

"Brady will hold her against the shore," Blades was saying. "We won't attempt to lower the gangplank. The moment we are close enough, leap overside and run for Barker and the stranger. Get them on board. That is all we shall attempt now, since to search for the cowardly scoundrel in that swamp would be futile. Get those men on board—that is all we can hope to do."

"But, captain!" the chief clerk exclaimed. "What is the meaning of it all? I can understand that an enemy might have been in pursuit of the stranger, and that he overtook and shot him. But why—in the name of God!—should the killer shoot Barker?"

"Somebody else will have to answer that!" the skipper snapped. "In the meantime, prepare to land!"

Red River signaled the engineer to shut off steam, and the big boat swung broadside on shore.

Pop! Pop! Pop!

The man in the brush, working the lever of his repeater rapidly, sent bullet after bullet crashing against the *Gray Eagle's* side. Back of the skipper a window-light was shattered, and a leaden slug rang against the port chimney.

Red River, on his feet, swept the tree-line with naked eyes. He was close enough to see the smoke plainly now, without aid of glasses. A cloud of white vapor boiled against the green of the woodland, and in the place where he had expected it to be.

In a rack back of him reposed a rifle. Snatching the arm, he fired into the brush where he knew the assassin to be. Once—twice—

Pop!

A single report this time—and Red River Brady dropped across the wheel, a trickle of blood running down his face.

At that moment Captain Blades and his officers leaped ashore, and started on the run for the two men who lay so still about thirty feet away. Blades fell, a bullet in his shoulder, before he had gone ten feet.

Carter, second mate, dropped to his knees and emptied his magazine into the foliage back of which the marksman was concealed, while Barton, the clerk, seized Blades under the armpits and dragged him to cover behind a tree.

The tube whistle in the pilot house was then wailing insistently. The engineer was pleading for orders.

For, incomprehensible though it was to the engine crew, the *Gray Eagle* was drifting back into the current. Already there was a space of fifty feet between her and the shore!

But Red River Brady, whose hand should have held the boat true in her berth, lay upon the floor of the pilot house, his life blood slowly ebbing away. He could not answer.

Tom Lyle, second pilot aboard, who had come sleepily from his quarters when the yells and shrieks of the passengers warned him that something was wrong, cast a glance shoreward, perceived the state of affairs exactly, and took the pilot deck companionway in one bound. Crashing open the pilot house door he bent for a moment above the still form of his fellow officer, determined that he still lived, then seized the wheel with firm hands.

"Half speed ahead!" was the jangling order he sent below.

The *Gray Eagle* regained her lost ground, swinging again in to the shore.

But the man in the brush evidently did not intend for the big boat to lay along shore, or to send another landing party off. Bullet after bullet splintered through the pilot house walls and windows. Lyle, crouching low, held his position, while lead sang in the air about him.

Carter, the mate, who had gone ashore, having emptied his rifle into the brush, ran for cover while he reloaded. At the base of the tree behind which he would have been safe, he fell—a bullet through his body.

In the absence of the skipper and his two mates, command of the boat fell upon the chief engineer. Perceiving the perilous situation of those ashore who yet lived, he determined to risk a rescue. It was a foolhardy move, no doubt.

The marksman who had created such havoc had all the best of it. He lay concealed in the brush, while those who attempted a rescue would be compelled to expose themselves to his fire. Yet—what else was there to do? Captain Blades and his party had need of assistance.

"Hold 'er down, MacAnany!" he ordered his second. Then, addressing his two assistants and the four stokers then off duty, he said: "Lads, the cap'n is shot, over on the Point, and we've got to get him aboard! Some of us may get ours while we are doing it. How many are willing to go?"

Apparently there were no cowards among the crew of the *Gray Eagle*. They answered yes, to a man.

"On deck, then!" the chief commanded, and, followed by his crew, he hastened forward along the port side of the freight deck, where the chief steward and several passengers were in the act of lowering a boat.

"We'll take the boat, men!" the chief told them. "It's our turn, now—"

He broke off short. Again the big boat was drifting. A wide gap lay between her and the shore. Another bullet had found its mark in the pilot house.

"Take command, Redmond!" the chief called to the steward. "I've got to take the wheel!"

He ran toward the boiler deck companionway—but paused at its foot.

Near at hand, almost alongside the *Gray Eagle,* rose a high, shrill wail—the siren of a government river patrol boat. It came with a suddenness almost paralyzing. The chief engineer hesitated a moment only, then mounted to the pilot deck and took the wheel.

Tom Lyle was crouching on the floor of the pilot house, clutching a shattered arm in his left hand.

"Ahoy, aboard the *Gray Eagle!*" came a hail from the river.

The chief glanced over the *Eagle's* bows and saw a long, low, dingy craft—a disreputable boat, if ever there was one afloat—bearing alongside. A number of men in brown uniforms were grouped about the deck, while a tall soldierly looking young man stood on the bow, trumpet in hand.

"Ahoy, aboard the *Clipper!*" came an answering shout from the steward, then in command. "We are in distress! Come aboard!"

The tall man on the bow of the little steamer, the *Clip-*

per, gave an order, the boat lay to and berthed easily beside the *Eagle.*

A moment later Inspector Jack Calhoun, of the United States Rangers, leaped to the *Gray Eagle's* boiler deck—followed by half a dozen of his crew.

3

WHAT THE KILLER WANTED

A FEW DEFT questions informed the inspector of what had occurred, and, after instructing one of his men to render aid to the wounded men in the pilot house, he turned his attention to those beleaguered ashore. His practiced eyes took in the possibilities of the situation at a glance, and he acted accordingly.

Three rangers manned a small boat and rowed upstream under cover of the shore; they landed at a spot near the base of the Point, and slipped into the timber. A second boat, containing three men, dropped downstream, and its crew also landed where they would not be under fire from the hidden killer.

Calhoun leaned against the guard rail and waited calmly.

In the meantime Captain Blades, the chief clerk, and Windom, the oarsman, remained under the cover they had gained. The arrival of the *Clipper* had been witnessed by them, and they realized that it would be only a matter of moments until the man in the brush was captured, killed, or driven off.

Fifteen minutes passed, then a brown figure stepped from the foliage at the point where the marksman had been. He was followed by two others. The first ranger to appear signaled his chief aboard the *Gray Eagle.*

"He's gone," Calhoun informed those about him. "Ran when he saw us arrive. We'll get your men on board now."

He leaped overside and made his way, first, to where the mate and the strange man lay.

"Dead," he told the deck steward briefly as he lifted the body of the mate from that of the unknown. "Shot through the head—at a hundred yards. Good shooting. You say there appeared to be only one man in the brush?"

"Only one, sir," the steward replied. "All the bullets came from the same point. I am sure that one man held us all helpless! What I cannot fathom is why he sought so desperately to prevent any one reaching the body of the stranger.

"Judge, sir, how determined he was to keep us from getting to the man! He deliberately shot Barker, Captain Blades, Carter, and the two pilots—held the *Gray Eagle* away! Why?"

Calhoun was examining the body of the stranger patiently, intently, and made no answer.

"Captain Blades has a bad wound in the left shoulder, inspector."

It was Ranger Richmond, first-aid man of the *Clipper,* reporting.

"Fatal?" Cal queried.

"Not necessarily. I am sending him aboard his boat. The mate, Carter, is dying. A bullet pierced his right lung, and a bad hemorrhage resulted. Nothing can be done in his case. One of the pilots has a shattered arm; he probably will lose it. Brady, the other pilot, has a head wound, and should recover.

"Any further casualties?"

"None."

"Get the wounded on board," Calhoun ordered. "Run on to Memphis, making no stops save for wood. They will be taken care of there. You accompany them. Get statements from all who are able to give them, as soon as possible. I'll join you later."

He placed a retaining hand on the steward's shoulder, as the latter turned toward the boat.

"I shall need you here," he said. "You can be spared, and I shall want to question you later."

"Very well, sir. What of the dead stranger?"

"We will look after him," Cal replied. "The mate, however, may be taken aboard the *Eagle*."

Fifteen minutes later the *Gray Eagle* steamed away under a full head, bound for Memphis, leaving the *Clipper* berthed against the Point where the *Gray Eagle* had been.

The body of the dead stranger was taken aboard, and Calhoun began an exhaustive examination. About thirty years of age, he was. The clothing marked him as one more used to city life than that of the wilderness. The contents of the pockets were such as most men carry: A pocketknife, cigar-case, plain handkerchief, keys, billfold. The billfold contained fifty-odd dollars in currency, and the bills were thoroughly wet.

The identification card usually to be found under celluloid in a compartment of the ordinary fold, had been filled out, but it was wet and illegible. Some letters, found in the inner pocket of the coat, also had been reduced to a pulp by the action of water.

From the condition of the clothing, shoes, and the contents of the pockets, it was evident that the man had been subjected to a thorough soaking a short time prior to his death.

"Probably swam a long distance," was Cal's conclusion. "Ought to be some marks on the linen, surely. This chap spent a good deal of time in some city or other—maybe Memphis. Had his laundry done there, too. No native wash woman would suit so fastidious a man.

"Yet he has been in the woods a good while, too. Wears heavy, woodsman's shoes, which show signs of hard usage. A blue pencil and a red one in his breast pocket—lumber checking pencils. Probably was connected with a sawmill somewhere in the interior."

Close scrutiny disclosed faint markings on the under-shirt and inside the collarband of the outer shirt.

"R-J-B," Cal deciphered. "Humph! Now, what was the motive back of the killing of this man, R.J.B.? I thought, at first, that he must have possessed something his slayer wanted—else why was he so determined to prevent Blades and his men from removing the body?

"The pursuit must have been a long one, since there are no mills or settlements anywhere within a radius of twenty miles of this spot. Yes, the unfortunate chap carried something of value to the killer—that is certain. Nothing significant on him, however. May have thrown the thing—whatever it was—away. Not likely—"

His glance rested upon the cigar-case which had been

taken from the dead man's pocket, a metal affair, and a moment later he snapped it open.

"A-h-h-h!"

What caused the ejaculation was a folded bit of paper which had been tucked inside the case. It was dry, since the metal was impervious to water. Cal had it out in a twinkling.

What the inspector found was a plain white envelope— or rather half of an envelope. Inside was a folded sheet of paper, also torn in half. It had evidently been a letter intended for mailing, and the half Cal held in his hand was that upon which the stamp had been placed.

Both the envelope and the sheet of paper were creased and crumpled, as though the man had held it tightly— probably while some one else was trying to wrest it from his hand.

Calhoun spread the fragment of paper on the table and bent over it intently. At length he straightened and turned to Tom Murdock, his chief aid, who stood beside him.

"This," he said, tapping the fragment of letter lightly with a long forefinger, "is what the killer was after. He succeeded in getting the other half, but that was not enough. Rather than have this fragment fall into other hands, he was willing to kill not only this victim, but Captain Blades and his entire crew as well!"

4

HALF OF A MESSAGE

MURDOCK NODDED. "TYPEWRITTEN," he commented succinctly.

In the early '90s, typewriting machines were something of a novelty, save in the larger centers. Few small towns boasted more than one, and they were seldom found in the backwoods. Calhoun acknowledged his aid's pointed comment with a nod of his head.

"That narrows our field, in so far as the source of the letter is concerned. It is well typed, arguing that the writer was no novice with a machine. The paper used is unruled bond, note size.

"If it originally carried a printed head, that portion is missing. Likewise the end of the envelope which may have borne a return address. However, the thing is very informative, despite the fact that we have only half of it."

Murdock took the torn sheet up and ran his eyes down the printed fragment, attempting to piece out the missing lines. Presently he handed it back to Calhoun, with the remark:

"You may be able to get something positive from it, but I confess it gives up very little to me. But then, I'm not especially good at such puzzles. Suppose you interpret."

Cal spread the sheet on the desk, and scanned the following:

No. 2,

Eye, Ark.

he 4th, 1891.

as I believe my life

n knowledge that the

y are not merely cutting

re after the big timber.

worked, and it is very

tection proof; those who are

disposing of it to certain

ard-wood mills, and once in

s no way of identifying the

ay in a letter, since I know

am watched, and have been

t two weeks. I may not leave

sure this letter will ever

try to send it. If you get it,

force to this place at once,

d protection to me after I

ow. Otherwise I will be slain.

is reaches you, I am

Yours truly,

mond J. Barwick

pt. Mill No. 2

"Well," Cal queried after a bit, "just what do you get from it?"

"I gather that the writer had something important to tell somebody, and that he was known to have such intentions," said Murdock. "He feared death, was unable to get away from wherever he was, and desired somebody to send a force of men to his rescue. That's about all."

Cal eyed his subordinate quizzically, the corners of his wide mouth lifting humorously.

"There's a lot more on that sheet of paper, Tom," he declared. "Here is what I glean:

"The letter was written by the superintendent of blank Mill No. 2, which is located at blank Eye, Arkansas, on June 4 in the present year—1891, two days ago. Now, mills are scarce in the Sunken Lands. No. 2, the letter says. That argues that this mill is one of a string belonging to the same concern.

"The Arkana Mill and Lumber Company is the only concern operating a number of mills in the swamps. Therefore it is safe to say that the writer was at the Arkana Company's mill number two.

"It is easy enough to fill in the blank before 'Eye.' Needle's Eye, Arkansas. There we have the place ticketed. Arkana Company's mill number two; at or near Needle's Eye, Arkansas.

"Let us take the name of the signer. We have 'mond J. Barwick.' Edmond, Redmond, Armond, Raymond—any of those will do. Let us choose the latter name as being the most common. The initial R from the man's underclothing will go a long way to confirm this.

"Raymond J. Barwick, then, in his capacity as superintendent of Mill No. 2, learns something damaging to some man or group of men in the swamp country. The men concerned are aware that he has such damaging knowledge and that he intends divulging it to the authorities, and they set a watch upon him.

"Realizing this, Barwick writes a letter, intending to get it out to a mail station in ways best known to himself. He attempts to do so, is detected in the act and part of the letter wrenched from his hand.

"There is a fight. I know that because there are bruises on the head and face of the corpse yonder which clearly show it. I am assuming, of course, that the corpse is that of Barwick. The superintendent flees from his assailant, and takes to the timber in an effort to escape. He reaches the Mississippi, but is shot down by someone who was close on his heels.

"Now the man who shot Barwick knew about the fragment of letter. He meant for no one to get possession of it. Therefore he stood off all who tried to approach the body, meaning to drive the *Eagle* and her crew away, then retrieve the damaging fragment from the dead man's person. He would have succeeded, no doubt, had we not arrived when we did.

"Important? I'd say that we have fallen onto something big, Tom. So big that, rather than have the least inkling of it leak out of the swamp, any number of human lives would be sacrificed. Barwick, Barker and Carter were slain, and three others wounded, all to prevent that bit of letter from falling into alien hands."

"Any idea what it is?" Murdock asked.

"Well, yes," was the slow reply. " 'Big timber, hard-wood mills'—that appears in the letter. The Arkana people are operating a number of mills in a corner of the Sunken Lands where we have never been—the deep Lake country.

"They operate under a concession from the government, which permits them to cut and remove all the cottonwood timber on certain tracts of land. Cottonwood, mind you, and nothing else. Big timber, to my mind, refers not to size, but to quality—value. Woodsmen allude to the valuable hardwoods, such as maple, walnut, oak, and the like, as 'big timber.'

"The lesser woods—cottonwood, gum, cypress—are 'small timber.' Small because comparatively low in value. I may be wrong, but such is my interpretation of the reference to 'big timber.'"

Murdock nodded comprehendingly. "Right, of course," he agreed. "This fellow Barwick must have been an honest man, and when he found that the big timber was being cut, he wanted to let the government know about it—say," he exclaimed, "isn't the government on the job in the big woods? Don't the Arkana people operate under United States inspection? How the devil could anything such as the letter hints at be carried on, anyhow?"

"Tom," said Cal, "if you wanted a nice, big, red apple, and had the money in your pocket, what would you do?"

"Why, I'd buy the apple, of course!" the big ranger replied.

"Exactly. You would buy the apple. Suppose you wanted a man, and had plenty of money—what then?"

"I see!" Murdock exclaimed. "Apple or man. Money buys all things—or nearly all. Yeah, I get you."

"Exactly. Let us see now what we can get from the envelope."

Cal spread the piece of wrapper on the desk, smoothed it out and studied the few word-endings it bore.

"Of the superscription, we have 'ford,' 'ock,' 'sas,'" he remarked finally. "The last two are easy. Little Rock, Arkansas. Now, in view of the knowledge we have gained from the letter proper, we should be able to arrive at the identity of the gentleman whose name ends in 'ford.' Put yourself, Tom, in Barwick's shoes for the moment.

"His company operates under concession from the government, and the United States Land Office, at Little Rock, has jurisdiction over all government wild lands in the State. But the swamp lands are especially administered by the United States Swamp Land Commissioner, residing at Little Rock.

"In Barwick's dilemma, you would, without doubt, seek to communicate with the commissioner, since his authority in the section is supreme. John Rexford is the commissioner.

"So, we have learned that Barwick addressed a letter to John Rexford, at Little Rock, Arkansas, and we know, in part, what the letter sought to convey."

"By jove!" Murdock exclaimed. "With that much to go on, we ought to get somewhere in a hurry!"

Cal nodded, and glanced through a window toward the shore. "I see that Ramsay and his men are crossing the Point," he said, rising. "We'll get their report—though I dare say it won't help us much."

5

SEEING THE UNSEEN

RANGERS RAMSAY, TILLMAN, and Ballard, all of whom had remained in the timber, scouting in an effort to pick up the trail of the killer, came aboard and entered the cabin.

"We easily located the spot where the marksman stood," Ramsay reported. "There are foot-prints about, though so imperfect as to be of no value, other than to mark the place where he operated. Also, we found these."

He placed a bandanna handkerchief upon the desk in front of Cal. It was tied at the four corners, and contained twenty metal jackets which had once been loaded cartridges.

"All forty-five-ninety," Cal announced after a brief inspection. "Winston make. Doesn't tell us much, of course, since there are a lot of such rifles in the big woods. We know, however, that the man we want is a crack shot with a forty-five-ninety Winston.

"Not all men who use rifles are crack shots. That is something to go on. Anything else?"

"Yes," Ramsay replied. "He ran north and west for three-quarters of a mile and entered a dugout on the north bank of Cypress Slough. There we lost him."

"A dugout?"

"Yes. The imprint is there in the end of the slough. No mistaking the mark left by a dugout."

"Right. Did you search the spot where he stood, with absolute thoroughness?"

"I think so, sir," was the answer. "Will you have a look?"

Cal nodded. "I think I shall," he said. "Lead the way."

Ramsay retraced his way across the Point and into the timber, followed by Cal, Murdock, and two others. Just back of a screen of buckbrush and blackberry sprouts he halted.

There was no need to point out the spot on which the killer had stood. The turf was torn by boot-heels in a circle perhaps three feet in circumference, indicating that the man had changed his position many times in order to bring his rifle to bear on his chosen victims.

Cal stood where the other had stood, and found himself well protected by the screen of underbrush. A bush larger than the rest attracted his attention, and he examined it closely. After a bit he dropped to his knees and went over the ground slowly and with extreme thoroughness.

Presently, just outside the trampled circle and lying upon the thick fronds of a blackberry shoot, he found an object which interested him greatly—interested and puzzled him.

It was nothing more or less than an oblong bit of slate, perhaps two inches wide and five inches long. That it had been carefully cut to its dimensions, and was not merely a chance fragment, was patent. Cal looked at it long, then slipped it into a pocket.

"The man who did the shooting," he said, turning to his companions, who had been watching him absorbedly, "is a native. He is about six feet and two inches tall—my height. A hunter, I take it, with a leaning toward the taking of wild turkeys.

"He wore gaiters instead of boots, and is a constant chewer of tobacco. In addition, we know that he is an expert with a forty-five-ninety Winston, and that he is as ferocious as a hungry panther.

"I know his height because he rested his rifle across this limb," he went on, indicating a branch of a blackjack. "The bark is worn there, and you can see where the flame from his rifle withered the leaves in a straight line with the limb.

"Once he knelt on the ground—probably when Red River Brady fired into the brush. He knelt with his left leg straight out behind him, and the rubber in the side of his gaiter left its imprint in the damp soil."

He pointed out the spot, and all saw that what he said was true.

"As for the tobacco habit," the inspector went on, "you can see that he continued to chew and spit"—he indicated numerous brown spots on the green foliage—"even while doing his murderous work. He is, then, a habitual chewer."

"All that is clear," Murdock remarked, "now that you have made it so. But, about him being a turkey hunter—how do you know that?"

Cal was silent for a moment, seeming not to have heard the query. Then, with a start, he brought his thoughts back from wherever they had been.

"Turkey hunter?" he repeated. "Oh, yes. Well, I'm not quite so sure of that point as I am of the others. If, however, no other man has stood in this spot recently with the exception of ourselves, then the killer is a hunter of turkeys, and no mistake about it. Just mark that and remember it. A turkey hunter, or I miss my guess."

With that he led the way out of the jungle and onto the *Clipper,* where he gave orders to run for Memphis, under full steam.

"Ain't we going into the jungle after that killer?" Murdock, pilot of the *Clipper,* wanted to know of Cal, who sat silently against the wall of the pilot house while the little boat made her run, his gray eyes holding a far-away look.

"I'm not particularly interested in that killer," was the surprising reply. "Though we'll get him, no doubt.

"Speaking of 'big timber,'" he went on. "There's big timber among men, as well as among trees. This killer is a mere sapling. There are other saplings in our particular forest, no doubt.

"They must all be cleared away—in order to enable us to reach the big timber we are going after. Yes, a lot of saplings, sprouts and parasitical underbrush mask from view the big, very big trees we are going to throw—if it is possible to throw them—and I'm betting it is!"

6

CALHOUN GRINDS HIS AX

KIMBALL'S POINT LIES forty miles above Memphis, on the Arkansas shore, and was, in 1891, as lonely a spot as could be found on the Mississippi. Two miles above it Frenchman's Bayou enters the river, and one mile below it is the mouth of Cypress Slough.

Both streams afford a waterway clear to the St. Francis River, which divides the Sunken Lands from north to south, like a long, tangled white thread.

Cypress Slough flows through the Deep Lake region, and north of Deep Lake, in a wild and virgin portion of the swamp, the Arkana Mill and Lumber Company operated.

The concession had been granted a year previous to the tragic events which occurred on Kimball's Point, and during the first year of operation the company had merely begun to nibble at the tremendous tracts of cotton wood it was privileged to cut.

As yet no logging railroad had been built from the outside to the Arkana's holdings. Construction of railways in the swamp country present almost insurmountable difficulties. All logs which the company's four mills did saw were floated out in rafts to various operators nearer the railway points.

Some of the logs found their way to the Mississippi, by way of Cypress Slough; others were rafted down the St. Francis at high-water time in the spring, where the mills at Marked Tree turned them into boards and timbers. Huge flat boats were employed to convey the company's finished product to the outside.

From any viewpoint, the Arkana Company had a difficult task in getting its logs and lumber on the market. Yet there were certain very tangible compensating features. For instance, the government, desiring to have the cotton wood areas cleared, preparatory to reclaiming and colonizing the land, practically gave such timber away. So low was the stumpage it might well have been called a gift.

But in granting the concession the government had no intention of allowing its vast hardwood tracts in the district to be touched. To the north and west of the Deep Lake region were thousands of acres heavily grown with maple, walnut, and the various members of the oak family.

Many of those trees, particularly in the maple forests, were of rare quality and great value. A single maple, of the quality of those to be found so plentifully in the Sunken Lands, would bring from two to five hundred dollars, delivered to the proper market.

So, in the contract between the Arkana people and the government, it was stipulated that should other timber than cotton wood be cut by the company, the concession would forfeit to the government, immediately proof of a breach of faith was forthcoming.

The government concession had, therefore, teeth in it.

When Hubbard Wheeler and his force of rangers were sent into the Sunken Lands to safeguard the government's interests and teach the widely scattered inhabitants respect for law, the Deep Lake district lay far outside the district occupied by Wheeler.

Three million acres of forest, innocent of ax or saw, flooded once each year by the overflow of the Mississippi and the surplus water of innumerable rivers, sloughs and bayous to be found in the place itself, was the rangers' territory.

But it must, of necessity, be occupied gradually, each appointed district won before another was invaded. The patrolling of Deep Lake had not been undertaken. Until the Arkana people entered the section it had not been considered important.

With the coming of the mill company, Wheeler had crossed the Deep Lake region off his list of future operations. The company could handle its own. Besides, government inspectors were stationed there, and should be amply able to cope with any situation which might arise.

Jack Calhoun, Inspector of Rangers, second in authority only to Hubbard Wheeler himself, sat against the pilot house wall while night dropped down upon the river, and considered his problem from all angles.

He had, in the four years since he came to the Sunken Lands, been confronted by many difficult situations which had to be handled, and handled with thoroughness and dispatch. Many problems had arisen, some of them shrouded in mystery which had to be penetrated and cleared away. So successful had he been in unraveling such puzzles, Calhoun at length found himself assigned almost wholly to the duties of what might be called a forest sleuth.

The little launch, the *Clipper*, had been turned over to

that branch of the ranger service, and the inspector had been on patrol when his attention had been drawn to the *Gray Eagle.* Now he found himself with another mystery to solve, and one which he instinctively felt would not be easy to fathom.

"Big timber," he said to himself. "Well, the biggest of trees are vulnerable to the ax."

Closing his eyes, he devoted the passing hours to perfecting plans for his first important move—in effect, he began grinding his ax. He knew that a false step in the big woods means, almost invariably, the loss of the game one is stalking. He meant to make no false steps. No twigs should be allowed to snap beneath his feet, to startle the wary game he was about to hunt.

Exhaustive questioning of Redmond, the steward whom Calhoun had retained aboard the *Clipper,* had elicited not one item of positive value. He related meticulously what had passed on the Point and under his eyes, but beyond the bare facts involved he could not go.

"We sent a boat ashore to pick up a passenger who seemed to be in trouble," he summed up. "Then the shooting began. I never saw the man who did the shooting, nor do I believe any one else aboard the *Eagle* caught so much as a glimpse of him."

Cal dismissed the man. He had nothing important to offer.

The *Clipper* docked at Memphis shortly after dark, and the body of the stranger was taken to the morgue at once. Half an hour later it was positively identified as that of Raymond J. Barwick. The young man's brother made the identification, and from him Cal elicited the following information:

Young Barwick was a recent graduate of a well known technical school, having specialized in engineering and industrial management. Three months before, he had left his home in Memphis and accepted a position as superintendent of employment for the Arkana Mill and Lumber Company, and, in addition, was resident superintendent of the company's mill number two, near the inland village of Needle's Eye, in Arkansas.

"I know of no trouble between Ray and his employers," the brother stated. "He came home about twice a month, spending Saturday and Sunday with myself and wife. He appeared quite satisfied with his work, and had hopes of later becoming interested as a stockholder in the Arkana Company.

"Upon the occasion of his last visit, nearly three weeks ago, he did, I recall, seem greatly preoccupied. When my wife asked as to his health, he replied that there was nothing wrong.

"Nevertheless, while I attached no importance to his rather morbid condition at the time, I can see, now, that something was troubling him. What it was I have no inkling of."

Calhoun had more than an inkling. Barwick had become suspicious. The fragment of letter went unmentioned. Having gotten all the information the brother was able to give him, the inspector departed for the river front, boarded the *Clipper*, and sat down to think.

Later, Ranger Lee Cardwell took the night train for Little Rock, bearing a long letter from Calhoun to United

States Commissioner John Rexford. Still later, Calhoun himself departed for Marked Tree, thence on up the St. Francis to Oak Donnick, headquarters of Hubbard Wheeler, chief of the rangers.

And later still, the *Clipper* cast off and, under Tom Murdock's command, departed swiftly northward toward Kimball's Point.

Calhoun's ax had been ground to a razor-edge.

7

IN ANOTHER MAN'S SHOES

CALHOUN'S INTERVIEW WITH his chief at Oak Donnick was brief. Daylight found him returning to Marked Tree. There he took a room at the Harris Hotel, with nothing to do apparently, save loaf on the depot platform and watch the trains roll by. He was not in uniform, and not many of the citizens connected the tall, sandy-haired, gray-eyed young man who haunted the railway station, with the forceful and ever active inspector of rangers.

On the morning of the third day of Cal's stay in Marked Tree, Train Number Four, out of Memphis, was half an hour late—but when it finally stopped at the station Cal knew that his period of idleness was at an end.

Among the few passengers for Marked Tree was a young man dressed in all the regalia figuring in a city man's mind as suitable for a sojourn in the big woods. Knee-breeches, laced boots, belted jacket over a flannel shirt, wide-brimmed Stetson—he had them all. Brand new, too, testifying to a comparatively recent decision on the wearer's part to risk the adventure.

There was much luggage accompanying the young man. Two valises, a raincoat, rolled and strapped, and two cases containing rifle and shotgun, respectively.

Calhoun looked the newcomer over, heard him ask for a guide to the Deep Lake section, then faded away to the St. Francis, entered his dugout and headed post haste for Oak Donnick.

The boat bearing the newcomer and his impedimenta to the swamps, was not far behind him. It came upriver an hour after Cal's arrival, driven by the powerful paddle of "Wildcat" Broadus, a native. By right Wildcat should have passed by the donnick, since there was no apparent reason for a halt there. He did not, however.

Instead, he headed to shore just below Headquarters House, beached his boat, and sat grinning in the stern while he Watched Calhoun's approach down the path.

"Here it is, Mr. Calhoun!" Broadus cried, his grin spreading. "I done fotch it along lak you-all tol' me to—fine fixin's an' all! Whut air you gwine to do with it?"

Cal grinned. "Don't know, just yet, Wildcat," he replied. "You wait here, and maybe there'll be a passenger for you to take on to Deep Lake."

The stranger, indignant over the ridicule to which he had been subjected by his guide, then broke into speech:

"What sort of an outrage is this?" he demanded, stepping ashore. "I employ a guide to take me to Needle's Eye, wherever the place may be, and I find—"

"You find yourself in good hands, sir," Cal assured him courteously. "I am Inspector Calhoun, United States Ranger Service, and you are now at our headquarters in the Sunken Lands. If we are compelled to detain you for a short period, it is because the interests of law and order demand it, and not because we do it of our own choice.

Just go up to the house and answer a few questions—that may be all we shall require of you."

There was something likable about the tall, homely ranger—a something which invited confidence. The stranger felt it, and, though it cannot be said that he did so with good grace, he walked beside Cal to the house.

Hubbard Wheeler waited at his desk in his office, and when the two entered he arose, shook hands cordially with the stranger and invited him to be seated.

"You are, I take it, the new superintendent for Mill Number Two, Arkana Lumber concern?" he said, after the young man had taken a seat.

"I am," was the reply.

"Name, please?"

"Robert Keene," came promptly.

Wheeler turned to Cal. "Take him," he said shortly.

Calhoun drew out a chair and sat down directly in front of the uneasy young man, eyed him sharply for a moment, then began:

"Mr. Keene, how did you come by your present job?"

"My job, please understand, is more in the nature of a position—"

"We'll grant that!" Cal snapped. "How did you get this position then?"

The stranger's face grew suddenly red and his eyes sparkled with anger. "Say, what is this, anyhow?" he demanded. "What business is it of yours—"

"Do you want to sit in that chair all night long, without the privilege of smoking—I have noted that you draw a long pipe—and without food or drink?

"Do you want me to sit here and ask you that identical question over and over until your eardrums ring with it?" Cal demanded. "If not, then answer—and answer promptly!"

The young man stared at him long and hard, his face losing most of its red. "You wouldn't dare do that!" he hazarded.

Cal shrugged. "Try me and see," he said. "Though, for your information, I assure you that we dare anything here—anything at all. Understand?"

"Well," came the reply, "I can't see any harm in answering your question. My uncle got the job for me. You see, the former incumbent got mixed up in a quarrel with a native over a girl, and the native killed him. So they had to have a super—"

"Yes, we know about that," Cal interrupted. "We were expecting you, or some one, to arrive in your avowed capacity. Who is your uncle?"

There was immense pride in the young man's voice when he answered.

"My uncle is George Hackett Spangler, Representative in Congress, from the Third Congressional District of Arkansas!"

"So," Cal commented, "you are George's nephew? And Uncle George got a nice fat job for you! Know anybody up in the Deep Lake country?"

"I do not. I've only been out of the tech a year."

Cal nodded toward Wheeler. "That sounds fine," he said. "I think we may go ahead with our plan. Any questions?"

Wheeler shook his head, and Cal resumed his pumping. At the end of an hour he was in possession of every detail connected with young Keene's employment, and most of his past history. Then he arose from his chair.

"Mr. Keene," he said soberly, "you are going to have a new experience. You are going to be the guest of the United States Government for a while—a short while, I hope. A week, let us say. You will be treated royally by Captain Wheeler and his men, but you will be virtually a prisoner.

"Perhaps, after the matter is made quite clear to you, you will lose all feeling of outrage and injury, and acquit us of taking unwarranted advantage of you. I hope to see you later, sir, and under pleasanter circumstances."

Before the amazed Keene could frame an answer, the tall ranger passed through the door and down to the river.

"Mr. Robert Keene's shoes may pinch most horribly before I see the end of this," was Cal's thought as he took his place in Wildcat's boat and started up the river. "But I reckon I can wear 'em!"

8

THE TROUBLE BEGINS

JUNIUS B. TRASK, general field superintendent for the Arkana Mill and Lumber Company, might have given his dog an occasional bone, albeit, sans meat and marrow, had he permitted himself the extravagance of a canine dependent, but one could hardly vision him giving a neighbor's dog anything but a kick. He was hard—hard as the heart of a red-oak tree.

It was his invariable habit to "say it" with pig-iron, rather than with flowers. He did not manage the men under him; he herded and drove them. Drove them methodically and without mercy. It was significant that very few native woodsmen were on his pay rolls.

The native swamper does not, as a rule, take kindly to any kind of steady employment, and he certainly will not be driven. Most of the company's employees were shipped in from the outside, and, once on the job, they found it extremely difficult to get off it again.

Circumstances of location, aided materially by certain practices in the matter of payment of wages, had a good deal to do with keeping men on the work. In the first place, the Deep Lake country lies fifty miles from a railway. Secondly, the company did not pay its men in cash, but used tokens of brass of its own coinage.

The tokens were worth face value at the commissaries owned by the company, and at its boarding houses, but they could not be exchanged for cash save on the first day of each month. Usually the worker had very few of those tokens to "cash in" when the first of the month rolled round, since commissary goods came high, and wages were low.

To buy or hire a boat for the trip out to a railway required a considerable sum, hence the hands were constrained to remain on the job.

They were not, however, satisfied workers. Far from it. That made very little difference to Trask, however, who was interested solely in getting out logs and sawing them into rough lumbers. That he did. He got results.

The Arkana's holdings were flanked on the west by the St. Francis River, on the south by Cypress Slough; northward its territory extended for fifteen miles, and a like distance to the east.

On the south bank of Cypress Slough, on a bit of high ground, through which the slough was confined to something like banks, was the village of Needle's Eye. It consisted of two general stores, a fur buyer's warehouse, and two saloons.

All the buildings were constructed of unbarked logs, and life there was fully as primitive as outward appearances unmistakably indicated. Two dozen native families were domiciled there, also, dwelling in crude log huts which stood upon pilings about four feet above ground. All the buildings were thus erected, in fact, since the country was flooded each spring.

A mile east of Needle's Eye, on the south bank of Deep Lake—one of a chain of lakes lying eastward, and through which Cypress Slough took its course—stood a log building of many rooms, wide and deep verandas, which had an appearance of wellbeing unusual in the swamps.

This place was the Arkana Club, maintained by the officers of the company for themselves, their families and their friends. During the fishing and duck-hunting seasons, the club was very popular, and was served by a launch which plied the waters of Cypress Slough, to and from the Mississippi.

On a morning several days subsequent to the tragedy on Kimball's Point, Superintendent Trask paced up and down the main veranda of the club. He was not nervous; merely in a high state of displeasure.

Far across Deep Lake he could observe the smoke and steam from the boilers of Mill Number Two, and it was toward that point his glance was directed most often. Mill Number Two was the direct cause of his discomfort, and for various reasons.

For one thing, a large party of guests would be in on the following Saturday, three days off, for the bass fishing. Half a dozen stockholders—important ones—accompanied by their families and friends, were due to arrive. For a very personal reason, Mr. Trask desired to be free and untrammeled by business cares during the stay of the outing party. He wanted nothing to interfere with his leisure.

But he was not to have the desired freedom, it appeared. Mill Number Two was responsible. Lacking a superintendent, Mill Number Two required his watchful eye if it was to be kept at the top of its capacity—and anything short of capacity output caused Trask to shudder.

He was strictly a capacity-output man. Such was his nature and training. At the age of forty he had climbed higher than the average man could have done, had he possessed as little to begin with as Trask—which was exactly nothing. Nothing, that is, save determination.

"Barwick, damn him!" the superintendent muttered wrathfully, as he paced back and forth. "Just at a time when we partially do not want undue attention directed this way, he very nearly wrecks everything!

"Killing was what he deserved! Now there'll be investigators of all kinds and qualities overrunning the swamp, poking their noses into things that don't concern them, and causing us no end of trouble and worry!"

That was the biggest, most obnoxious fly in the ointment. Trask knew that an investigation into the cause of Barwick's murder was certain to be made—and Trask wanted anything but that.

In his hand was a Memphis paper, issue of the previous morning. It had informed him that the people of Memphis were thoroughly aroused over the dastardly slaying of Barwick, Barker and Carter, and the wounding of three more of their citizens.

A large reward, raised by popular subscription, had been posted by the city, and already sleuths, amateur and professional, were headed for the swamps.

Trask spat viciously, got up, tore the paper in two, slammed it on the floor—and turned quickly to answer a summons.

"Trask," said a soft, drawly voice just behind, "thar's

a dude feller a comin' up th' slough. Wil'cat Broadus is a paddlin' of him, an' I reckon it's th' new boss fur Mill Number Two.

"I reckon it mought be him—then, agin, it mought be one of them spies you-all says air due to come pokin' inside right soon. Thought you-all ought to know about him."

"Damn it all, Hooper!" Trask snapped irritably. "I wish you wouldn't sneak up on me and speak so suddenly! I was thinking, and you gave me a start! Confound it, man! Can't you come around to my face, when you have business with me, instead of soft-shoeing it up behind?"

The man addressed was a native, tall, and extremely slender. Despite the slenderness, he had a look of power—such as a lithe and tawny panther possessed.

His hair was long, touching his shirt collar in the back, and black as a ripe muscadine; his eyes matched his hair in color, and were round and seemingly lidless, flanking a long, high-bridged nose. The mouth was wide, and almost concealed by a long, drooping mustache.

In dress he resembled most of the natives of the section. Like his fellows, he wore blue-jean trousers, light gaiters, a striped cotton shirt and a black slouch hat. In the crook of his left arm he carried an old-fashioned single-shot, breech-loading rifle, of thirty-eight caliber.

The native eyed the irate speaker calmly for an instant, his jaws working methodically while he pulverized a cud of "home-cured." Then he spat copiously over the veranda rail, grinned good-humoredly, and answered:

"I reckon I could come 'round to yore front, Trask," he said softly. "Seein' that you-all air skeerd of somethin' er nuther. 'Scuse me, this time, an' I'll blow a horn afore I come clost to you-all agin."

"You needn't take liberties, Hooper!" Trask reproved. "I allow you considerable familiarity when we are alone—but don't go too far!"

The native laughed—a soft, irritating laugh. "You-all done got up on th' wrong side of th' baid, this mawnin', Trask," he gibed. "Better come out of it—thar's apt to be business to 'tend to, afore th' day gits much older. I ain't told you-all somethin' else which I heered this mawnin'."

Trask's anger evaporated suddenly, and he became absorbedly attentive.

"Well, Hooper," he asked slowly, "what did you hear?"

The native came a few steps nearer, sat down on the edge of a table, rested the butt of his rifle on the floor, spat over the veranda rail again, and answered in low tones:

"Jigsaw Simpson, which has been nosin' eround down Cypress to'ads th' big river fur reasons you-all is acquainted with—hollered me up outen my baid this mawnin' an hour afore sun.

"He says thar's a mangy-lookin' steamboat which air called th' *Clipper,* tied up in Fishbone Lake, ten miles to th' east, an' that thar's a whole passel of them damn rangers a-board of her. Soon as he seed 'em, he snook away an' repo'ted th' matter to me.

"Now, Trask," he went on, his dark, heavily-lined visage becoming grave, "city detectives, amachoor an' perfessional alike, air jist so many pesky muskeeters a buzzin' an' singin' about. They ain't hardly wuth loosin' no sleep over.

"But them straight-shootin', never-quittin', woods-wise rangers air pure an' ondiluted hell. Plumb hell, that's whut!

"Now, Trask, seein' they air undoubtedly comin' in here, whut air you-all goin' to do erbout it?"

Trask was both surprised and disturbed by this bit of news. His hamlike hands were gripped tightly, and his thick lips were firmly compressed. Presently he opened his mouth to reply, but before he could put his answer in words, a newcomer appeared on the veranda steps.

It was Jack Calhoun, and, judging from the easy stride of him as he crossed the floor toward Trask, Robert Keene's shoes had not yet begun to pinch.

9

FACING DISASTER

TRASK, UPON SEEING the approaching stranger, immediately became Junius B. Trask, general field superintendent for the Arkana Mills—which is to say, his austere and overbearing manner asserted itself.

"We will talk this matter over later, Hooper," he said loudly, waving a hand in dismissal of the native. "I think my company has enough oxen for its present needs, but it may be that we shall have need of your herd later on. I shall advise you, should we decide to take them."

"Oxes is apt to die off, you knows, Mr. Trask," Hooper reminded him, getting up. "Mine is fust-rate critters, an' well broke. I'll sell th' whole passel of 'em cheap, if you-all decides you wants 'em. Good day, sir."

He left the veranda by the front steps, just as Calhoun, having arrived from the rear, paused before the superintendent.

"Mr. Trask?"

Trask eyed the speaker slowly, calmly and minutely, before he acknowledged his presence by word. He saw a tall, soldierly young man of near thirty. His face was homely, tanned and freckled, and his hair had been sun-bleached until it resembled ripe wheat-straw.

His eyes were gray and, Trask thought, altogether baffling. Rather fastidious in the matter of clothing, he also perceived, marking the new suit of corduroys the young man wore, and the immaculate handkerchief which protruded from the upper left hand pocket of the belted jacket.

"I am Mr. Trask," the superintendent acknowledged, having looked his fill. "Who may you be?"

"I'm Robert Keene," was the answer. "Mr. Banning, your general manager in Memphis, instructed me to report to you for duty as employment manager and superintendent of Mill Number Two."

"Humph! You have a letter from Banning to that end?"

"Yes, sir!"

The new boss presented the letter, which Trask perused and placed in a pocket. He nodded, signifying satisfaction.

"Young man," he said, and his manner was inexpressibly stern, "I shall ask you no questions concerning your qualifications. Banning hired you, and doubtless he would not have done so had he not been satisfied that you are fit. Time, however, will disclose your fitness, if you are fit; likewise time will disclose your unfitness, if you are unfit.

"You will enter upon your duties tomorrow morning, and Huggins, your mill assistant, will see you over the first day." He paused, placed the tips of his fingers together, and considered the young man thoughtfully for a full moment.

"There is one piece of advice which I shall give you—and only one. You will do well to make it your slogan while here. It is this: See nothing outside of your own circle of duties. Doubtless you will have enough to do to keep you busy.

"My quarters," he went on to explain, "are here at the

club—the west wing of the building is, in fact, the local general office. You may occupy a room here, and cross the lake to your work, or you may occupy a cabin over there. Suit yourself in that."

"I prefer to live at the clubhouse, since you permit," Cal answered.

As a matter of fact, he desired greatly to be where he could observe Mr. Trask and his activities closely. To live in the same building with him was rather more than he had hoped for.

"Very well," Trask assented. "Now, er—you have, no doubt, heard about the tragic fate which overtook your predecessor. Coming from Memphis, you could hardly have failed to get the news reports of the matter at least."

Cal nodded. "Yes," he replied. "The papers have been full of the thing for several days."

"What is the most accepted version of the killing?" Trask asked.

"Well, it seems that it is certain Barwick had trouble with a native, name unknown, over a girl here in the swamps," Cal replied. "There was a fight, and Barwick fled. The native, it seems, was crazed with jealousy, and pursued him clear to the Mississippi, slaying him there. Such is the newspaper version."

"Humph!" Trask ejaculated thoughtfully. "That does not, however, account for the native's ferocity—his killing others. How about that?"

"Well, it is thought that the killer feared pursuit and capture, so he shot the men who were in reality only seeking to aid Barwick. Crazy with hatred and jealousy, no doubt."

"Ah, yes," Trask agreed. "No doubt. Ignorance, plus utter lack of appreciation of the value of human life. Such is the swamper, Keene. I advise you to have little to do with them. Keep away from Needle's Eye. It is a tough place—a native gathering place."

Cal bowed. "I shall observe all you say, sir," he replied. "And thank you. I have no desire to mix with the tough element in the swamps. I am a man of peace, and devote most of my spare time to pursuing a hobby—that of collecting specimens of forest flora. I am greatly interested in botany from the standpoint of an amateur. Outside of my duties here, I have no other interest save the one mentioned."

"That is very good," Trask applauded. "I feel that we shall get along well. By the bye, who recommended you to Banning?"

"My uncle," was the prompt reply. "George Hackett Spangler, the Congress—"

"Hell!"

Trask's body stiffened, and he eyed the speaker keenly. Cal, realizing that his disclosure possessed elements of surprise and annoyance for the superintendent, waited for him to speak.

"So you are Spangler's nephew?" Trask said. "I've heard of you, but the name, Robert Keene failed to register at first. Your uncle's ward, Miss Lambert, has spoken of you to me. In fact, she seemed very desirous of obtaining some sort of position here for you when you finished school. Yes, very desirous. Nan Lambert seems to think an almighty lot of you!"

A slight tightness of shoe in the region of the instep

warned Cal that Keene's footgear was on the verge of pinching. His face was lit with a pleased smile, however, when he answered:

"Oh, yes!" he exclaimed. "Nan is a dear girl—very smart, and all that. She does take a very flattering interest in me, I am glad to say. Are you very well acquainted with her?"

"Not as well as I should like to be," was the answer. "I'm going to have a chance to further our acquaintance soon, though."

"You are going out to Memphis for a protracted stay, perhaps?"

"No. She's coming here for a week," was the answer. "Be here Saturday, along with a big crowd, Spangler included."

"Hell!"

The ejaculation was Cal's, and it was only mental—but it came, nevertheless, straight from his heart. His face still wore a pleased expression when he commented:

"I recall hearing Uncle George say something about an outing in the Deep Lake country, some time ago," he said. "It had slipped my mind, though. Coming Saturday, you say?"

"Yes. Coming Saturday."

"Hem, er—" Cal hesitated, then went on: "On second thought, I believe I shall occupy the cabin across the lake for the present. Such a large crowd will require considerable room, and I can cross the lake every evening and spend some time with Uncle George and Nan. Do you approve of that?"

Trask did.

"That's generous of you, Keene," he replied genially. "It

will be crowded when they get here. After the party goes you can select your quarters to suit yourself."

"Yes," Cal agreed. "Surely. Now, if there is nothing else, I shall look up my cabin and get straightened around."

"See you to-morrow then," Trask told him airily, dismissing him with a wave of a hand. "Hope you find things comfortable."

Cal, having had a good square look into the mocking face of disaster, desired more than all things else in the world to be alone. He wanted to think, to plan, and he did not delay his going.

Those shoes of Keene's were beginning to send warning pains up his ankles!

10

ON THIN ICE

"WILDCAT," SAID CAL when he returned to where the native waited in his dugout, "I have just had startling news. My Uncle George is to be with us soon. Nan is coming, too. The prospect is plumb shattering! On top of all that, my shoes hurt!"

"Why in hell don't you change yore shoes, then?" demanded Wildcat. "Dang me if I'd wear no shoes which didn't fit. My idear of hell on earth is shoes which makes me plumb mizzable to walk in!"

"Mine hurt, walking or sitting," Cal told him lugubriously as he dropped onto the bow seat. "But I've got to wear 'em!"

"Hell!" Wildcat commented disgustedly. "I wouldn't do it fur love ner money! Whar to, now?"

"Straight across the lake to where you see the smoke on the far shore," Calhoun directed. "Tell me, do you know a man—a native—in these parts who is as tall as I am, chews tobacco constantly, and is a dead shot with a rifle?"

"I knows a whole caboodle of jist sich pussons," was the answer. "Most of us swampers is tall, we all chaws tobak-ker without let-up, and we most p'intedly air crack shots with a rifle gun. Whut other marks does this here man of your'n carry?"

"He's meaner than hell, for one thing," Cal went on. For another, he's a game hunter by profession—when he's not busy killing human beings."

Wildcat shook his head. "You-all ain't disclosed no onmistakable year-marks yit," he said. "Lots of us swampers is mean as hell, when we gits riled up. Course, they ain't many of us which would kill a lot of folks, without they war aimin' to do us dirt.

"Reckon you-all will have to ax somebody else about this gent you refers to. I don't know him, or, leastwise, I ain't got no means of knowin' whether I know him or not!"

Calhoun gave up. The boat plowed on toward the far shore of Deep Lake.

For all of Cal's seeming lightness of mood, his mind was anything but easy. That he was on thin ice he was well aware. At best his venture into the region in his borrowed character was a dangerous procedure.

Yet there were certain very good reasons why he was warranted in taking the risk. It was only in the capacity of a boss, or some other official position, that he would have a chance to gain access to certain quarters from which he hoped to learn much.

At best he had only hoped for perhaps a week's freedom to come and go as Robert Keene. Sooner or later the impersonation would be discovered, since Keene's connections in Memphis would naturally expect to get letters from him. Failing to do so, they would doubtless inquire into matters. Keene could not be kept in durance long.

But Cal did not want more than a week for his operations in the mill district. At the end of that time he would have established one of two things: His own mistake, or the existence of one of the most colossal robberies the government had ever been subjected to in the timber lands.

A week. That would be sufficient.

But he was not to have a week in which to work. Three days, at most, was all he could count on. For, with the arrival of George Spangler and the outing party, discovery of his imposture would inevitably occur.

Fast work. That was the only way out. He must compress within the short period of three days all the labor he had expected to invest in a week. Not impossible, he thought, but certainly uncertain of accomplishment.

The big mill loomed ahead, with its huge piles of sawdust, waste heaps and dry-kilns. To the right, in rows ten deep, were the board shacks of the laborers, with the commissary in their midst. Above the mill, at a distance of perhaps two hundred feet, were several other shacks, one of them obviously the mill superintendent's office.

Saws screamed shrilly and without cessation, as their long, sharp teeth tore through the resisting fiber of their prey. In the edge of the lake, clad in rolled trousers, caulked shoes on their sockless feet, and their torsos bare to the parching sun, men leaped about from log to log where they floated in the water.

With pike-poles they sorted and shifted the trunks, steered those desired at the moment into the clutch of the carriers, thereafter to go shooting up steep inclines into the mill house, thence upon the teeth of the saws.

Truckmen scurried here and there along the elevated platforms, shoving loads of newly cut boards before them.

Tall stacks of those boards were everywhere to be seen, awaiting their turn in the kilns; Activity everywhere— hard-driven activity.

"This is the place, Wildcat," Cal remarked, staring up toward the high floor of the main mill room where shirtless men sweated and strove. "I'm boss of all this. Don't want a permanent job, do you?"

"Naw! Not in that hell pit, I don't!" Wildcat declined with heat and vehemence. "Whut you-all reckon I'd sweat my life away in sich a torment for, when thar's all th' whole wide swamp fur me to git my livin' in? Hell! Why will folks be sich fools!"

Cal chuckled. He knew Wildcat of old. A square man, he was, and one who had often been useful to the rangers. He could be trusted to keep his tongue still, and many lucrative jobs fell to him at the hands of Wheeler's men. But he was not to be begged, hired or forced into steady toil of any sort whatsoever.

"I war bawn free, an' my pappy an' grandpappy afore me war likewise bawn free," he was wont to assert. "I most p'intedly don't aim to do nothing slavish. I don't hire my body to no man. I works fur myself, an' nobody else!"

His attitude was but a reflection of that of the average native. He was in nowise to blame for it. He came by it honestly.

"Then," said Calhoun, stepping ashore, "I guess we part here. I'll take care of the luggage. Go directly back to Oak Donnick and say this to Captain Wheeler: 'Three days.' Just that. He'll know what you mean. Also, he will take care of you on this deal. Tell him that I am well pleased with your performance. So long."

The native started to push off, thought better of it, and hailed Cal back to the water's edge.

"Look here, Mr. Calhoun," he said hesitatingly, "I don't exactly like leavin' you-all up here by yoreself. Somethin' sort of tells me you ain't goin' to have no picnic of it. If you-all wants me to, I'll stop with you a spell. At leas' ontel you gets things lined up.

"I ain't hongry fur no job of work—but I ain't got no objections to doin' a little shootin' with a rifle gun, if so be it's needed. I won't charge only day wages fur it neither."

Cal considered the native soberly. It entered his mind that Wildcat, a skilled woodsman and an expert with a rifle, might come in handy there. Second thought, however, warned him that the presence of the native with him would likely lead to questions. Questions which might lead to something else.

"Thank you, Broadus," he said. "I shan't keep you, though. There are reasons why I must play a lone hand. Go back to Wheeler."

The native pushed off, and Calhoun turned to see a short sandy-haired young man approaching from the mill. He waited.

"I'm Huggins," the young man stated, pausing near Cal. "You're the new super, I take it?"

"Right, Huggins," Cal affirmed, grinning and offering a hand. "My name is Keene—Bob, for short. Trask told me you would whip me into line."

"Sure thing. Glad to. This job is too big for one man. Sure glad you are here. You'll be wanting to arrange a shake-down for the night, and I'd recommend the back room of the office. Nobody there since poor Barwick dropped out. He slept there, you know."

"That will suit me," Cal told him "Got a key?"

Huggins fished out a key and tendered it. "I'd go with you, old man," he said, "only I've got to stay on the job. Trask drives me, and I drive the men. Pretty soon you'll be driving, too. I know of pleasanter situations," he added, giving Cal a straight look from a pair of indescribably tired eyes, "but they are a long ways off!"

He turned on his heel and hastened back to the mill.

Five minutes later the inspector found himself within the four walls of the dead Barwick's former office—the place he had risked wearing another man's shoes to gain. Barwick's office had been his chief objective all along.

"Well," he said to himself in silent communion, as his eyes ranged about over desk, chairs and filing cabinets, "I'm here!"

11

IN THE EYES OF HUGGINS

CAL PASSED INTO the lean-to back of the main room of the office. In a corner beneath a window was a single bunk, on the foot of which lay two neatly folded blankets. A shelf held a tin bucket and washpan; above was a small mirror. Two splint-bottom chairs and a home-made table completed the furnishings.

Barwick's personal effects had evidently been removed, since they were nowhere to be found. But the dead man's personal belongings held no particular interest for the ranger.

He returned to the office and approached the window in its front wall. His attention immediately concentrated upon a man who sat on a stump a short distance away—a tall native, clothed in blue-jean trousers, a striped shirt, and slouch-brimmed hat. Across his knees rested an old-fashioned, single-shot rifle.

The man's jaws moved slowly and methodically, and streams of amber shot from his mouth at intervals. He appeared to be intent upon the lumberjacks who worked in the edge of the water.

"That's the chap who left Trask when I came onto the veranda," was Cal's thought. "Evidently I am not to be accepted as safe until I've been watched for a spell. Well, watch on, my tobacco chewing friend," he silently admonished the man on the stump. "You haven't got a monopoly of that sort of thing.

"A tall native who chews tobacco constantly, and spits frequently and copiously. He seems to fit, all save the rifle—and that may well be exhibited for a stall.

"And yet—hang it all! He's too prominently in the picture! Hasn't the look of a born killer, either. The man I am after hasn't a soft spot in his make-up.

"He's a demon, with no more regard for human beings than a sawyer has for the trees he fells. Yonder chap will bear close watching, though, while he's keeping tab on me!"

He left the window and sat down near a wooden filing cabinet in a corner.

"He wouldn't have been so thoughtless as to have filed it," the inspector reasoned, as his glance ranged down the row of drawers in the case and came to rest on one lettered "R to Z."

"But there's nothing like being certain."

He arose, looked out the front window again, saw that the man on the stump had not changed his position, then crossed swiftly to the cabinet. Withdrawing the lower compartment noiselessly, he ran through its contents with nimble fingers. Then he replaced it and sat down at the desk. Two minutes sufficed to disclose that what he searched for was not there.

Some sheets of carbon-paper next attracted his attention. They were in the upper right hand drawer of the desk.

"All old," he remarked, after examining the carbons.

"Nothing there—only, the corner of one is folded in. That's in line with what I expected."

He sat for a while in deep thought. He had, upon examining the fragment of Barwick's letter, noticed a dark smear on the back of the sheet—such a smear as might have been left by an illy inserted sheet of carbon paper. One with a corner folded down, thus bringing the treated side in contact with the original sheet.

Common sense had assured Cal that Barwick would not have made a carbon copy of the letter for filing. That would have been foolish, and would have served no purpose whatsoever. Yet he had made such a copy. Why?

There was only one satisfactory answer: Barwick was not alone in his knowledge of whatever it was he had discovered. Some one else who, like himself, rebelled and desired to act with him, shared his knowledge.

Barwick had, therefore, written his letter in duplicate and intrusted the copy to his co-plotter. Should Barwick fail to get his communication outside, as he had reason to fear he should be unable to do, the other was to have a try at it.

So Cal had reasoned, and so he yet believed.

Why, then, had not the other man acted? Doubtless he had been unable to do so. Had been too closely watched. Perhaps the silent tobacco chewer on the stump was even then—

A steam-whistle sounded hoarsely without, and there was an immediate cessation of the bedlam in the mills, resulting in a silence that was almost painful.

Cal got up. The sun was down behind the westward wall

of trees, and shadows were beginning to invest the lake. It was quitting time at Mill Number Two.

Huggins hurried from the big building, crossed the sawdust littered clearing which lay between the mill and the office without so much as a glance toward the native who still sat on the stump, and entered the office.

"Time to eat," he told Cal, dropping into a chair. "I'm so damned tired, though, I had rather pass the grub up than go and get it!"

Cal looked him over closely, noted the lines of worry about his mouth, the creases between his brows and on his forehead, and said:

"You haven't been sleeping well lately, have you, Huggins?"

Huggins flashed him a swift glance, then lowered his eyes.

"No," he answered sourly. "Too much work, and the mosquitoes are bad."

"So. I thought maybe you might be worried about something."

Huggins started, and raised his eyes again to Cal's. This time he found the keen gray orbs of the latter full upon him, and, though he tried to do so, he found it impossible to shift his gaze.

In complete silence the two men sat and stared straight into each others' eyes, while slowly there dawned in those of the assistant superintendent a look of sheer, stark fear.

After a bit Cal nodded slowly, and spoke:

"I think I understand," he said quietly. "You are desperately afraid of—mosquitoes. The sting of certain kinds of mosquitoes means death—the kind you fear. The kind that stung Barwick."

Huggins leaped to his feet, his face white, eyes wide with terror.

"In God's name, man," he cried, "what do you mean? What do you know?"

Sit down," Cal bade him, "and don't raise your voice again. This is what I mean:

"Barwick wrote a letter, and got out with a fragment of it, only to be slain before he could board a boat for Memphis. The papers did not mention the fact that he had that bit of letter upon his person, because the papers know nothing about it. Nevertheless he had it. But that letter was not the only one in existence, treating the same subject. He made a carbon copy."

Cal ceased speaking, his eyes once again probing those of Huggins.

"You are not good at dissembling your feelings, Huggins," he said. "You have the kind of eyes which are truly 'windows of the soul.' You are frozen with fear—and you can't hide it. I saw it this afternoon when you came to greet me. Suppose you hand that duplicate letter over to me!"

Up to the moment of Huggins's entrance, Cal's high-crowned Stetson had been on his head. When the assistant superintendent came into the room, he had removed it, placing it upon his lap where he fingered the brim gently, as though molding the turned edge into a different form.

His eyes dwelt now upon the crown of the hat, as though something there absorbed him.

"Hats tell some people lots of things," he said quietly,

during the pause after his last words—a pause which Huggins had failed to fill. "For instance, yours bulges a trifle on the left side, beneath the band. Wouldn't wonder, now—"

Huggins leaped to his feet, his face ashen. "By God!" he ejaculated, albeit a repressed ejaculation, while he cast fearful glances around the darkening room as though expecting something to leap at him from the shadows. "You—why, damn you—"

"Sit down and take it easy, my friend," came Cal's voice softly from the shadows. He had chosen his position well. The section of the room in which he sat was now almost in darkness, while the last light of evening sifted through the front window across the person of the thoroughly aroused assistant.

"You are in more danger right now than you have ever been before in your life. You just don't realize it. Take my word for it, keep your hands out of your pockets—and—sit—down!"

Huggins caught the significance of the words addressed to him, and sat down.

"Will you tell me who you are?"

"No. The letter?"

"You are assuming too much! Even if such a letter should be in my possession—

"The letter, Huggins! Or shall I take it?"

Cal arose, his powerful figure looming threateningly in the gloom.

Huggins snatched the hat from his head, withdrew a tightly folded sheet of paper and hurled it upon the desk.

"Take it!" he gasped. "It has lain there scorching my

brain ever since the night poor Barwick gave it to me! I'm glad it's gone! No matter what happens to me now, I'm damned glad I don't have to keep it any longer!"

Cal's eyes held nothing but pity for the man. "Nothing will happen to you at my hands, Huggins," was his assurance, as he crossed to the window and held the unfolded sheet to catch the faint light which yet came through. "Get a grip on yourself, man! The thing you fear may not happen after all!"

12

THE FAT'S IN THE FIRE

THE WANING LIGHT was yet sufficient to enable Calhoun's keen eyes to decipher the letter. He picked it up from the desk where Huggins had thrown it. Slowly, yet carefully, he allowed his eyes to roam over the message. It ran:

> Arkana Mill No. 2,
> Near Needle's Eye, Ark.
> June the 4th, 1891.

Mr. John Rexford,

Commissioner Swamp Lands,

Little Rock, Arkansas.

Dear Sir:

I write this in haste, as I believe my life is in danger. I have certain knowledge that the interests back of my company are not merely cutting the cottonwood here, but are after the big timber. I know how the scheme is worked, and it is very shrewdly done, almost detection proof; those who are getting the timber are disposing of it to certain supposedly legitimate hard-wood mills, and once in their possession there is no way of identifying the logs. More I cannot say in a letter, since I know beyond any doubt that I am watched, and have been spied upon for the past two weeks. I may not leave the mill, and I am not sure this letter will ever go out. I can only try to send it. If you get it, please send a strong force to this place at once, strong enough to afford protection to me after I have divulged what I know. Otherwise I will be slain.

Hoping that this reaches you, I am

Yours truly,

Raymond J. Barwick

Supt. Mill No. 2

A disheartening sense of failure assailed Calhoun when he had finished reading the letter. He could scarcely believe that that which had promised so much really fulfilled so little.

"Not a thing in it that I had not already suspected," he thought. "Nothing definite. The interests back of the Arkana company are stealing Uncle Sam's fine trees. The fragment told me that much. And I was fool enough to think the balance of the letter might mention names—or at least suggest some one whom I might pin something on!"

He stood beside the window, gazing out. The native was still on the stump, his long figure barely discernible. He had changed his position, now, and was faced toward the office door.

"Look your fill, damn you!" Cal muttered under his breath. "The time may come soon when you won't be able to look!"

The inspector was not used to giving way to fits of temper, and the one now possessing him passed swiftly.

"Well, I didn't exactly fail," he assured himself with a grin. "I set out to get a letter—and I got it." He swung about toward Huggins's chair, intent upon questioning him, but emitted a long, low whistle of surprise instead.

The chair where the assistant had been sitting three minutes before was empty. A quick survey of the room failed to locate him. Cal entered the lean-to, and a draft of air fanned his face. The back door stood ajar.

Huggins, taking advantage of Cal's preoccupation, had flown!

Bang! Bang! Bang!

The noise came from the front. Some one was banging on the door. Cal remembered having locked it after Huggins came in. He hurried into the office and swung the door open.

The tobacco-chewing native stood upon the step, his rifle in the crook of an arm.

"Whar at is Huggins?" he demanded.

"Who the hell are you?" Cal snapped in retort.

"Lissen!" the native ordered, his voice low but threatening. "I done axed you-all a question! Whar at is Huggins?"

"Listen!" Cal's voice was equally as low, equally as threatening. "I asked you a question! Who the devil are you?"

The native drew back from the door, his blazing black eyes surveying Cal from head to feet. The inspector stood in the doorway, nonchalantly fanning the swarming mosquitoes away with his hat. After a moment's scrutiny the native spoke again.

"I'm Nate Hooper," he said evenly. "I may not look lak I amounts to much, but folks ginerally does what I tells 'em to do around here. If you-all wants to git erlong good in these parts, jist remember that. Now—whar at is Huggins?"

"Glad to know you, Mr. Hooper," smiled Cal genially.

"Honestly, you kind of scared me, banging on my door like you did. I am not used to the woods, and you can't blame me for being jumpy my first night here. Won't you come in?"

"Hell!" blazed Hooper. "Air you-all a damn fool? Does you think I come here to pay you-all a visit? Say—whar—at—is—Huggins?"

There had been method in Cal's foolery. He was playing for time—time for Huggins to go wherever it was he meant to go. Somehow, he felt that the assistant was in deadly danger, and from the man who stood before him.

He did not want the assistant to fall into Hooper's hands. Rather, he hoped to get hold of him himself. He felt, however, that he had gone as far as was safe with the native, and answered:

"I can't tell you where Huggins is," he said. "I could have told you five minutes ago. At that time he was right here. Now he's gone—and I haven't the least idea where. He left while I was standing by the window, looking out at the lake. Kind of lonesome—"

Hooper crossed the threshold in a stride, Cal stepping back to permit his entrance, "I think you air a damned fool!" he snarled over his shoulder, as he passed into the lean-to. A moment later Cal heard the back door slam, and he knew that Hooper had taken up Huggins's trail.

Would the latter make good his get-away? Cal felt sure it was a get-away. That look of terror in the assistant's eyes meant flight. The ranger had not, however, expected it so soon.

"Well, I guess I'll eat," Cal decided. "No use starving in a land of plenty. Besides," he reflected as he circled the mill house and steered toward the long building which housed the mess hall, "I may get real hungry before morning dawns."

13

AMBUSHED

THE NOISES OF man cease early in the big woods, almost with the coming of night. At moon rise the animals and birds of the forest move about, the fish in the streams awake and go leaping and plunging in search of food, while countless frogs bellow the long night through.

Man, however, sleeps. Worn with the toil of the day, he seeks his bed early.

Calhoun rolled into his blankets directly he had finished his after supper pipe. He made his intention quite clear at the boarding house, where he dined at a table reserved for the bosses, timekeepers, and other so-called better class employees.

His kerosene lamp glowed against a curtainless window while he undressed, and ten minutes after he extinguished it he was snoring in his bunk.

At eleven o'clock the blankets stirred slightly, and he slid noiselessly from under them—leaving the pile bunched as though they still wrapped a human form.

Dressing required no more than two minutes. In the moonlit area of a window he carefully examined a pair of forty-five caliber revolvers, making certain that the mechanism was working to perfection.

One gun was thrust into the bosom of his shirt, where a shoulder holster lay under his left arm; the other was shoved two-thirds of its length inside his right bootleg.

Calhoun had reason to expect action before the sun rose again.

Letting himself out the rear door, he stood in the shadow of the cabin for five minutes, during which time he did not so much as move a finger.

Satisfied that no one save himself was stirring, he made his way slowly, taking advantage of every shadowed place which offered, into the fringe of trees which grew on the west side of the clearing above the mill. After gaining the trees it was an easy matter to circle the mill site and reach the lake shore below the clearing.

A boat was then to be found. No easy task, stealing a boat from among the fleet which lay at anchor higher up the shore and near the dwelling quarters. There were watchmen about the mill, and, what was more to the point, about the extensive yards as well. But Calhoun needed a boat, and needed it badly.

Following the shore toward where the boats lay he came to the edge of the growth of timber, and his objective was yet a hundred feet away, bathed in the light of the moon. He crouched down, eyes directed toward the mill and the yards.

After what seemed an interminable time a hand lantern came bobbing along an alley way between high stacks of lumber, and a watchman passed along the shore line and into the mill.

Cal arose, after the watchman had disappeared, and walked boldly to where the boats lay. Untying the painter of a long dugout, he got in and poled the craft noiselessly down the shore into the shadows. If any one observed the theft, he failed to raise his voice.

Cal might, indeed, have been a mill hand going about business of his own and in his own boat. At any rate, he believed he had worked unseen.

Hugging the dark shore line of Deep Lake, the ranger sped swiftly toward the point where Cypress Slough tailed off toward the second of the lakes in its chain—Blue Gill Pond, it was called. Not another craft was to be seen on the water.

The inspector's purpose was to communicate with Murdock on board the *Clipper,* which lay at anchor in Fishbone Lake, second in the chain.

The duplicate letter having failed him, Cal was at the moment without plans. He had hoped to be able to complete his case before Saturday, thus avoiding exposure by Spangler; now all that was changed.

But there was a way whereby the danger of exposure could be eliminated. He meant to take that way. He proposed, in fine, to have Murdock detain the launch bearing the outing party when it showed up.

There would be no aftermath because of such detention, for Cal was convinced that most of the men aboard, officials and stockholders in the Arkana Company, were up to their eyes in the deviltry going on in the big woods. At any rate, he meant to take such action, let the consequences be what they would.

At the supper table that night he had been introduced to the two government inspectors attached to the Arkana operations. Redding, the chief, had not made a very favorable impression upon him. Perhaps that was because Cal expected to find him crooked. Time would tell.

Roberts, the second inspector, was a small, meek man, evidently of not much force. Thefts of the proportions undoubtedly going on could not be perpetrated without the connivance of one or both. That was certain.

"They are just saplings," Cal ticketed them in his mind. "When the really big trees are thrown they will go down in consequence."

At the extreme east end of Deep Lake, Cypress Slough leaves that body and crosses a flat: the flat, being mostly a level stretch of mud and slime, grown up with water-shrubs and grass through which the channel of the slough winds.

Cal left the lake and entered the slough, pushing forward rapidly. He had to make the ten-mile trip and return before dawn.

To negotiate the intricate channel, beset as it was by treacherous mud banks, submerged logs and concealing brush, required strict attention to the business in hand. Because of that Calhoun shot his boat into a zone of danger without having the least warning.

He did not see the two long dugouts lying in the shadow of a huge clump of river flags until it was too late to avoid them. His first intimation of other presences on the water was when a command came to halt—a command backed by two men whose boats suddenly appeared from the shadows, and whose rifles were trained steadily upon him.

"Drop that paddle!" ordered the first of the boatmen. "Put your hands high, an' keep 'em high!"

14

TRAPPED

CAL'S FIRST IMPULSE was to draw and give battle, but a movement in the shadows from whence the boats had come informed him that a third man loitered there.

It was that third man, hidden by darkness and commanding the situation as he did, that caused the inspector to yield. To resist, under the conditions, would have been voluntary suicide—nothing less.

Cal's paddle dropped overside, and his hands went up.

"A pleasant night for boating, gentlemen," he commented politely. "I trust you are enjoying yourselves?"

There was silence for a moment. Then:

"Hell!" exclaimed a voice from the shadows, that of the unseen man beyond. "That ain't Huggins!"

"Looking for Mr. Huggins?" Cal queried. "Then perhaps you will allow me to take my hands down," he went on suggestively. "My arms ache in such an awkward position. Since it is Huggins—"

"Keep them hands up!"

Cal obeyed. He had no illusions about the situation. Death was threatening him, and he knew it.

The third boat at that moment came out of concealment, driven by a tall, heavy-set man in native attire. It crossed the moonlit water and rested across the bow of Cal's dugout, held stationary by means of a long paddle thrust against the slough's shallow bottom.

The third man was Trask. Trask in the dress of a native swamper, his heavy face shadowed by the brim of a black slouch hat, but recognizable for all of that. For a moment he did not speak, simply sat and surveyed Cal coldly.

"Well, Keene," he said at length, "what have you to say for yourself?"

"Is it necessary to say anything?" Keene countered. "Is boating at night prohibited on Deep Lake?"

"No. I was just thinking, though, that for a young man who is confessedly out of his element in the big woods, whose years have been spent mostly in school, you are remarkably skillful in handling a dugout—the trickiest craft afloat. I thought botany was your specialty, not boating."

"I'm getting tired holding my hands in the air," Cal snapped. "What are you afraid of? You are three against one!"

"See if he's got a gun, Hank," Trask ordered.

"A gun!" Hank cried, a moment later. "Danged if he ain't plumb weighted down with hardware! Two of 'em—an' big as cannons at that!"

The speaker exhibited a pair of forty-fives he had removed from the ranger's person.

"Search him good!" Trask commanded, sudden suspicion in his voice. "He may have another!"

"Nope!" announced Hank, after running his hands over Cal's person, and minutely searching the boat. "Them two air all!"

Trask's voice now became bitingly sarcastic.

"Botanizing with a pair of six-guns!" he gibed. "What did you mean to shoot? A water lily?"

"No," Cal retorted evenly. "A water-moccasin."

Trask edged his boat closer, and Cal, catching an imperfect view of his features, thought at first that the man's face was working with passion. Such was not the case, however, as he soon perceived.

Trask's face muscles were working, right enough, but anger was not the cause. He was slowly, and with apparent relish, masticating a cud of tobacco.

There was a difference between the Trask of the morning and the individual the moonlight disclosed. A subtle change which Cal felt, but could not define.

But that Trask was in his element there on the slough, garbed in native dress and grinding a hunk of "home-cured" between his strong, yellow teeth, was, to Cal's mind, inescapable. He had no time, though, in which to ponder over that.

"Keene," Trask said coldly, "under ordinary circumstances you would do your botanizing henceforth in the mud and ooze of the slough. But the circumstances are not ordinary. You may be the harmless half-wit I took you for this morning. You may really be George Spangler's nephew—and that last possibility saves you for the present.

"Personally, I think you are something quite different from what you pretend to be. I think it because, right on the heels of your coming, Huggins runs away. That is suspicious. Then you steal a boat, late at night, to go, er—botanizing in. That is also a suspicious circumstance.

"If you are really Bob Keene, you won't in the least

understand what I am getting at. If you are not Keene, then you do get it. You see, I'm rather frank with you— since you will never have a chance to use anything I say against me. Spangler's nephew wouldn't. Keene's counter- feit won't be able to."

"What makes you think I'm not what I seem?" demanded Cal, distress in his voice. "I've given you no reason to think I'm not. And, I assure you, Uncle George will not be at all pleased if you misuse me! He will be very angry, and when he is angry he does things!"

"To hell with your Uncle George!" Trask blazed. "I've got a damned good notion to sink you here and now! I'm that sure you are a sneaking spy! But, on the chance that I may be mistaken, and that you are really Spangler's nephew, I'm going to postpone the pleasure I'd get out of filling you full of lead!

"But don't congratulate yourself too hastily. Spangler will be here Saturday, and then we'll know all about you! In the meantime, fearing that your love for forest flora— and your hatred of water-moccasins—might lead you into danger, my two friends here will look after you—and look after you most capably!"

"Thank you, Mr. Trask!" exclaimed Cal innocently. "But I have not yet had the pleasure of being introduced to the gentlemen you are assigning to me for companions—"

"Oh, hell!" Trask spat over the side of his boat in deep disgust. "You make me sick! Take him along, boys—you know where. Keep him close, and I'll let you know after Saturday what to do with him."

One of the boatmen retrieved Cal's floating paddle and restored it to him with the order:

"Head your boat about, and keep its nose as close to the stern of Kinney's as you can. Remember, I'm following right behind, and if you start any monkey business your light goes out! Get it?"

"How can I start anything?" Cal asked mournfully. "You got both of my pistols! This isn't fair, Mr. Trask!" he cried, turning toward where the superintendent had been. But Trask was gone. His dugout had slipped back into the shadows.

"Shut up, an' git goin'!"

The man called Kinney, paddling the leading boat, shouted the order over his shoulder, and it was seconded by a forceful prod from the muzzle of the rifle in the hands of the man behind.

Cal dipped his paddle in the water, and obeyed. Less than five miles away, the *Clipper* lay at anchor in the waters of Fishbone Lake. The *Clipper*, with Murdock and a crew of ten.

But, insofar as any aid coming to Calhoun from that source was concerned, the rangers' boat might as well have been a thousand miles away!

15

THE CABIN ON MULBERRY BAYOU

IN SINGLE FILE, the three boats threaded the morass of Cypress Slough into Blue Gill Pond, and Kinney, in the lead, laid a course toward the distant north shore.

Calhoun, whose bump of location was highly developed, took careful note of the changes in direction. The country thereabouts was new to him, but he had no difficulty in marking the course. He was due for a surprise, however, when the dugout ahead was bow onto the margin of the pond.

The north shore was heavily timbered, looming dark and forbidding, and thick water-growths stood rankly in the shallow water. Kinney did not slacken the speed of his boat upon approaching the shore, but drove the bow straight into a mass of undergrowth, seemingly with the intention of beaching there in the mud.

No such thing occurred. The light shell slid through the seeming obstruction and floated free upon the bosom of a bayou, the mouth of which was completely hidden by the weeds.

Cal followed on up the bayou, careful to give the man in the rear no cause to use the rifle he felt sure the fellow was only too willing to use. The inspector, upon entering the hidden water, felt certain that he was on the verge of important discoveries and, while it seemed just then that nothing he might learn thenceforward would avail him in the least, he was far from hopeless of escaping. He had been in tight places before.

A quarter of a mile from its mouth, the bayou angled toward the northwest, followed that direction for a mile, then straightened in a due western course.

"We are traveling back toward Deep Lake," Cal decided. "Only farther north. This bayou probably has its source close to the St. Francis, draining some marsh or other near it. Humph! Therein lies food for thought!"

His companions traveled in complete silence, and Cal made no effort to draw them out. He knew it would be but wasted time. Hour after hour passed, and a hint of dawn was in the cooling air.

The bayou continued to follow a course almost due west, and Cal judged that they had long since passed the position of Mill Number Two and the Arkana Club.

He recognized, too, that the course of the stream lay within a couple of miles of the north shore of Deep Lake. On all sides of him great trees loomed—and they were hardwoods all. Maple, mostly, with here and there a tract of enormous oaks.

"Millions of dollars' worth of trees!" he thought. Isolated as this place is, a small, busy crew would reap a golden harvest in a very short while, with little chance of discovery!

"Fine specimens of maple, oak, walnut, selected carefully and in singles here and there, and the practice kept up steadily for a couple of seasons, would yield huge returns.

And that is exactly what has been going on in here, the Lord only knows how long!"

Not a single sign of human habitation had Cal seen during the long journey. The section was the wildest he had yet found in the Sunken Lands. Just when he was beginning to wonder if the boat trip was ever to end, he caught sight of a dim, red glow among the trees two hundred yards ahead.

As they pushed on, the glow became a flare and disclosed its source in a number of gasoline torches attached to trees on the south bank of the bayou.

Then a strange procession greeted his eyes—strange in that Cal had never seen the like at night before.

Along a rutted rail which came in from the south and which was lit at intervals by gasoline torches, toiled an eight-yoke team of oxen, drawing a stout wagon on which lay two sixteen-foot maple logs.

The oxen, under the goad of a lank driver, turned up the bayou's bank and came to a stand where a group of loggers waited. In the water below that group a raft was in process of formation.

Cal's opportunity for further observation came to a sudden end.

Kinney beached his boat a hundred yards short of the group ahead, and stepped ashore.

"Git out!" he ordered, and Cal, only too glad to stretch his cramped body, instantly obeyed. "Follow me," the native continued, leading off through the timber. "Keep close behind him, Howit," he cautioned his mate. "He might try to make a sneak into the brush."

"If he does try it," Howit replied ominously, "he'll walk right into his own grave, before he gits ten foot off th' trail!"

Cal made no comment. Had there been but one man, there would have been a different ending to that journey. But there were two—one in front and one behind, and Cal knew without being told, and without the least desire for a demonstration, that they were both dead shots with a rifle. Had they not been, Trask would not have employed them for their present task. He walked along a dim path close upon the heels of Kinney.

They had not far to go—less than a quarter-mile. Presently Kinney halted before the door of a cabin which was so nearly hidden by trees it could hardly be seen fifty feet away. It was a squat cabin—a single room built of logs. The door was of thick, rough lumber, studded with the heads of cut-steel nails, and secured to a large staple by a stout chain and a padlock of formidable size.

"You ain't th' fust man which has took up housekeepin' here," Kinney assured the ranger with a grin, as he fitted a key into the lock. "Thar's been two or three afore yore time. Whar at air they now? Axe Trask—he knows!"

"There are a number of things I intend to ask of Trask—later," Cal replied evenly. "Just now, though, I am rather in need of sleep—and damned sick of the company I've been in for the past three hours. Do we part here?"

The reply was in the nature of a stunning blow between the shoulders from the butt of Howit's rifle—a blow which sent Calhoun staggering through the narrow doorway to land in a heap upon the floor.

The door slammed, the chain rattled, and Cal, in a daze,

heard the laughter of his jailers as they departed. After a bit he got up, struck a match and looked about him.

When the match flared up an observer would have noted that his eyes were almost black in the reflected light, and that his lips were tightly drawn. The face of Inspector Jack Calhoun was not, indeed, a nice thing to look upon.

"Howit," he muttered between clenched teeth, "I shan't forget you—nor your prowess with a rifle butt!"

Presently the ache between his shoulders grew less poignant, to be banished altogether by Cal's complete mental submergence in matters of greater moment.

There was no lamp of any sort to be found in the cabin, and Cal was compelled to make an examination of the place by match-light. This he did.

There was only one door, and it so strongly constructed as to defy even Calhoun's skill. The windows, of which there were three—one in the rear wall and one in each of the sides—were only narrow slits high above the inspector's head. Evidently they were for purposes of ventilation only.

The floor and ceiling consisted of "puncheons"—small tree trunks, adzed smooth on one side and laid as ordinary floors and ceilings are laid, with this difference: spiked into place, the puncheons could not be removed with anything legs powerful than a crowbar.

Cal had no crowbar. He was, therefore, helpless. The cabin was as stout a jail as even the most careful of jailers could wish for.

On a bunk in a corner was a roll of fairly clean blankets, and Calhoun stretched himself upon them, calmly thinking over his position.

"It's Friday morning," he reflected. "To-morrow the

Arkana launch will arrive. Any way you look at it, I'm done in the Deep Lake region, even though I succeed in getting away from here.

"I can, of course, stop the wholesale theft of timber that is going on, but can I connect the Arkana crowd with those thefts—prove it on them, beyond doubt? Not yet. Maybe never.

"Lacking proof, Rexford will be unable to bring about a forfeiture of their concession—and Arkana will get off with hardly a scratch.

"Maybe not, though. This is only Friday—and a lot can happen within a few hours. Guess I'll sleep on it."

He was not to sleep that night, however. Voices outside roused him from the first doze of what promised to be deep slumber. The chain rattled, the door creaked on its iron hinges and, in the light of a lantern outside, Cal saw that his two jailers had returned. They were accompanied by two others.

One was Hooper, the tobacco chewing native, who had dashed so unceremoniously through the mill office the evening before.

The other was Huggins—scarcely recognizable under a bloody bandage which shrouded his head.

"Here's company for you-all!" Hooper remarked derisively.

He thrust his captive into the cabin, shut the door and locked it. Cal could hear the low murmur of voices outside for a moment, then silence ensued.

He got up and struck a match—just as Huggins, who exhibited many outward signs of having been badly maltreated, dropped in a heap on the floor.

16

TRASK ENTERTAINS

SATURDAY AFTERNOON AND a drizzle of rain falling steadily. The outing party, expected to reach the clubhouse that day, had arrived on the *Speedy* at noon. Regardless of the gloomy weather, everybody seemed to be in excellent feather.

That is to say, the women of the party—of whom there were half a dozen—were gay and high of spirit. Miss Lambert, the pretty ward of Congressman Spangler, proved to be a very engaging young woman.

She asked concerning the whereabouts of her cousin, Robert Keene, during the first five minutes after reaching the club, demanding that he be produced forthwith. It was easy to see that she had more than a cousinly interest in the young man.

Trask dissembled his irritation, replying that Keene had been sent to the interior on an important mission, and that the date of his return depended entirely upon his ability to expeditiously transact the business claiming his attention. Mr. Trask was sorry, but it could not be helped.

Miss Lambert pouted. She was, Trask thought, even more charming when in a temper than when amiable and gay. Perhaps the fact that her personal fortune ran into the hundreds of thousands helped the superintendent to view her mood so leniently. Trask, of course, knew about that fortune.

At any rate, he thought, nephew or not, the man calling himself Robert Keene should not be present on the clubhouse porch during the party's visit, if he could prevent it—and he thought he could.

Miss Lambert's spell of pouting was of short duration, and soon her smiles were again helping to drive away the gloom of the rainy afternoon.

The Honorable George Hackett Spangler was a large, fat man who loved his ease and the good things of life. A past master in the intricacies of "inside" politics, he was also a shrewd financier.

Just how much he was worth, in dollars and cents, no man knew but himself. At the lowest estimate, he was a very wealthy man.

Five minutes spent in Trask's office, in conference with the latter and the four other male guests, who constituted the full tale of Arkana's stockholders, took some of the joy of living out of the Congressman's immediate present. He came out of the conference room looking a bit nervous and uneasy.

He was not alone in his state of unease. Roscoe Banning, prominent Memphis banker, and a heavy stockholder in Arkana, appeared even paler than was his wont. Banning was a shrewd man, a good banker—but he had a longing for great wealth, and his desire chafed at delay. He wanted much money, and he wanted it now.

Banning and Spangler retired to a small room off the main lounge, where could be had drinks of all kinds. They sat down in silence, drank in silence. Each wanted to talk, but neither appeared willing to open the conversation. Presently Banning said:

"Let's not worry until we are sure there is cause for it," he urged, attempting a light tone. "This chap may be your nephew after all. Who else could it be?"

"That's what I'd like to know," Spangler rasped. "Who? The description Trask gives doesn't tally out in all particulars with that of Keene. Though, I'll admit, it may well be he. We'll know to-night, at the earliest possible moment— or perhaps this afternoon. That is, of course, up to Trask."

They were joined in the little room by the other men of the party, all of whom appeared uneasy.

"Let's know the worst right now, Trask!" Banning demanded, setting his glass of whisky down untouched. "A bit of rain won't hurt us, and I am frank to say I am most damnably uneasy!"

Trask gave him a glance of half veiled contempt. "Why worry?" he asked. "If the man is not Keene, he is, at any rate, powerless to harm us. So, I repeat, why worry?"

Spangler brought a heavy fist down upon the table before him, causing the glasses thereon to rattle and jump. "If the man you have confined is not my nephew, Robert Keene," he asserted positively, "then we may as well expect trouble. How do you know that he has not means of communicating with the outside, and that he has not already done so?"

Trask shrugged, and his dark face grew ugly. "What, may I ask, could he have communicated? What chance has he had to learn anything damaging?" he inquired.

"Do you think I am a fool? That I have not taken every precaution against him, or any other man who has not been proven, learning anything about us and our business? I tell you that this chap is as harmless now as Barwick is!"

A shudder ran through the group.

"Careful, Trask!" Banning warned. "That is a name that should not be mentioned here!"

"You have let us into a terrible thing, Trask!" complained Havens, the insurance man. "That was illy done—"

"Shut up!" snapped Spangler. "Get off that topic! Let's have a drink all round, and then go and see this man who claims to be my nephew. If he proves to be an imposter—" He paused, glancing significantly toward Trask.

The latter's yellow teeth showed in an evil grin. "You can forget all about him, in that case," he said reassuringly. "He won't ever trouble us again."

"Shall we go?" Banning asked, rising.

"Not the whole crowd of us," Trask objected. "I'd suggest that you, Banning, and Spangler accompany me. We won't attract attention so. Besides, the ladies would not understand a wholesale desertion."

"Quite right, Trask," Spangler agreed.

"How shall we travel?"

"By launch to the west side of the lake, then a two mile walk to the spot. Better put on boots, and dig out your slickers."

A few minutes later the group departed, Banning and Spangler booted and wrapped in slickers, Trask making a not unattractive figure in the native rig which he wore for the occasion.

The remaining members of the Arkana concern formed a silent group in the little room off the lounge. They consumed an astonishing amount of raw liquor, and plainly

betrayed the fact that they were, to a man, under tremendous nervous strain.

The rain, which began falling in a torrent half an hour
after the departure of Trask and the others, did nothing
to lighten the gloom.

"We can only wait," Havens said with a sigh, as he
drained his fifth glass of whisky.

17

HUGGINS'S STORY

FRIDAY WAS A long, hard day for Calhoun. He spent it watching over Huggins, who became feverish in the early morning hours and babbled incessantly and incoherently.

An examination of the wound in his head assured Cal that it was superficial, and Huggins's poor condition was due more to exhaustion than loss of blood.

Shortly after daylight the door opened just wide enough to permit some one outside to shove in a can of water, a pot of coffee and a pan of fried bacon and potatoes. Then the door was locked again.

Cal's appetite was not one whit impaired, and, since poor Huggins was unable to partake of food, he ate both shares. After a bit he felt remarkably cheered.

In the late afternoon more food was set inside the door, but the man who brought it addressed no word to the occupants of the cabin, in spite of the fact that Cal offered him a rapid fire of highly insulting remarks. He was not to be coerced into talking.

Again the ranger fed well, saving the choicest portions, however, on the chance that Huggins would be able to eat later on. His fever had spent itself, and he slept.

About twelve o'clock that night Cal also went to sleep,

and, so exhausted was he, the sleep lasted until near noon the following day. He was awakened by Huggins, who asked for water.

Cal gave him a drink, then sat down on the bunk beside him.

"Old man," he said, "you and I are in one devil of a fix. If you had any thought in your mind that I was going to make trouble for you, as your sudden flight from the mill office indicated you had, you surely know better now. Do you feel like talking?"

"Yes," was the answer. "I'd like a smoke first. Then I'd like to know just who you are."

Cal filled a pipe and gave it to him.

"My name is Calhoun," he said in an undertone. "I'm a United States Ranger. My mission in these parts is to get the man who killed Barwick, and find out why he was killed. Does that satisfy you?"

"Yes. What do you want to know?"

"In the first place, how did you happen to fall into Hooper's hands?"

"He knew I would have to steal a boat in order to leave the swamp, and, outside of the fleet at the mill, I could get one only at Needle's Eye.

"I was a fool to try to get away, since I had about convinced Trask that I was willing to stay here and play his crooked game. But you gave me a real scare. I think I have been half crazy these last few days.

"Hooper laid for me at Needle's Eye, captured me after clubbing me with his gun, and brought me here. I was, of course, unarmed."

"Now, how does Trask operate his steal?"

"The stolen trees are floated into Blue Gill Lake by way of Mulberry Bayou, where they are mixed in with the cottonwood logs of the drive. Both inspectors are aware of what is going on, but they get well paid for shutting their eyes.

"The logs are delivered, along with the cottonwoods, to a string of mills on the Mississippi below Kimball's Point. There the big timber is worked up into veneer. Those mill owners know that the timber is stolen, but they get it at a much lower price per foot than they would have to pay for legitimate logs, and are safe in buying them, since to identify them as stolen stuff is practically impossible."

"I suspected as much from what I saw on Mulberry Bayou that night," said Cal.

"Yes. They operate at night mostly."

"Now describe what occurred the night or day Barwick tried to escape," Cal requested.

"Barwick and I found out what was going on," Huggins related, "in an accidental manner. Some tally-sheets used by Hooper, who is the man who checks the stolen timber, got mixed in with the regular mill sheets. How, I do not know. We investigated—and got caught at it by Hooper.

"From that moment on we were watched closely. All mail was gone over carefully before it was sent out of the swamp. It may seem odd to you that we should find it impossible to escape, but that demon, Trask, is a superman in some respects. He never left us alone for a moment, and foresaw and guarded against every possible avenue of escape our position offered.

"Just what he meant to do with us in the end I do not know. Doubtless we were slated to find a grave in some slough. He needed us at the mill, however, and so long as he could keep us he would not have to import strangers. He felt sure he had us blocked, and could finish us whenever he chose.

"I am not the arrant coward you quite likely believe me to be, Mr. Calhoun," Huggins went on. "Trask's system of browbeating and constant espionage, together with poor Barwick's terrible fate, simply got the best of me. Broke me, you might say.

"Barwick, let me say here and now, was a man of high courage. He resolved to get word of conditions out of the swamp. He wrote a letter, planning to elude Hooper and his spies, and get it out to Needle's Eye. A difficult undertaking, but not an impossible one, he thought.

"He wrote the letter one night, and gave me the duplicate you saw. If he failed, then I was to try. Two days thereafter he saw what he took to be his opportunity. Trask has one weakness—a human one. He likes to hunt, and this is the wild turkey season.

"It is his boast that he has killed more wild turkeys, and the largest specimens, than any other man in the Sunken Lands. Trask went hunting.

"Something later in the day took Hooper across the lake to the clubhouse, else he chose the period of Trask's absence to make a call on his own account. At any rate he went over, leaving a man called Fletcher to watch us.

"That was Barwick's chance. Fletcher was not so good a watchdog as Hooper, and Barwick got away.

"Poor chap! He ran squarely into Trask, who was returning from his hunt. There was a fight, and Barwick went down. The unlucky letter fell out of his pocket, betraying him. He snatched it up and Trask tore part of it from his hand.

"Barwick was a slight man in stature, but he had nerve. It was nearly dark, and he somehow managed to get hold of a billet of wood which lay near by.

"With that he struck Trask on the head, and while he lay partly stunned, Barwick fled. He leaped into a boat and fled down the lake toward the Mississippi.

"That was a mistake. Trask, a regular hound at trailing, recovered and followed. What happened when he overtook Barwick you already know."

"Yes," said Cal when the other finished. "I already know. Barwick must have capsized his boat somewhere down the bayou. He made a game swim for it, gained the shore and almost got aboard the *Gray Eagle*. Where was Hooper, while the pursuit was in progress?"

"He followed down the lake on Trask's heels."

"Then it is by no means clear who did the killing," Cal mused. "Hooper, or Trask."

He thrust a finger into a pocket of his vest, and brought out a bit of slate—an oblong slab.

"Maybe I have the means of finding out, though," he said to himself.

He got up from the bunk in answer to Huggins's request for food, but stood stock still as the chain rattled and the door of the cabin was swung open.

18

CALHOUN DOFFS HIS LID

HOOPER AND HOWIT, followed by Trask, Spangler and Banning, trooped into the room. All were dripping water. Night was closing down and the lantern Hooper carried cast but a feeble light.

"Git up, feller!" the native ordered gruffly. "Stand whar th' light kin shine on you, so yore betters kin git a look at you!"

"Which is Uncle George?" Cal asked, grinning widely as he stepped into the circle of light.

"Damn your impudence!" Spangler shouted, taking a step toward the ranger, his fat face red with rage. "You are no more Robert Keene than I am Pontius Pilate! What have you done with my nephew?"

"At my last view of him, Mr. Keene was doing very well," Cal answered easily. "He was somewhat nonplused, a bit frightened, and not in the best of temper. However, give yourself no uneasiness about Bobbie. He's safe enough."

Spangler swore. "Where is my nephew?" he demanded.

"Sorry I can't offer you seats, gentlemen," Cal remarked apologetically, ignoring Spangler, "but our keepers neglected to furnish us with chairs. There's a bit of cold coffee left, and a few scraps—"

"Fellow," Trask interrupted, his voice calm and even,

"you are a game man, I grant, but you are a damned fool with it. You can gain nothing by refusing to tell the whereabout of Robert Keene, and you may profit by so doing. I advise you to speak up."

"When your advice is desired, Trask," Cal retorted, "it will be asked for. In the meantime, what is your further pleasure, gentlemen?"

"Won't tell, eh?" Trask growled. "Well, maybe before the night is over you will be glad to do so. Come, gentlemen," he went on, addressing the others, "there's nothing for it but to leave him to the tender mercies of Hooper and Howit. I know his type. He won't talk—unless he is made to. Hooper, you can do as is customary in such cases, then report to me aboard the *Speedy*."

Trask turned on his heel and walked out, followed by all of the party except Hooper and his mate.

Howit, rifle ready, leaned against the closed door, his eyes watchful. Hooper stood in the center of the room, a six-shooter in his right hand.

"Feller," he said grimly, a look of ferocity in his eyes, "I am a dead shot. In about one minute more I am going to shoot a hole through yore left hand, then one through yore right. After that, if you-all haven't talked, I'm goin' to begin on yore years. Air you goin' to tell what th' gent wants to know?"

Cal sank back upon his bunk, his face wearing a look of fright. With trembling hands he removed his high-crowned Stetson, laid it in his lap and fingered it nervously.

"I say, now, Hooper," he said pleadingly, "give me a chance. Suppose I don't really know where young Keene is—"

"Hell, Hoop!" growled Howit. "Sink a slug in his head, and be done with it! That's whut he's goin' to git in th' end, any ways! Him an' th' other sneak in th' bunk! Otherwise we'll be foolin' around all night with a job which ought'n to take more'n a pair of minutes! We can say he wouldn't talk, an' we done whut we was ordered to do!"

"Air you-all goin' to talk, feller?" came fiercely from Hooper, whose black eyes now blazed with an insane light. "Fur th' las' time, air you goin' to talk?"

Cal's right hand slipped under the brim of his hat, there was an ear-splitting explosion, a spurt of flame and smoke, as the crown of his Stetson was torn into smoking shreds.

Hooper, with a shriek of agony, crumpled to the floor, his heavily shod feet beating a loud tattoo on the puncheons.

With a movement so swift Howit, at the door, was unable to follow it, Calhoun threw himself prone on the floor, swung the derringer, which had been concealed in the crown of his hat, upon the latter and sent its second bullet squarely between the gunman's eyes.

Howit pitched forward on his face, his rifle under him.

Cal was on his feet in an instant, and the revolvers of both men were his in the next.

"Quick, Huggins!" he ordered. "We've got to move! Those shots probably will not attract attention, since they were expected! But we won't take chances! Can you make it?"

Huggins got to his feet. "I've got to!" he declared. "Give me one of those guns!"

"Take the rifle," Cal ordered. "Cartridge belt, too!"

Huggins dragged the repeater from beneath the fallen Howit, and an instant later both slipped out of the cabin into the rain-drenched night.

19

THE CHIPS FLY FAST

CALHOUN STRUCK OFF through the downpour in the direction of Deep Lake, on a path intermittently disclosed by the lightning. Huggins was following close upon his heels.

"What are you going to do?" the latter called, when they had put a mile behind them.

Cal halted, allowing Huggins to gain his side. "You heard Trask say that he would wait aboard the *Speedy*. That means the Arkana launch is lying somewhere on this side," he said. "It is not likely that our escape will be discovered immediately.

"The pistol shots, if heard either by Trask and his party, or the logging-crew in their shanties on Mulberry, would signify only that Hooper was about his business. But, at best, we have only an hour or two. Trask will not rest easy until Hooper has reported, and he won't wait very long for him to do so.

"Now, here is what I propose to do. I am going to pay Mr. Trask and his friends a visit aboard the *Speedy*. What I do afterward depends upon circumstances. Are you with me?"

"Good God, man!" Huggins exclaimed. "We'll be running right back into danger! Why not take Hooper's dugout—the one he brought me over in, and which I'm sure I can find—and make our get-away while we have the chance?"

"Do as you like," Cal told him shortly. "Find the dugout and go, if that appeals to you as being the thing to do. As for me, I came here for a purpose, and that purpose is yet to accomplish.

"A delay of a couple of hours might prove fatal to my chances of ever accomplishing it. I'm going to act now—alone, if you haven't got the nerve to lend your aid. Now decide, and do it quickly!"

"I owe you a debt!" Huggins declared after a moment's hesitation. "And I'm going to pay part of it at least! Go ahead, and I'll follow wherever you lead!"

"Good!" Cal approved. "Now let's make time!"

Fifteen minutes of swift walking brought them to the shore of Deep Lake, where the *Speedy* lay at anchor, her gangplank down. Lights shone from the cabin, and from the engine-room below. Cal paused in the fringe of woods and considered the situation. Presently he spoke in a whisper:

"The pilot is probably in the engine-room, gassing with the engineer while he waits for orders. There's at least one stoker aboard; maybe two. We'll have to look sharp for them.

"Come on—and don't shoot unless I give the word. This whole business depends absolutely upon our being able to take them by surprise. Ready?"

"Yes!"

Cal crept across the gangplank, Huggins following closely. Along the port guard they made their way and stopped beside the open door of the engine-room, where a dim light burned far back.

Two men sat smoking and talking in low tones, ten feet inside the room. They were pilot and engineer. A third man was sprawled on the deck, asleep. The stoker, Cal reasoned.

"Ready!" he whispered, and stepped inside. "Up with your hands, men!" he ordered, bringing the muzzles of a pair of six-guns to bear upon the two officers. "Make the least sound," he went on, "and I'll shoot you where you sit!"

"What—what is this?" demanded the engineer. "A holdup?"

"Open your mouth again," Cal warned, "and I'll fill it with hot lead!"

Within ten minutes the three men in the engine-room were securely bound and gagged, Huggins attending to that part, while Cal commanded the situation with his guns.

"Now what?" Huggins asked.

"The cabin," Cal answered briefly. "Bring along the balance of that coil of rope. If all goes well, there'll be some more tying to do!"

They mounted to the boiler-deck, the rain helping to drown any noise they may have made, and Cal peered through a port into the lighted cabin.

Trask, Banning and Spangler sat at a table in the center of the room. Trask was speaking, though it was impossible for the ranger to make out what he said, and the others were listening intently. Cal would have given much to have heard what was being said, but time pressed and he must act.

"Follow me!" he whispered to Huggins. "Do just as I tell you, after we get inside!"

Creeping to the cabin door he tried the knob gently and found that it turned easily. An instant later he strode into the room, both guns drawn.

"Hands on the table, all of you!" the ranger ordered the astonished trio. "A move for a gun will be your last on earth! You, Trask, reach for the ceiling—quick!"

Banning and Spangler, too amazed for speech, placed trembling hands on the board before them. Trask, with an oath, half rose from his chair. It looked as though he meant to obey.

Then with a swift upward thrust of his right knee he struck the table from beneath, overturning it. At the same instant he swung a clenched fist toward the lamp which hung above his head, in an attempt to plunge the room in darkness, whipping out a gun as he did so.

One of the guns in Cal's hands spoke with a whiplike crack. Trask; whose fist was yet an inch short of the lamp, stiffened, quivered for a second, then collapsed heavily upon the floor.

Cal waited, eyes upon Banning and Spangler. Both cowered in their chairs, faces livid. He had nothing to fear from them.

Crossing to where Trask lay, the ranger bent over and thrust a hand into a pocket of his shirt, after unbuttoning the flap. That pocket, he had noticed, bulged.

From the pocket he abstracted an oblong wooden block—perhaps six inches long, one inch thick and four inches wide. It was a bit of basswood, and had been reduced to a shell by gouging the fiber out at one edge.

He tossed the block of wood upon the table, which Huggins had restored to its legs. "Part of a turkey-caller," he commented, eyes upon the blanched faces of Banning and the Congressman, neither of whom had yet regained the power of speech.

"Here's the rest of it," he went on, placing an oblong bit of slate beside it. "Trask had been hunting turkeys the day he did the shooting on Kimball's Point, wearing the same clothing he is dressed in now. That bit of slate, drawn across the thin edge of the hollow block, creates the illusion of a wild turkey's call.

"You will note," he continued, taking up both block and slate, "that the two belong together—the slate fits snugly inside the hollow space. Trask lost the slate out of his pocket, there in the brush of the Point.

"If there was any doubt before as to the identity of the fiend who killed three men and wounded three on Kimball's Point, that turkey-caller settles the matter. Trask is—or rather was—the inhuman monster who shot them all!"

20

WHEN THE BIG TREES FELL

THE CANCELING OF Arkana's timber concession, shortly after the facts were in the hands of the government authorities, is a matter of record in the files of the United States Land Office. But that did not end the case.

Spangler, in spite of all the political influence he was able to bring to his aid, received a long sentence in the government prison at Leavenworth, whereupon he promptly killed himself.

Banning escaped with a short sentence, as a reward for turning upon his associates and giving his evidence at their trials—evidence resulting in putting a dozen men in stripes.

While it cannot be doubted that Spangler, Trask and Banning were the ringleaders in the swindle, the lesser criminals whom they had gathered about them also had to pay.

As is always the case when big trees are thrown, the saplings near them are crushed by their fall.

Robert Keene, who turned out to be a very good sort after all, was in no way involved, and his marriage to Nan Lambert a few months after his trying experience probably wiped any grudge he may have harbored against the rangers out of his mind.

As for Calhoun, his adventure into the land of big timber was merely an incident in his active life. Having swung his ax and thrown his trees, he promptly forgot the matter and began looking for other things to do. Needless to say, he found them.